传世经典桥梁书

灯塔之家

1

暴风雨中的灯塔

[美] 辛西娅·劳伦特 著

[美] 普莱斯顿·马克丹尼斯 绘　栾述蓉 译

21 二十一世纪出版社集团
21st Century Publishing Group

献给格蕾丝，深爱大海的人。

——辛西娅·劳伦特

献给鲁斯，他曾带我航行。

——普莱斯顿·马克丹尼斯

奇想国童书

项目策划　奇想国童书
责任编辑　刘晨露子
特约编辑　郑应湘　孙金蕾
装帧设计　田丽丹

目 录

1. 潘朵拉

在一座孤零零的、远离城市村庄、远离朋友关心的灯塔里，住着一只心地善良的猫，名叫潘朵拉。

她已经独自在灯塔中生活了四年之久，灯塔日渐破败。她发现自己时常不自觉地发出长长的、深深的、寂寞的叹息。她坐在岩石上，久久地俯瞰着远处的海浪。因为坐得太久，有几次把鼻子都晒伤了。

晚上，她想在灯下读会儿书，却总是走神，一连几个小时地回想童年——那时候，她有很多朋友，很多伙伴。

为什么潘朵拉甘愿忍受这种孤独的灯塔生活呢？

因为曾有一座灯塔救过她的命。

潘朵拉小时候，曾和爸爸跟着一艘大帆船出海，前往一个新的国度。她的妈妈带着刚出生的婴儿留下了，计划日后再与他们会合。

大船在海上航行。一天深夜，突然，一阵剧烈的震动把潘朵拉和爸爸从床上掀了下来。庞大的船头猛烈地摇摆着。

"待在这儿别动，潘朵拉！"爸爸命令道，"待在这儿等我回来。"

他们遇上了可怕的暴风雨。狂风怒号，海浪劈头盖脸地砸向他们。更糟糕的是，一场大雾在海上弥漫开来。这样的大雾对航船来说是致命的。雾气会遮挡水手的视线，使船撞上岸边犬牙交错的礁石而粉身碎骨。

潘朵拉的爸爸对此一清二楚。潘朵拉在床上瑟瑟发抖的时候，他和其他人一起竭尽全力拉住船帆，避免它们被狂风吹落——他知道他们正处于极度的危险之中。

潘朵拉的爸爸是一只勇敢无畏的猫，绝不

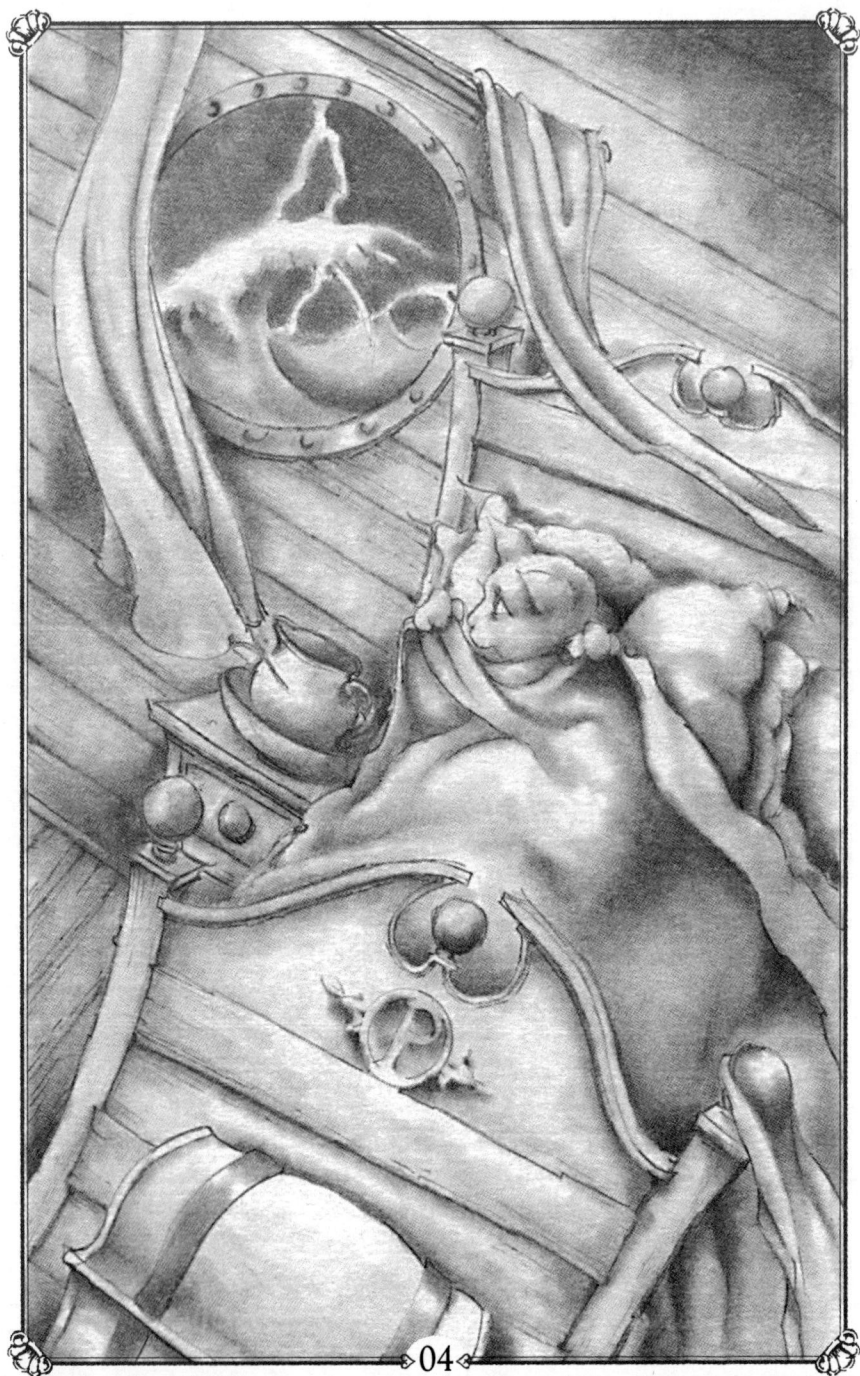

放弃希望。他和大家一起紧紧抓住船帆的绳索，等待救援到来——不管这救援以何种形式到来，会来自何方。

时间流逝，风渐渐消停，浪也越来越小，浓雾却一直不散。

船长满脸焦虑。他知道这片水域的凶险，知道长久以来有多少船只在此沉没。

对于或许会有救援到来，或许会有人带他们离开这一片致命的海域，他已不抱任何希望。只有灯塔能给他们指明方向，然而上百年来，这片水域从没有亮起过灯光。

所以，当船长先是听到一声深沉而清晰的雾角声，紧接着看见前方亮起了一束光——是的，一束光！他感到既困惑不已又惊讶诧异。那绝不是过路船只发出的光，只有灯塔的强光才能穿透这样的浓雾。只有灯塔之光！

"向下风方向行驶！"船长高声喊道，"远离灯光！"

所有人使劲拽着绳索，让船转弯，驶离了

那段危险的海岸。

这艘船，还有船上所有的人，都得救了。

从那以后，潘朵拉经常梦见灯塔。虽然她没有亲眼见过那座救命的灯塔，但她的爸爸见过，并且常常谈起它。他一直想知道，是谁点亮了那盏明灯。

潘朵拉慢慢长大了，她自己也开始思考这个问题。她到图书馆搜集关于灯塔的书，在速写本上画各式各样的灯塔，就连晚上做梦都会梦见它们。

一天清晨，她一觉醒来，觉悟到有件事势在必行——她要成为一个灯塔看守人！这，是她的使命。

没用多久，潘朵拉就找到了一座需要守护的灯塔。这份工作艰苦又孤独，很少有谁愿意干。灯塔大多建在荒无人烟的地方，在陡峭险峻的悬崖之上。冬天里，一场暴风雪可能会把守护者困在塔里几个星期；而等他终于脱困，却找不到一个可以说话的人。人们都住在别的地方，在大城市里，或者小村镇里，没有谁愿意在这么荒凉的地方生活。

但是这种生活吓不倒潘朵拉，因为她有一颗善良、纯洁的心，恐惧永远无法靠近这样的心灵。那些在危险莫测的水域上航行的船只，载着无数的父母和孩子，他们需要指引。潘朵拉知道自己能行。

就这样，潘朵拉尽心尽力地工作了四年。在这漫长的四年中，她目睹了许多场可怕的

风暴来了又去。她在无尽的冬夜中不眠不休地守护着那盏了不起的灯，吹响低沉回旋的雾角。

她数不清自己到底救了多少人，但她知道那数目不算少。

长期孤独的生活已经令潘朵拉疲惫不堪，不过，她即将再次拯救一个生命。

2. 海 勇

探险号

有一种人，他们是如此热爱大海，以至于一天都无法跟它分开。这只名叫海勇的狗就是这样一个天生的水手。

当海勇到了可以离家自立的年龄时，他动手为自己造了一艘船。他给这艘船取名"探险号"，然后，他告别父母和姐妹，启程远航，去探寻属于自己的生命意义。

他是个不错的水手，了解关于风的相关知识，会观测星象，并且深信自己的直觉。

在过去的五年中，海勇驾船去过世界各个大洋。他的直觉从未出错。他一路劈波斩浪，顺顺利利，无忧无虑。

然而，有一天，一切都变了。

一直以来，靠着自己灵敏的鼻子，海勇总是能提前感知到暴风雨的到来，然后找到一个避风的海湾或港口，直到风浪平息。

但是这一天，他感冒了。他的鼻子因为感冒而堵塞，嗅觉变得异常迟钝。此外，他还很疲倦。他在船舱里打了个长长的盹儿，没有注意到海鸟在他头顶上方紧张不安地盘旋，惶惶地叫唤着，互相传递着坏天气即将到来的消息。

海鸟们都明智地向陆地飞去，只有身陷梦境的海勇，仍然停留在开阔的海面上。

随后，猛烈的暴风雨到来了。

闪电刺耳的噼啪声，低沉的雷鸣，还有滔天的巨浪，把海勇从睡梦中惊醒。"探险号"被风暴肆意抛掷，忽上忽下。海勇只能用尽全力紧紧抓住小船，除此之外毫无办法。

一向对他非常友善的大海，此刻却翻脸无情。开启水手生涯以来，第一次，海勇感到了害怕。

他在风浪中低声祈祷："安全港，但愿有个安全港。"

海勇的话音未落，一道耀眼的光芒穿透了黑暗，紧接着，海面上远远地传来一阵悠长的雾角声。

"安全港！"海勇重复道。

这是勇敢的海勇说出的最后一句话。随后，他被风浪抛了起来，翻滚着，翻滚着，落入幽深黑暗的大海。

海勇就这样永远地消失了吗？

不，海勇的故事并未就此结束。

3. 安 慰

当海勇再次醒来时，他怀疑那场暴风雨或许只不过是一场梦。

他发现自己正躺在一张小木床上，身上盖着一条鲜艳的格纹棉被。他已经不再置身海上，而是正透过身边的一扇小窗望着大海。一朵雏菊插在窗台上的罐子里。

海勇拍了拍脑袋，确定自己不是在做梦。正当他准备伸腿试着在光亮的木地板上站起来时，房门开了，一只猫走了进来。

她脸上挂着微笑，腰间系了条围裙，手里端着一个盘子，里面放着茶和饼干。

"早上好！"说着，她把茶盘放在床边的桌子上，"我想着你该醒了。我叫潘朵拉。"

虽然不确定自己是不是在做梦，海勇还是

伸出爪子跟她握了握。"我叫海勇，"他说，"至少，我记得是这样。"

潘朵拉笑了。"你经历了一段艰难的旅程。"她说。

"我还以为那是我的最后一段旅程了。"海勇回答。

潘朵拉给他倒了一杯茶，茶闻起来有花香味儿，海勇感激地一饮而尽。"谢谢你。"他说，"能再给我倒点儿吗？我渴极了。"

潘朵拉点点头，又给他倒了一杯。"是海水的缘故。"她说。

"我不知道自己怎么活下来的。"海勇说。

"我也不知道。"潘朵拉回答说，"三天前，我在岸边看到你时，还以为你已经死了。"

"我已经在这里三天了？"海

勇惊讶地叫道。

"是的。"潘朵拉微笑着说，"你睡得像个婴儿一样。"

海勇摇了摇头说："我只记得掉到了水里。"他好像突然又想起了什么："对了，我的船，你见到我的船了吗？"

"没见到。"潘朵拉说，"也许在岸边更远的地方。等你能走了，我们一起去找找看。"

"能走？"海勇问道。

"你的腿……"潘朵拉说。

海勇掀开被子，吃惊地看到自己的左腿缠着绷带，从膝盖到脚打了夹板。"我的天！"他叫道，"但我不觉得疼。应该很疼不是吗？"

潘朵拉高兴地笑了。"我想我算得上半个医生。"她解释说，"我对植物有一些研究，知道哪些有治疗功效。我用车前草的叶子包住你的腿来消肿，打上夹板是为了防止它再度受伤。"

"你可真厉害！"海勇说。

潘朵拉骄傲得涨红了脸。

"你一个人住在这里吗？"海勇小口喝着茶问。潘朵拉给自己也倒了一杯。

"是的，就我自己。"她说，"不过，过那么一段时间，就会有朋友在这个岛暂作停留——应该说，过很长一段时间。他们季节性地来。"

"季节性？"海勇问道。

"他们长途迁徙，"潘朵拉解释说，"所以我只有在春秋时节，在他们北上或南下时，能看到他们。比如环礁，他是一头灰鲸……"

"你认识一头灰鲸？"海勇问。

"是的。"潘朵拉回答说，"一旦熟悉起来，鲸鱼很健谈。如果你问起他们的孩子，他们就会说个不停。"

"还有燕鸥亨利，"她接着说，"他一向行色匆匆，甚至都不会降落，只是在我头顶盘旋一会儿，问问我的身体、我的花园等情况，然后就飞走了。他每年要飞近一万千米。"

"真的吗？"海勇问。

"真的。"潘朵拉说，"他很强壮。"

“就是说，你几乎总是一个人？”海勇问。

“几乎总是。”潘朵拉回答道。

海勇摇了摇头说：“我从没想过，有一天会遇到一个像我一样的人。”

“像你一样？”潘朵拉疑惑地问。

“一个喜欢独自生活的人。”海勇回答，“我几乎总是在海上漂泊，几乎总是独自一人。像你一样。”

潘朵拉笑了，她沉思了一会儿。“我不大肯定自己喜欢独自一人生活，”最后她说，“我只是这样生活而已。”

“为什么？”海勇问道。

“为了挽救生命，”潘朵拉说，“比如你的生命。”

她再次为他斟满一杯茶。

4. 伙 伴

海勇到来后，灯塔里的一切都不一样了。

每天早晨潘朵拉醒来，第一个念头就是有人可以说话了。她从床上跳起来，准备上一顿丰盛的早餐：有热乎乎的奶油燕麦粥、苹果司康和几碗越橘酱。然后她用托盘端着，去到海勇的房间，两个人能聊一整个上午。潘朵拉的花园里，渐渐杂草丛生。

后来，当海勇能够借助拐杖，一瘸一拐地走路时，他们把聊天的地点转移到了户外。潘朵拉和海勇坐在海边的大礁石上，互相讲述自己的人生故事，分享所见所闻，还有各自的爱憎。

海勇聊起自己的父亲，他害怕水，不肯踏上船板半步。

潘朵拉则说起自己的妹妹，她曾给女王们缝制结婚礼服。

他们俩小时候都爱读童话，也都认为比起那些善良的动物来，童话里那些坏的动物要生动有趣得多。

他们还聊到过这个世界上各自最喜欢的是什么。

"北极光。"海勇回答。

"企鹅。"这是潘朵拉的回答。

那么最不喜欢的呢？他俩一致认为，是海难。

正值夏天，这是潘朵拉的守塔工作相对比较轻松的时节。七月和八月这两个月很少下雨，也几乎不会起雾，行船十分安全，潘朵拉也可以休息一下。

事实上，也只是稍作休息罢了。她仍然要为即将到来的寒冬做准备。她知道，自己得种植和采摘蔬菜，把玉米和小麦磨成粉做面包，把海上漂来的木头劈成块留着生火，用补给船运来今年灯塔要用的煤油。所有这些都需要靠

潘朵拉准备妥当。

白天，潘朵拉在菜园忙碌的时候，海勇会忙着修复自己的船——拖着仍然不便利的腿脚，尽自己最大的努力。他竟然在离岸较远的地方找回了船——虽然不是完整的船只，但至少找回了大部分船体。看到船破损得那么严重，他的心都要碎了，不过他相信自己可以修好它。

潘朵拉在菜园里一边干活儿，一边看着远处在修船的海勇。她感到心中有些怅然若失，这是人们看到一个亲爱的朋友准备离去时会有的那种失落。

到了傍晚，他们两个会在山坡上野餐。雏菊开满了小山，一直蔓延到海岸，他们一起看着太阳慢慢落山，世界被涂染成粉色和红色。

第二天，是同样的一天。

海勇很想知道灯塔是怎么工作的，但他的腿不允许他爬上四段陡峭的楼梯，然后踩着梯子进入灯室，直达那盏巨大的玻璃灯。由于没有暴风雨，用不着那盏救命的灯，海勇有时会把灯塔的存在忘得一干二净。

　　但是九月初的一天，就在野鹅、绿头鸭和林莺从头顶飞过，开始它们漫长的南迁之旅时，海勇终于切切实实地意识到那座巨大的灯塔所肩负的使命。

　　以及这使命又是被谁真正肩负着的。

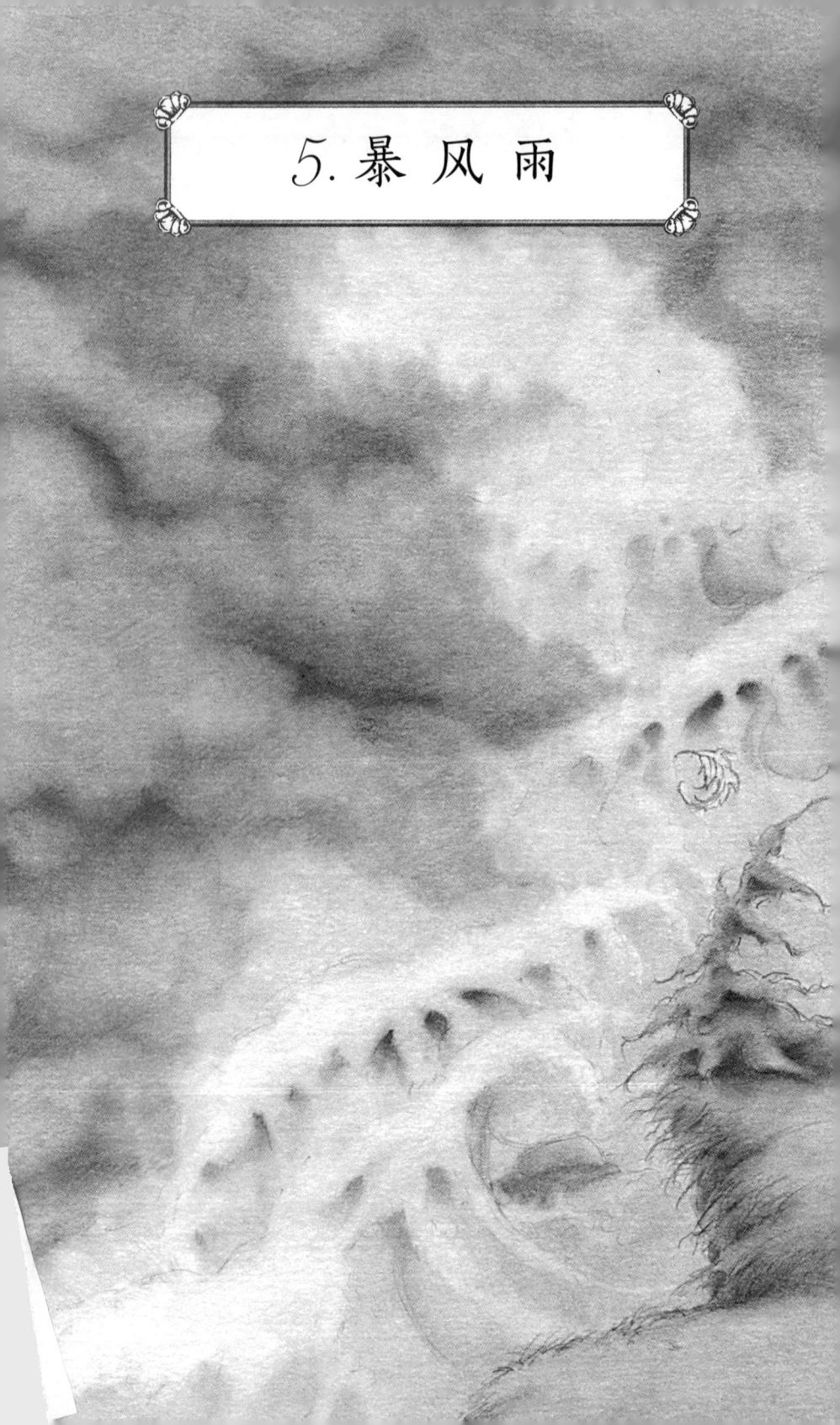

5. 暴风雨

潘朵拉本以为，这个季节还远远没到刮风暴的时候。没错，现在是雾季，但海上的大风暴……通常要到深秋的时候才会来啊。

"可是为什么天空变得这么黑？" 九月初的一个下午，她正在采摘枝蔓上的西红柿，心里不禁纳闷儿，"为什么风这么冷？为什么海鸥盘旋着飞得越来越高？为什么他们的叫声越来越紧张不安？"

因为海上的天空喜欢变化莫测，喜欢让人措手不及。

这天，它显然跃跃欲试，有所意图。

海勇和潘朵拉给海勇的船钉上板条，加固了小屋窗户的护窗板，在厨房的火炉里生起火。

"今天可真冷啊！"海勇说，"昨天还很暖

和来着。"

"海上吹来了异常的风。"潘朵拉说，"我觉得，这风充满危险。我得去上面的灯室点上灯，看顾它。"

海勇郁闷地看了看自己仍然绑着夹板的腿："我应该上去帮你才对。"他说。

"不，千万别这样。"潘朵拉说，"要是你的腿再受伤，又得多花上一个月才能长好。我工作时，你照看着炉火就行。"

海勇在厨房为火炉添柴，并泡好一壶热茶，准备两个人一起喝。潘朵拉则爬上了最上面的灯室。她修剪好灯芯，点燃了塔灯。她检查了煤油罐，擦了防风玻璃。然后，她爬下来进了值班室。

晚饭时分，一片巨大的浓厚雾层滚滚而来。潘朵拉站在高高的灯塔上，眼看着大雾像翻滚的棉花一样朝着陆地席卷而来。于是，她拉响警铃，吹响雾角，指引小船靠岸，帮它们逃离即将到来的暴风雨。

在灯室下的厨房里，海勇坐立难安。他听到了警铃和雾角。"我也能做这些，"他想，"我本可以帮忙的。"可眼下他只能坐在火炉旁干等着，这让他很不好受。

接下来的几个小时，风速越来越惊人，狂风摇撼着潘朵拉值守的灯塔。她毫不畏惧。现在，夜幕已经降临。对于航行在海上的任何船只来说，这都是一场可怕的风暴。大雾、闪电、瓢泼大雨和狂风，所有这些都可能使船只触礁沉没。

潘朵拉守在值班室里，一遍又一遍地吹响雾角。在她头顶上，那盏巨大的灯将明亮的光束直射到海面上。她冷得要命——她没来得及穿暖和点儿，也没时间为值班室的炉子准备木柴。但是她已经顾不上这些，她不能停下来。这是场可怕的暴风雨，她很清楚一场肆虐的风暴会带来什么后果。

海勇坐在厨房的窗户边，望着闪烁的明亮灯光，听着雾角发出的警报声。一小时、两小时、

三小时、四小时……潘朵拉是怎么做到的？她从哪里获得的力量？此时的自己只是照看着厨房的炉火，就已经感到疲倦了。

最后，睡意占了上风，他睡过去了。风暴肆虐，而他未能目睹。

第二天早晨，明亮的阳光照进厨房，惊醒了海勇。他整个晚上都躺在火炉边。潘朵拉在哪里？他朝窗外望去。

她在那儿！远远地，站在悬崖边缘，肩上裹着一条披肩，爪子在空中挥舞着。

远处的海面上有一条船，看上去像是地平线上的一个黑点。船静静地泊在那里，安然无恙。

她救了他们，海勇心想。

他惊叹不已地注视着这位朋友。

6. 目　标

海勇原本计划在十月底，在冬季风暴开始肆虐前，赶在冰冻和大风到来之前驾船离开。他是一名水手，大海是他的家。他清楚这一点，潘朵拉也清楚这一点，因此，两个人也都为即将到来的悲伤离别做好了准备。

只不过命运另有安排。

海勇的船并没有像他希望的那样迅速修好。船只还缺少一些关键的小部件，他只能自己手工制作。这需要时间，也许要花上一个漫长的春天和一个漫长的夏天，说不定还有整个秋天。

海勇很能干，可是他变不出时间来。

他的腿好得也很慢，当初的骨折很严重。尽管潘朵拉有神奇的草药和管用的夹板，但这条伤腿仍然很虚弱，海勇要借助拐杖才能行走。

所以，当风越来越凛冽，迁徙的鸟儿布满天空时，海勇站在岸边，意识到这个冬天他没法儿启航了。

他本以为自己会很失望，会非常沮丧。

然而，他并没有。

他目睹了潘朵拉为拯救他人做出的可贵的努力，目睹了她为了更崇高的目标舍己为人，这让他在不知不觉中发生了改变。

海勇受到了启迪。他想，也许，至少在这一个冬天，他也能像潘朵拉那样，让自己的生命变得有意义。

于是他问潘朵拉，自己是否可以继续待到春天。

她的回答当然是肯定的。其实，这正是她心底暗自期盼的。

他们一起收集冬天生火用的木柴，还有过冬的食物。海勇终于能够爬到灯塔上面看看那盏巨大的灯。看到它的第一眼，海勇震撼万分。"太壮观了！"他对潘朵拉说，"真是个奇迹！"

海勇和潘朵拉把那盏巨大的灯的黄铜配件擦得锃亮，把灯罩拆下来做了清洗，更换了用完的灯芯。待在灯室里让海勇异常激动，那感觉不亚于最美妙的航海日（尽管他不愿对潘朵拉承认这一点）。

晚上，潘朵拉给自己和海勇编织暖和的帽子、连指手套和袜子，海勇则用捡来的漂流木制作工具。两个人一边干活儿一边聊天。

"我很惊讶，"一天晚上海勇说，"这次我竟然没有晕陆地。我以前可不能在岸上待这么久，待得稍久，我会感觉自己的腿变成了石头。"

潘朵拉微笑着，转动了一下正在给他织的帽子，说："我希望这种孤独的灯塔生活不至于让你太难熬。"

"不，一点儿也不，"海勇说，"我对此满怀期待。希望我能帮上点儿忙。"

"你能帮上很多忙。"潘朵拉回答。

"我希望随着时间的推移，我们能交到一些新朋友。"海勇说，"哪怕他们只是路过也好。

我特别想结识一头鲸鱼。"

"大海充满惊喜，"潘朵拉说，"新朋友是其中之一。"

她冲海勇眨了一下眼睛："别问我是怎么知道的。"

"等春天来了，"海勇说，"在'探险号'完工之前，我准备在那座开满雏菊的小山上建一个凉亭，我们可以在那儿坐下来，看看会发生些什么。"

"哦，"潘朵拉回答说，"我相信会有很多、很多美好的事情发生。"

她往火中添了一根木柴。

两个人都觉得异常温暖。

7.营救

冬天确实很漫长。过去，当冬天来临，海勇总是去到阳光明媚的地区航行，以度过寒冷的月份。他几乎已经忘记了脚指头被冻僵是什么滋味。

在潘朵拉的灯塔，从十一月到三月，他每天都在体会这种滋味。

在最冷的日子里，整座小岛被寒冰覆盖。海水喷溅的浪花打湿了每一寸土地、每一株灌木、每一块岩石，结成坚硬的冰。有一阵子，潘朵拉和海勇连续几周都没敢出门。

这倒也无妨。由于猛烈的暴风雨，海勇和潘朵拉需要夜以继日地守护在塔灯旁。他们不分昼夜地照管着灯塔，让警示的灯光闪耀在海面上。

他们挽救生命，但却不知道被救者是谁，以及被救者在何时被救起。如果在灰蒙蒙的海上，有人向他们发出由衷的感谢，他们也无从得知，无从听闻。

尽管如此，当这两只筋疲力尽的猫和狗倒头短暂睡去时，他们心满意足，睡得非常香甜。

春天刚刚到来时，总是有些阴晴无常。头一天可能还碧空如洗，阳光照耀在潘朵拉门前的小小白色番红花上；紧接着第二天，就可能狂风肆虐，暴雨袭来，大雨压得所有初绽的花儿都垂下了脑袋，倒伏向地面，万物都在颤抖。

海勇想建造凉亭，尝试了几次都没有成功，直到太阳终于露出脸来，并且停留足够长的时间时，才终于能够干点儿活了。

正是海勇在开满雏菊的小山顶上敲敲打打搭建凉亭的某一刻，他看见远处的海面上漂着样东西，看上去像是个木板箱，箱子上依稀有面小旗子。

此时的海勇还不知道，潘朵拉孤独的灯塔

即将迎来一个美好的奇迹。

"潘朵拉！"海勇喊道，"快来看！"

潘朵拉两手抱着满满的木柴，从小屋后面走出来。她把木头放在门边，急忙跑向山顶。

"快看！"海勇指着海上漂着的木板箱说。他看不到任何生命的迹象。

"上面好像插着面旗。"他告诉潘朵拉，"你觉得那是个空箱子吗？"

潘朵拉盯着远处的海面，脸上的表情变得凝重。"我有种预感，"她严肃地说，"我觉得那里面有生命。"

海勇皱起了眉头："如果那里面真有生命，情况肯定不太妙。那只木板箱显然只能随着波浪载沉载浮。"

潘朵拉点点头。"我知道。"她说。

海勇深吸一口气，挺直了肩膀。"我得想办法把它拉上岸。"他说。

潘朵拉望向他问："你打算怎么做？"

"这个距离，我想我可以驾船过去。"海勇

说，"船虽然受损，但我觉得它还能浮起来。"

"你觉得？"潘朵拉重复了一句。

"我们要么站在这里，看着那面小旗漂走，天知道会发生什么悲剧。"海勇说，"要么，就让我驾着'探险号'下海。"

潘朵拉深深地叹了口气，下定了决心。"开船去吧，要快！"她说。

海勇朝岸边跑去。

8.孩子们

探险号

这只勇敢的狗没花多长时间就把破烂的小船开上了海面，很快就靠近了漂浮的木板箱。毕竟，他依然是位出色的水手。

"喂！"他一边划船靠近，一边喊道。他现在看清了，那面旗子其实是一件红色小衬衫，被绑在一根小木棍上。"有人吗？"

没有人回答。

他怀着沉重的心情把船靠到木板箱边，做好了最坏的打算。

他朝木板箱里瞥了一眼。"我的天哪！"他失声叫道。

木板箱里面，三只年幼的老鼠正瞪大眼睛看着他。事实上，其中一只还是个婴儿。三只小老鼠紧紧地依偎在一起。

"你们受伤了吗？"海勇问道。

其中一只老鼠是个男孩，他张开嘴想说话，却发不出声音来。另一只是个女孩，只是呆呆地看着海勇。那个婴儿睡着了。

"你们迷路了吗？"海勇再次问道。

男孩和女孩一起拼命点头。

海勇伸出爪子。"孩子们，你们得跟我来。"他说，"你们的处境很危险。"

女孩握住海勇的爪子，点点头表示同意。他把她抱上船。然后，那个男孩动作温柔地把婴儿递给海勇。这是个女婴。她那么小，那么轻，当海勇小心翼翼地把她放在女孩的膝盖上时，他连大气都不敢出。

"这个小宝宝是你妹妹吗？"他问女孩。

"是的。"小女孩点了点头回答道。

最后，那个男孩也上了船，依然说不出话来。

海勇赶紧掉头朝岸边划去。"你们肯定渴坏了，"他说，"得尽快让你们喝到淡水。"

当海勇用自己的毛线帽子兜着三只小老鼠

上岸时，潘朵拉拿着一条毯子，还有——谢天谢地——一大碗水等在那里。孩子们喝了又喝。那个女孩将两个小爪子合在一起，做成杯状，捧水给小宝宝喝。

等他们终于喝完了水，那个男孩清晰又郑重地说道："谢谢你们。"

海勇和潘朵拉脸上浮现出微笑。两个人都非常高兴，发自内心地高兴——是孩子们！

他们把小家伙们带回小屋，为他们准备好晚饭。

第二天早晨，男孩和女孩跟潘朵拉和海勇一起吃早饭。头天晚上，他们已经做过自我介绍，男孩名叫哨子，女孩名叫莉拉，他们俩是兄妹。那个婴儿，他们管她叫小不点儿。

"她的确是个小不点儿。"潘朵拉回答说。

"不，不是这个意思。"莉拉说，"她的大名就叫小不点儿。"

"嗯，"潘朵拉微笑着说，"这个名字非常合适。"

这会儿，一大清早，坐在暖乎乎的厨房里，面前是热乎乎的早餐，哨子和莉拉仍然觉得又累又饿，但比这更严重的，是满心担忧。

"小不点儿还在睡觉，"莉拉告诉潘朵拉和海勇，"她从来没有睡过这么久。"

"而且她整晚几乎没怎么动过。"哨子说，"她原来睡觉总是翻来覆去，还咯咯地笑或者吐泡泡，现在却很安静。"

潘朵拉立刻起身察看。

她从椅子上的毛线袜子里抱起了熟睡的小婴儿。

"这个小家伙发烧了。"潘朵拉担心地说，"我觉得她病得很重。"

莉拉望着潘朵拉，一颗大大的泪珠沿着她的脸颊滚落。

哨子忧心忡忡地望向海勇。

"海勇，"潘朵拉说，"我得到树林中去一趟，你得在这里照看宝宝。我要去找一种特别的柳树枝，也许要费些工夫。"

海勇点点头，伸出爪子。潘朵拉轻轻地把婴儿放在他的大爪子上。

"注意给她降温，"潘朵拉说，"但也别冻着她。窗边轻柔的微风对她有好处。她得多喝水，留神她什么时候想喝。"

潘朵拉慈爱地看着哨子和莉拉："你们把小宝宝照顾得很好。她是因为天气和大海才生病的，而不是因为缺少关心和爱。"

又一颗泪珠从莉拉的脸上滚落。

"我得抓紧时间。"潘朵拉一边说，一边披上羊毛披肩，走出家门。

9. 家 庭

潘朵拉到外面的树林里寻找柳树枝了，海勇让莉拉和哨子坐到了他自制的跳棋棋盘前，来转移他们的注意力，免得他们担惊受怕。

"我来照看小不点儿，"他温柔地对他们说，"你们俩试一下我的新棋盘。"

"蛤蜊！"莉拉拿起一个棋子，惊讶地说。

"还有海星。"哨子也拿起一个棋子。

海勇笑了："它们比普通的小圆棋子有趣多了。我自己雕刻的。"

"太棒了！"哨子说着，把海星拿在手里翻来覆去地看，"什么时候我也能试试刻点儿什么就好了！"

"你愿意的话，什么时候都可以。"海勇说，

"当然啦，除了现在。现在我需要照顾这个小家伙。"

他让哨子和莉拉两个下棋，自己抱着老鼠宝宝坐到了厨房窗边的椅子上。他用一只爪子捧着宝宝，旁边放了一点点水，开始履行自己的职责。

潘朵拉交代过他——需要给她降温，给她喝水。

这些海勇都照做了。

而且他做的不止这些。

坐在潘朵拉挂着格纹棉窗帘的窗户边，海勇注视着含苞的樱桃树、怒放的水仙花，他自己也在经历一场悄然巨变。

他说不上来到底是怎么回事，但当他轻轻晃着掌心上的婴儿，听着哨子和莉拉在旁边轻柔的说话声，还有火苗噼里啪啦燃烧的声音，闻到烤箱中烤成褐色的面包散发出来的芳香时，他意识到自己非常快乐，比以往任何时候都快乐，比他在海上度过的任何一个孤独的夜晚都要快乐。

他坐在窗边，轻声对着小宝宝说话，微笑着。

从那天起，一切都变了。

柳树枝非常有效，小不点儿好多了。莉拉种下了向日葵种子。潘朵拉和海勇发现自己拥有了一个家庭。有时候，潘朵拉看着自己灯塔中的所有这些住客，不由得惊叹："这一切到底是怎样发生的？"

这一切是这样发生的：因为一只年轻而高尚的猫立志挽救生命；因为一只勇敢的狗热爱航海；还因为，三个孩子渴望有个家。

在海勇发现海上漂泊的孩子们之前，哨子、莉拉还有小不点儿住在离潘朵拉的灯塔很远的一个孤儿院里。但是他们即将要被分开，被送到不同的地方。"我们永远不会分离。"哨子对莉拉说。于是，在一个漆黑的夜晚，莉拉把小不点儿裹好，背在背上，他们逃了出来。

他们一路来到城市的码头，找到即将启航

孤儿院

的大船，然后藏到了其中一艘船上，开往茫茫未知的远方。

但在海上，他们遇上了狂风。船翻了，三只可怜的小老鼠也跟着掉到了海里。

也许是他们在天堂的父母护佑着他们，哨子设法抓住了一只空木板箱，把他的两个妹妹拉了进来。

在海勇发现他们之前，他们已经又饥又渴地在海上漂了不知多长时间。

而现在他们在这里，雕刻水獭棋子，种植向日葵。

海勇对小不点儿的感情越来越深。他把她放在自己柔软的毛线帽的卷边上，走到哪儿都带着她，跟她分享所见的一切。

晚上，当潘朵拉把晚饭摆到餐桌上时，海勇把小不点儿放在他盘子旁边的小蛋杯里，吃饭的时候不时满怀爱意地拍拍她的脑袋。

而当孩子们肚子饱饱、快快乐乐地上床睡觉以后，海勇和潘朵拉会在客厅里喝着一天中的最后一杯茶，回忆往事。

"你还记得我们看见双彩虹的时候吗？"

"你还记得日食的时候吗？"

"还有那次鹈鹕被大风刮倒的时候！"

他们一边小口啜着茶，一边因为回忆不约而同地微笑起来。

然后，作为夜晚结束前的最后一个问题，

海勇一如既往地问道："你还记得我发现孩子们的时候吗？"

潘朵拉会点点头。

"他们真是棒极了！"海勇会这样说。

"是的。"潘朵拉会这样回答。

"谢天谢地，我们找到了他们。"两个人异口同声地说。

然后，他们会愉快地互道晚安，各自回到自己温暖的床上。在厨房里，靠近炉火边，三只小老鼠蜷缩在潘朵拉特意为他们织的袜子中，做着关于蔚蓝大海的梦，睡得正香。

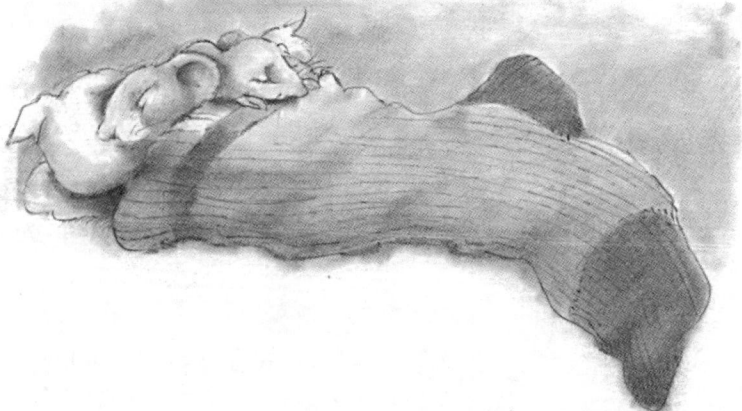

就这样，

灯塔中有了一个家庭。

故事从这里开始……

The

LIGHTHOUSE FAMILY

THE STORM

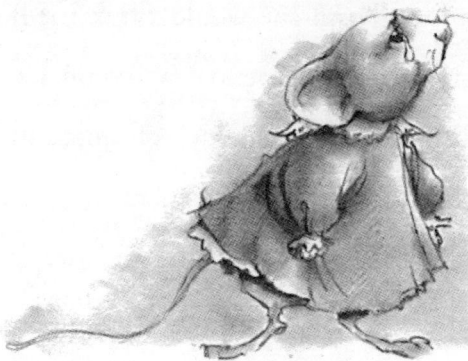

1. Pandora

In a lonely lighthouse, far from city and town, far from the comfort of friends, lived a kindhearted cat named Pandora.

She had been living at this lighthouse all alone for four long years, and it was beginning to wear. She found herself sighing long, deep, lonely sighs. She sat on the rocks overlooking the waves far too long. Sometimes her nose got a sunburn.

And at night, when she tried to read by the lantern light, her mind wandered and she would think for hours on her childhood when she had friends and company.

Why did Pandora accept this lonely lighthouse life?

Because a lighthouse had once saved her.

When Pandora was but a kitten, she and her father had gone sailing aboard a grand schooner, bound for a new country. Pandora's mother had stayed behind, with the baby, to join them later.

And while they were at sea, Pandora and her father were shaken from their beds one night by an awful twisting of the ship's great bow.

"Stay here, Pandora!" her father had commanded. "Stay here and wait until I come for you!"

They were in a terrible storm. The wind was howling, and the waves crashed hard upon them. Worse, a deep fog had spread itself all over the water, and it is fog that will bring a ship to its end. Fog that will blind a sailor's eyes until his ship has hit the jagged shore and torn itself to pieces.

Pandora's father knew this as he strained with the others to keep the ship's sails aloft and his daughter trembled in her bed. He knew what somber danger they were in.

But Pandora's father was a brave cat and he would not give up hope. He would hold tight to the riggings with the others until help, in whatever form, might come to them.

In time, the winds began to settle and the waves grew smaller. But the dense fog refused to lift.

The ship's captain was clearly worried. For he knew these waters they sailed in. He knew the long history of ships gone down.

And he carried little hope that help might come to them, that someone might lead them away from the deadly shore. For only a lighthouse might show them the way, and there had been no working light on these waters for a hundred years.

So it was with much bewilderment, and amazement, and overwhelming *joy* that he heard, first, the deep, clear sound of a foghorn, then saw before him a *light*. Yes, a light! And it was not the light of another ship or small boat. Only a very powerful lamp could make itself seen through a fog like this. Only the lamp of a lighthouse.

"Pull leeward!" cried the captain. "Away from the light!"

And everyone pulled hard on the riggings to make the ship turn, turn away from the dangerous shore.

The ship, and everyone on it, was saved.

Ever after, Pandora dreamed of lighthouses. Though she had not seen the beacon that had saved her, her father had, and he spoke of it often. He always wondered who had made the great light shine.

As she grew, Pandora herself came to think much on this. She went to the library and gathered books on lighthouses. She drew them in her sketch pad. She dreamed of them at night.

Then one morning she awoke and she knew what she must do. She must become a lighthouse keeper! She knew that this was her destiny.

It did not take Pandora long to find a lighthouse in need of keeping. It is a hard and lonely job, and few want it. Lighthouses are often built in unwelcoming places, atop sharp dangerous rocks. A winter storm can hold a keeper inside for weeks on end. And when she finally emerges, there is no one to talk to. They are all someplace else, living in little towns or big cities. They are not interested in desolation.

But Pandora was not afraid of this life, for her heart was so good and clear that fear would not creep inside it. The ships in those unpredictable waters carried fathers and mothers and children, and they needed guiding. She knew she could do it.

And Pandora had been doing it, faithfully, for four long years. She had seen many an awful storm come and go. She had stayed awake long winter nights, tending the great lamp, sounding the deep horn.

Pandora did not know how many lives she had saved. But she knew that she had saved some.

And now, weary with being alone for so long, Pandora was about to save one more.

2. Seabold

There are those who love the sea so deeply, they cannot bear to be away from it even for a day. A dog named Seabold was one of these. He was born to a sailor's life.

When Seabold was old enough to leave home and family, he built himself a boat—which he named *Adventure*—said good-bye to his parents and sisters, and off he went, in search of the life meant for him.

He was a fine sailor. He had a keen understanding

of the wind. He could read the stars. And he trusted his instincts.

For five years Seabold sailed the world's great oceans, and his instincts never failed him. He sailed safe and strong and free of worry.

But one day, this all changed.

Seabold had always known when a storm was coming. His nose told him so. And he had always found a sheltered cove or harbor in which to wait out the rough seas.

But this day, he had a cold. He had a cold and a stuffy nose, and his sense of smell was very bad. Added to this, he was tired. Seabold took a long, long nap in his bunk, and he did not notice the seabirds nervously circling in the air above him, agitated and calling to one another about the bad weather ahead.

The seabirds all wisely headed for land. But Seabold, adrift in his dreams, stayed out on open water.

Then the great storm hit.

Seabold was jolted from sleep by a sharp crack of lightning, a deep roar of thunder, and an enormous, crashing wave. As *Adventure* was flung here and there, up and down, Seabold clung to the little boat with all his strength, for there was nothing else he could do.

The sea, which had always been his friend, had turned against him. And for the first time in his sailor's life, Seabold was afraid.

He whispered into the wind, "Safe harbor, Let there be safe harbor."

Just as Seabold whispered these words, a magnificent light broke through the darkness, and the long, distant call of a horn sounded across the water.

"Safe harbor," Seabold repeated.

And this was the last thing brave Seabold said before he was lifted and rolled, over and over, into the deep black sea.

One might have thought the dog was forever lost.

But this is not the end of Seabold's story.

3. Comfort

When Seabold next awoke, he wondered if perhaps the storm had been just a dream.

For he found himself in a little wooden bed under a cheerful gingham quilt, and he was no longer *in* the sea, but looking out *at* the sea, through a small window by his side. A daisy stood in a jar on the windowsill.

Seabold tapped his head to be sure he wasn't dreaming. And just as he was about to try his legs on the shiny wooden floor, the door to his room opened and in stepped a cat.

She was smiling and had an apron tied around her waist. In her hands was a tray of tea and biscuits.

"Good morning," she said, setting the tray on the table beside the bed. "I hoped you might be awake. I am Pandora."

Still unsure whether he was dreaming, Seabold extended his paw to shake hers. "And I am Seabold," he said. "At least, I think I am."

Pandora smiled. "You have had a rather bad journey," she said.

"I thought it was my last," answered Seabold.

Pandora poured him a cup of tea, which smelled like flowers. Seabold drank it gratefully. "Thank you," he said. " May I have more? I'm so thirsty."

Pandora nodded and poured another cup. "All that salt water," she said.

"I don't know how I am alive," said Seabold.

" Nor do I," said Pandora. " When I found you on the shore three days ago, I was certain you were dead."

"I've been here three days?" exclaimed Seabold.

"Yes." Pandora smiled. "Sleeping like a baby."

Seabold shook his head. "I remember only going under," he said. " My boat—have you seen her?"

"Not yet," said Pandora. "But it may be farther down the shore. When you are able to walk, we shall go search."

"Able to walk?" said Seabold.

"Your leg," said Pandora.

Seabold drew back the gingham quilt. With surprise, he saw that his left leg was bandaged and splinted knee to foot. "Heavens," he said. "But, there is no pain. Shouldn't I be suffering?"

Pandora smiled with pleasure. "I am something of a doctor, I suppose," she said. "I have studied plants and learned those that heal. I wrapped your leg in plantain leaves to relieve the swelling. And the splint will prevent further injury."

"Amazing!" said Seabold.

Pandora blushed with pride.

"And are you alone here?" asked Seabold, sipping his tea. Pandora had poured herself a cup.

"Yes, all alone," she said. "Although I do have friends who stop by this island once in a while. In a *very* long while, I should say. They are seasonal."

"Seasonal?" said Seabold.

"They migrate," said Pandora. "So I see them only in spring and fall, as they make their way north or south. There is Atoll, the gray whale . . . "

"You know a whale personally?" asked Seabold.

"Oh yes," said Pandora. "Whales are very sociable once you break the ice. Ask them about their children and they'll go on forever."

"There is also Henry, the tern," she continued. "He's usually so pressed for time, he doesn't even land. He simply flutters above my head and asks after my health, my garden, and so forth. Then he's off. He flies six thousand miles every year."

"Really?" said Seabold.

"Yes," said Pandora. "He's quite fit."

"But you are alone nearly always?" asked Seabold.

"Nearly always," said Pandora.

Seabold shook his head. "I never thought I would meet someone else like me," he said.

"Like you?" asked Pandora.

"One who loves the solitary life," said Seabold. "I am nearly always at sea, nearly always alone. Like you."

Pandora smiled and thought a moment. "I am not sure I *love* the solitary life," she said finally. "I simply live it."

"And why?" asked Seabold.

"To save lives," said Pandora. "Like yours."

And she poured him another cup of tea.

4. Companions

Everything at the lighthouse was different after Seabold's arrival.

Mornings when Pandora awoke, she remembered she had someone else to *talk* to. She leaped from bed and prepared a big breakfast of hot wheat cereal with cream, and apple scones, and bowls of huckleberries. She carried the tray to Seabold's room, and there they chatted all morning. Pandora's garden grew very weedy.

Then, once Seabold was able to hobble about on his leg with the help of a walking stick, their talks moved outside. Sitting on large rocks by the water, Pandora and Seabold told each other stories of their lives and things they had read or seen and what they liked most in this world or least.

Seabold told of his father, who feared the water and would not set foot in a boat.

Pandora told of her younger sister, who sewed wedding

gowns for queens.

They both had read fairy tales as children and agreed that the bad animals were more interesting than the good ones.

And what did they like best in the world?

The northern lights, said Seabold.

Penguins, said Pandora.

Least, they both agreed, were shipwrecks.

It was summer, and Pandora's lighthouse responsibilities were small. For two months—July and August—there was little rain and hardly any fog. Ships traveled safely, and Pandora got a rest.

Well, somewhat. She still had to tend to preparing for the hard winter ahead. She knew she must grow and harvest vegetables, grind corn and wheat for bread, collect and cut driftwood for the fire. A supply boat had already delivered the year's kerosene for the lighthouse. All depended on Pandora being ready.

While Pandora gardened in the day, Seabold worked— as best he could, given his leg—on rebuilding his boat. He had indeed found it—at least, most of it—farther down the shore, and though his heart broke to see it so battered, he believed he could save it.

As Pandora gardened, she watched Seabold off in the distance tending to his boat, and she felt a small emptiness in her heart. The emptiness one feels watching a dear friend prepare to go away.

Evenings, the two made a picnic on the hill of daises leading to the shore and watched the sun go down, painting the world pink and red.

The next day, it all began again.

Seabold was very curious about the workings of the lighthouse, but his leg would not permit him to climb the four steep flights of stairs, then the ladder up into the lantern room to reach the great glass lamp. With no storms and no need for the saving lamp, Seabold sometimes forgot there was any lighthouse at all.

But one day in early September, just as the geese and the mallards and the warblers were beginning to fly overhead on their long journeys south, Seabold was awakened to exactly what that enormous lighthouse was meant to do.

And to just who was prepared to do it.

5. The Storm

It was much too early in the season, Pandora thought, for a storm to blow in. It was the season for fog, yes, but for serious ocean storms . . . those were due much later in the fall.

Then why, she wondered one afternoon in early September as she gathered tomatoes off the vines, was the sky growing so black? Why was the air so cold? Why were gulls circling higher and higher, their cries growing more and more frantic?

Because a sky above a sea loves unpredictability. It loves to surprise.

This day, it clearly intended to.

Seabold and Pandora battened down his boat, secured the shutters over the cottage windows, and set to building a fire in the kitchen stove.

"How cold it is!" said Seabold. "And yesterday was so warm."

"The sea is bringing us a different air," said Pandora. "One, I believe, full of danger. I must go up to the lantern room and attend to the light."

Seabold looked at his still-splinted leg in frustration. "I *have* to get up there to help you," he said.

"No, no," said Pandora. "Injury to your leg now will set you back a month of healing. Just keep the fire going while I work."

And while Seabold fed the fire in the kitchen and kept a pot of tea hot and ready for them both, Pandora climbed up to the lantern room. She trimmed the great lamp's wicks and lit them. She checked the kerosene vessel. She cleaned the storm panes. Then she climbed down to the watch room.

Just around suppertime, an enormous fog bank began rolling in. High in her tower, Pandora watched it spread toward land like creeping cotton, and she began to ring the bells and sound the horn that would guide smaller boats to shore, giving them escape from the storm that was surely about to hit.

Down in the kitchen, Seabold fretted. He listened to

the bells and the horn. *I could be doing that*, he thought. *I could be helping.* But he had to sit there by the fire and wait. He was miserable.

Over the next few hours the wind built to an astonishing speed, and its gusts rocked the tower Pandora worked in. She was undaunted. It was nightfall now, and this was a very bad storm for any ship at sea. Fog, lightning, lashing rain, hard wind—all could lead a ship onto the rocks and sink her.

Pandora worked in the watch room, sounding the horn again and again. Above her the great light kept its strong beam out upon the water. She was cold—she'd had no time to dress warmly or carry wood to the watch room stove. But she could not stop to remedy this. It was a terrible storm, and she knew what a terrible storm could do.

In the kitchen, Seabold sat at the window and watched the great light shine and listened to the warning horn. One hour, two hours, three hours, four hours . . . How did Pandora do it? Where did she find the strength? He was only tending the kitchen fire and already he was tired.

Finally, sleep got the better of him. The storm raged

on, without his witness.

Bright sun shining into the kitchen woke Seabold the next morning. He had lain beside the stove all night. And where was Pandora? He looked out the window.

And there she was, far out near the edge of a cliff, a shawl about her shoulders and her paw in the air, waving.

Off in the water, barely a spot on the horizon, was a sailing ship. At rest. Safe.

She saved them, thought Seabold.

He watched his friend in wonder.

6. Purpose

Seabold had planned to sail away by October's end, before the hard winter storms began, before the ice and wind. He was a sailing dog, the sea was his home. He knew this and Pandora knew this, and they both were prepared for the sorrowful good-bye.

But destiny had other plans.

Seabold's boat did not come together as quickly as he'd hoped. Small essential pieces were still missing and had to be made by hand. This would take time. It would take a long spring and a long summer and perhaps an entire fall as well.

Seabold was resourceful. But he could not invent time.

And his leg was very slow in healing. It had been a bad break, and in spite of Pandora's marvelous herbs and capable splinting, the leg was weak. Seabold still walked with the aid of a stick.

Thus, as the wind grew crisper and harder and the sky filled with birds going away, Seabold stood at the edge of the shore and realized that this winter he would not sail.

He thought that he would be despondent. He thought that he would be depressed.

But he wasn't.

Something had happened to him as he watched the noble efforts of Pandora save others, to serve a purpose higher than herself.

Seabold had been inspired. And he thought that perhaps, at least for one winter, he might also make his life count for something.

So he asked if he might stay on till spring.

And, of course, she said yes. It had been her secret wish.

Together they gathered wood for winter fires and food for winter sustenance. And Seabold was finally able to climb all the way up to the great lamp. He was astonished, seeing it for the first time. "It is magnificent!" he said to Pandora. "It is a wonder!"

Seabold and Pandora polished the brass fittings of the great lamp. They disassembled and cleaned the lanterns. They replaced worn wicks. Being in the lantern room thrilled Seabold as much as even the finest sailing day. (Though he would not admit this to Pandora.)

And in the evenings, as Pandora knit warm caps and mittens and socks for them both, and as Seabold fashioned tools from driftwood, they talked.

"I am astonished," said Seabold one night, "that I am

not land-sick by this time. I have never before been able to stay ashore so long without feeling my legs turn to stone."

Pandora smiled and shifted the cap she was knitting for him. "I hope you will not be too unhappy with this lonely lighthouse life," she said.

"Oh no," said Seabold. "I am quite looking forward to it. I am hoping to be useful."

"And you shall be," said Pandora.

"I hope we will meet new friends," said Seabold, "as the days go by. Even if they are only passing through. I should like very much to know a whale."

"The sea is full of surprises," said Pandora. "New friends among them."

She looked at Seabold with a twinkle. "I should know," she said.

"In spring," said Seabold, "before I finish the work on *Adventure*, I will build a gazebo at the top of the daisy-hill. And from there we may sit and see what comes our way."

"Oh," answered Pandora, "many wonderful things. There shall be many wonderful things."

She added another log to the fire.

They both felt wonderfully warm.

7. The Rescue

The winter was long indeed. Seabold had always spent the colder months sailing in sunny climes. He had nearly forgotten what it was to have frosty toes.

In Pandora's lighthouse, from November to March, he was reminded every single day.

In the worst of the cold days, the entire island was covered with ice. The spray from the sea washed over every piece of ground, every bush, every rock, and it froze solid. Pandora and Seabold did not venture out for weeks at a time.

It was just as well, for the storms were furious. Seabold and Pandora were needed day and night at the lamp. Day and night they tended the mantle and shone their beacon of warning across the water.

If they saved lives, they did not know whose, or when. And if anyone out in the gray waters sent them a prayer of thanks, they did not know it. They did not hear it.

Still, when finally the exhausted cat and dog laid their heads down to a brief sleep, they slept well, and with contented hearts.

Spring was never quite sure when She was arriving. One day the sky would be a clear, brilliant blue and the sun would shine its head on the small white crocuses around Pandora's door. Then the next day a wind would roar in like a hurricane and rain would bend all the new flowers to the ground and set everything a-shiver.

Seabold made several false starts on his gazebo before the sun finally came out and stayed out long enough for a soul to get some work done.

And it was while he was hammering on the gazebo atop the daisy-hill that Seabold saw what looked to be a floating crate far out upon the water. And above it what looked to be a small flag.

Seabold did not yet know it, but something wonderful was about to happen to Pandora's lonely lighthouse.

"Pandora!" Seabold cried. "Come and look!"

From behind the cottage, Pandora emerged with an armload of firewood. She set the wood by the door and hurried to the top of the hill.

"Look," said Seabold. He pointed toward the water where the crate floated. He could see no signs of life.

"It has some sort of flag," he told Pandora. "Do you think it is empty?"

Pandora gazed out across the water, and her face grew very serious. "I have a feeling," she said soberly. "I believe there is life out there."

Seabold frowned. "Well, if life *is* out there," he answered, "it is not at all well, you may be certain of that. For that crate is surely drifting at the mercy of the sea."

Pandora nodded. "I know," she said.

Seabold took a deep breath and straightened his shoulders. "I shall just have to go fetch it to shore," he said.

Pandora looked at him. "And how will you do that?" she asked.

"I think I can manage my boat out that far," said Seabold. "She's torn, but I think she will float."

"You *think*?" repeated Pandora.

"We can stand here and watch that small flag float away and goodness-knows-what tragedy with it," said Seabold. " Or I can make *Adventure* float."

Pandora sighed deeply, but with resolve. "Make her float," she said. " And be quick."

Seabold ran toward the shore.

8. Children

It did not take long for the brave dog to get his tattered boat upon the water, or to reach the drifting crate. He was, after all, still a very fine sailor.

"Hello!" he called as he steered nearer. He could see that the flag was actually a small red shirt on a stick.

"Anyone there?"

Silence.

Gravely, he pulled his boat alongside, expecting the worst.

He peered inside. "My *goodness*," he said.

For there, peering back at him, were three very young mice. One, in fact, was a baby. All three were piled close together.

"Are you injured?" asked Seabold.

One of the mice, the boy, opened his mouth to speak, but no sound came out. The girl-mouse simply stared. The baby was asleep.

"Are you lost?" asked Seabold.

The boy-mouse and the girl-mouse nodded vigorously.

Seabold extended his paw. "You must come with me, children," he said. "For your situation is very bad."

Nodding her head in agreement, the girl-mouse reached out for his paw. He lifted her aboard. Then the boy-mouse gently handed him the baby. She was so small and light that Seabold barely breathed as he carefully placed her in the lap of the older mouse.

101

"Is the baby your sister?" he asked the girl-mouse.

Yes, she nodded.

Finally the boy-mouse was on board, still unable to speak.

Seabold quickly turned back toward shore. "Thirst has gotten the better of you," he said. "We must get you to fresh water and fast."

When Seabold carried all three to shore, in his knitted cap, Pandora was there, waiting with a blanket and—blessedly—a bowl of water. The children drank and drank. The girl-mouse made a cup of her hand for the baby.

When they had finished drinking, the boy-mouse said, quite clearly and solemnly, "Thank you."

Seabold and Pandora smiled. For both were, deep down inside themselves, quite delighted. *Children!*

They took the little ones into the cottage and gave them supper.

The next morning the boy-mouse and girl-mouse joined Pandora and Seabold at breakfast. The evening before they had introduced themselves as Whistler and Lila, brother and sister. The baby they had introduced as

Tiny.

"Yes indeed, she is," Pandora had replied.

"No, no," Lila had said. "Tiny is her proper name."

"Well," Pandora had replied with a smile. "Perfect."

And now, in early morning, sitting before a warm breakfast in a warm kitchen, Whistler and Lila, still tired, still hungry, were, more than anything, *worried.*

"Tiny is still sleeping," Lila told Pandora and Seabold. "She never sleeps so long."

"And she hardly stirred all night," said Whistler. "She always stirs about and gurgles and bubbles. But she is so quiet."

Pandora rose immediately to see.

She lifted the sleeping baby from the knitted sock on the chair.

"This small one has a fever," Pandora said in deep concern. "I believe she is quite ill."

Lila gazed at Pandora, and one large tear began to roll down the small mouse's face.

Whistler looked at Seabold in distress.

"Seabold," said Pandora, "you will need to look after

this baby while I go out into the woods. I must find a special branch of willow, and it may take me some time."

Seabold nodded and reached out. Pandora gently laid the infant in his big paw.

"Keep her cool," said Pandora. "But not cold. A nice, low breeze from the window will help. And she needs much water. See if she will drink."

Pandora looked kindly at Whistler and Lila. "You have done very well, caring for this small child. She is ill from weather and sea, not from want of attention or love."

Another tear dropped down Lila's face.

"I shall hurry," Pandora said as, taking her woolen shawl, she stepped out the door.

9. Family

While Pandora went out searching the woods, Seabold sat Lila and Whistler down to a checkerboard he had made, to take their minds off their fears.

"I will look after Tiny," he told them gently. "And you may try out my new game board."

"Clams!" Lila said in surprise, picking up a game piece.

"And starfish," said Whistler, picking up another.

Seabold smiled. "They're much more interesting than little round circles. I carved them myself."

"Amazing," said Whistler, turning the starfish in his hand. "I should like to try carving sometime."

"Anytime you like," said Seabold. "Except just now, of course. This little one needs me."

He left Whistler and Lila to their game and carried the infant-mouse to a chair beside the kitchen Window. Settling her in one paw, with a thimbleful of water nearby, he went about his duties.

Keep her cool, Pandora had told him. Give her water.

And these things Seabold did do.

But he did something more.

There, beside Pandora's gingham-curtained window, in view of the cherry trees budding and the daffodils in bloom, Seabold transformed.

Exactly how, he could not say. But rocking the infant carefully in his paw, listening to the quiet and gentle voices of Whisder and Lila in the next room, hearing the fire crackle and smelling the good brown smell of bread in the stove, Seabold realized that he was happy. Happier than he had ever been. Happier than any solitary evening at sea had ever made him.

He sat by the window, cooed to the tiny baby, and smiled.

And after that day, *everything* was changed.

Tiny was made better by the willow bark. Lila planted sunflower seeds. And Pandora and Seabold found themselves with a kind of *household*. Some days Pandora looked about at all the dwellers at her lighthouse and she marveled. *How had it all happened?*

It had happened for many reasons. It happened because a noble young cat wished to save lives. Because a brave dog wished to sail. And because three small children wished for a family.

Before Seabold found them at sea, Whistler, Lila, and Tiny had lived in an orphanage far from Pandora's lighthouse. But they were to be separated and sent off to different places. "We will *never* be separated," Whistler had told Lila. And in the dark of night, with Tiny bundled onto Lila's back, they had escaped.

Finding the docks of the city, and all the great schooners ready to set sail, they had hidden aboard one of them, bound for they knew not where.

But out at sea, in a hurricane wind, the schooner had rolled itself under and the three poor young mice with it.

Perhaps their parents in heaven were watching over them. For Whistler managed to grab hold of an empty crate and pull his sisters in.

They floated, hungry and thirsty, for what seemed time unending, until Seabold found them.

And now here they were, carving otters, planting

sunflowers.

Seabold grew quite attached to Tiny. He put her in the soft roll of his knitted cap and she went everywhere with him, seeing all that he saw.

In evening, when Pandora set supper on the table, Seabold placed Tiny in a little eggcup by his plate and patted her fondly on the head as they ate.

And when, with full stomachs and happy hearts, the children were put to bed, Seabold and Pandora had their last cup of tea in the sitting room and reminisced.

"Do you remember when we saw the double rainbow?"

"Do you remember when the moon passed across the sun?"

"And the wind blew the pelican the wrong way?"

They would smile together in memory and sip their tea.

And, as always, before the night was ended, Seabold would ask, "And do you remember when I found the children?"

Pandora would nod her head.

"They are quite wonderful," Seabold would say.

"Yes," Pandora would answer.

"Thank goodness we found them," both would say in unison.

And with a happy good night, Seabold would go to his warm bed and Pandora would go to hers. In the kitchen, near the fire, tucked into the knitted sock Pandora had made just for them, the three mouse-children would sleep soundly, dreaming their blue sea dreams.

The lighthouse had a family.

The Beginning

图书在版编目（CIP）数据

灯塔之家. 暴风雨中的灯塔 ／（美）辛西娅·劳伦特
著；（美）普莱斯顿·马克丹尼斯绘；栾述蓉译. —— 南
昌：二十一世纪出版社集团，2023.4
ISBN 978-7-5568-6915-2

I.①灯… II.①辛… ②普… ③栾… III.①儿童故
事—图画故事—美国—现代 IV.①I712.85

中国版本图书馆CIP数据核字 (2022) 第195960号

THE LIGHTHOUSE FAMILY: THE STORM
Simplified Chinese translation copyright © 2023 by TB Publishing Limited
Original English language edition:
Text copyright © 2002 by Cynthia Rylant
Illustrations copyright © 2002 by Preston McDaniels
Published by arrangement with Beach Lane Books,
an imprint of Simon & Schuster Children's Publishing Division.
All rights reserved.

版权合同登记号：14-2022-0064

灯塔之家 暴风雨中的灯塔
DENGTA ZHI JIA　BAOFENGYU ZHONG DE DENGTA
[美]辛西娅·劳伦特／著　[美]普莱斯顿·马克丹尼斯／绘　栾述蓉／译

出 版 人	刘凯军	
项目策划	奇想国童书	
责任编辑	刘晨露子	
特约编辑	郑应湘　孙金蕾	
装帧设计	田丽丹	
出版发行	二十一世纪出版社集团	
	（江西省南昌市子安路75号 330025）	
网　　址	www.21cccc.com	
经　　销	全国新华书店	
印　　刷	固安兰星球彩色印刷有限公司	
版　　次	2023年4月第1版	
印　　次	2023年4月第1次印刷	
开　　本	710 mm×1000 mm 1/16	
印　　张	7.25	
字　　数	32千字	
书　　号	ISBN 978-7-5568-6915-2	
定　　价	198.00元（全8册）	

赣版权登字-04-2022-662　　　　版权所有，侵权必究
购买本社图书，如有问题请联系我们：扫描封底二维码进入官方服务号。
服务电话：010-64049180（工作时间可拨打）；服务邮箱：qixiangguo@tbpmedia.com。

传世经典桥梁书

灯塔之家

2

小鲸鱼塞巴斯汀

[美] **辛西娅·劳伦特** 著

[美] **普莱斯顿·马克丹尼斯** 绘 **栾述蓉** 译

21 二十一世纪出版社集团
21st Century Publishing Group

献给 D. P. 和他船上的小狗。

——辛西娅·劳伦特

献给我的妻子，伴着我的爱。

——普莱斯顿·马克丹尼斯

项目策划　奇想国童书
责任编辑　刘晨露子
特约编辑　郑应湘　孙金蕾
装帧设计　田丽丹

目 录

1. 家

在一座孤零零伫立着的灯塔中，住着一个动物家庭。他们，和孤零零的灯塔正相反，一点儿也不孤独。

他们的灯塔坐落在海边一座岩石嶙峋的悬崖顶上，就那么形单影只的，看上去仿佛是世界上最荒凉、最空旷的存在。

但是一旦你靠近灯塔，走到近前，你的感受会大为改观。

灯塔旁边有一座小屋，小屋窗台的花箱中种着蓝色的牵牛花。

院子里，向日葵沿着可爱的尖桩篱笆排成一排，菜园里生长着西红柿和胡萝卜。

灯塔基座边，停着一辆手工制作的木头推车，车里堆满了玩具。这些玩具也是手工制作的：有走路摇摇摆摆的企鹅，有大嘴一张一合的鹈鹕，还有腿会活动并发出咔嚓咔嚓响声的螃蟹。

如果再靠近灯塔看守人小屋的大门一些，就能闻到随风飘出的，刚出炉的面包或浆果布丁的香味。

透过敞开的大门朝里面望去，就会看到世界上最幸福的一家。

他们是：猫咪潘朵拉、大狗海勇，还有三个老鼠孩子——哨子、莉拉和他们年幼的妹妹小不点儿。

他们一起住在这里还不到一年，却已经把这里变成了一个温暖的家。

在这个特别的夏日，哨子和莉拉准备沿着海滩来一场"捡贝壳之旅"。哨子有一个计划。

"我们要去捡一些碎蛤蜊壳。"当潘朵拉再一次为他倒满一杯热气腾腾的姜茶时，哨子对她说道，"我打算做一个鸟巢，用贝壳来装饰它，然后放在花园的一根柱子上。"

"好主意。"潘朵拉赞叹道,"那样会有大海的感觉,小鸟肯定喜欢。"

"这是我想出来的。"哨子的妹妹莉拉插嘴道。

"是的。"哨子说,"是莉拉的主意,我只不过负责实施。"

"好极了!"潘朵拉说。

"我可以帮着捡贝壳。"莉拉说,"回来以后,我会继续缝我给娃娃做的围裙。"

莉拉说着,举起一个小小的木制老鼠娃娃。娃娃有着一双画上去的大眼睛,戴着一顶蓝色小软帽,穿着一条样式简单的印花裙子,样子跟莉拉有点儿像。

"我喜欢夏天,你们也是,对吧?"潘朵拉一边切了一片褐色的面包给哨子,一边愉快地问道。

"没错。"莉拉回答。哨子则用力地点点头。

"还有,我喜欢这里的夏天胜过世界上任何其他地方的。"莉拉说道。

莉拉的话让潘朵拉感到心里暖洋洋的。有

时候，潘朵拉都不敢相信自己能如此幸运，拥有这样一个小家庭。起初，她独自住在灯塔里。在漫长的四年中，她烤出来的面包只能自己一个人吃，沏好的茶也只能自己一个人喝，在孤立无援的情况下守护着这盏重要的灯，让它长明不灭。

而那一天，当那只名叫海勇的狗和他残破的船被冲上岸来，一切从此改变。海勇因为腿伤还没有愈合留了下来。从秋到冬，再到第二年春天，他一直跟潘朵拉住在一起。在修复他心爱的小船时，海勇还确信自己会重返大海，在宽广的海天之间航行。

然而，有一天，他们发现了躲在木板箱里，漂浮在海上，迷失了方向的孩子们——孤儿们。潘朵拉和海勇收留了他们。他们精心照顾和呵护这些小孩子，给他们做饭，晚上给他们掖好被角，早晨迎接他们起床。

随着时间的流逝，一些重要的变化发生了：他们的心被融化了。三只小老鼠把这间小屋，

还有孤独的灯塔变成了真正的家——一个有故事要讲、有面包要烤、有花儿要生长、有游戏要去玩的真正的家。

原以为自己会孤独一生的海勇，发觉自己已经无法离开——因为现在他是有家人的大狗了，他被这个家所需要。

这个夏天的清晨，在哨子和莉拉吃完面包，喝完茶之后，海勇带着小不点儿到环礁上去看巨型太阳海星。这是一种相当神奇的生物：他们奇大无比，有整整二十条腿——没错，海勇数过。他们在浅水区或者潮湿、冰冷的礁石上休息，沉浸在属于他们自己的思绪中。小不点儿坐在海勇软帽的卷边上看着海星们，那是她最喜欢待着的位置，一边看，一边高兴得咯咯直笑。

海勇满脸微笑。他非常疼爱小不点儿。

回小屋的路上，他们遇见了哨子和莉拉。两个孩子用小爪子拎着编织袋，正要去海边。

"多么美好的早晨，孩子们！"海勇说，"你们今天打算做些什么？"

兄妹俩跟海勇说了自己的计划。

"好极了！"海勇回答说，"可惜我得清洁灯塔的灯室，不然我会跟你们一起去。祝你们玩得开心。还有，"他补充说，"敏锐地发现冒险的机会！"

不管孩子们去什么地方，海勇总会这样对他们说。难怪他给自己心爱的小船取名叫作"探险号"。

只是，灯塔中的大多数日子都是简单而宁静的，幸福快乐却平淡无奇。

然而，今天，将是个幸运日。

今天将会有一场冒险。

2. 鲸　鱼

哨 子和莉拉正沿着布满礁石的岸边高高兴兴地捡拾贝壳，忽然，远处的水域传来一声拖着长音的、悲伤的哭喊。

"那是什么声音？"莉拉停下来，朝海面望去。

她和哨子静静地站在那里，侧耳聆听。

声音又一次响起。他们从没听到过如此悲哀和孤独的哭声。

哨子从地上捡起一根长棍子。莉拉也学着这样做。

"谁在那里？"哨子尽力抬高嗓门儿喊（只不过一只小老鼠的嗓门儿高不到哪里去）。

"谁啊？"莉拉跟着喊道。

对所有人来说，最最幸运、最最好运、最

最神奇的是——那个哭哭啼啼的家伙有一双灵敏的耳朵。

水里冒出来一个闪亮的白脑瓜。

"是我！"那个家伙说完，又开始哭起来。

"天哪！"莉拉惊呼道，"是个鲸鱼宝宝。"

她说得没错。确切地说，是头小白鲸。哦，他哭得可真伤心。

"我们马上过去。你待在那里别动。"哨子喊道。

紧接着，两个孩子跑向他们的小船（这是海勇给他们造的），驾船朝小白鲸划去。

等他们抵达小白鲸身边时，他已经筋疲力尽，甚至没有力气再哭喊了，只是用惊慌、害怕的眼神看着他们。

"我找不到妈妈了。"他啜泣着说。

"哦，小可怜！"莉拉难过地说道。身为一名孤儿，莉拉对于那些失去妈妈的孩子有着强烈的共情能力。

"你在哪里跟她失散的？"哨子问道。

小白鲸看上去好像又要哭了，不过他还是忍住了。

"我也不知道。"小白鲸说，"我们正在游泳呢，来了一大群座头鲸，他们的数量非常多。然后，我看见一头小座头鲸，就想跟他一起玩，于是跟着他游啊游，然后……然后……"

小白鲸呜咽着。

"然后那些座头鲸突然就游走了，只剩下我自个儿。"

"哦，可怜的宝贝。"莉拉说道。

小白鲸一声不吭地浮在水面上，看上去非常凄惨。两只小老鼠满怀同情地看着他。

突然，哨子说道："我们会帮你找到妈妈的。"

莉拉吃惊地看着他。

小白鲸的眼睛亮了起来。

"真的吗？"小白鲸问道，"你们能找到她？"

"千真万确。我们是寻找走失妈妈的专家。"为了安慰小白鲸，哨子撒了个谎。

莉拉看着哨子，更加吃惊了。

"我想请你……"哨子对小白鲸说，"对啦，你叫什么名字？"

"塞巴斯汀。"小白鲸回答。哨子也介绍了自己和莉拉。

"很高兴认识你们。"彬彬有礼的、眼含泪水的小白鲸说道。

"我想请你这么做，"哨子接着刚才的话说道，"你看到那边的环礁了吗？"

小白鲸点点头。

"我想请你到那边休息一下。"哨子说，"那里很舒服，水很暖和，有时候还会有一只水獭过来，讲个有趣的故事。"

小白鲸再次点了点头。

"好的。"他回答说。

"你妈妈叫什么？"哨子问道。

"妈妈。"小白鲸回答。

"不对，不对。"莉拉说，"他问的是她的名字。"

"哦，"小白鲸回答说，"大家都叫她蜜糖。"

"蜜糖。"莉拉重复了一遍，"这名字真好听！"

"她是个好妈妈！"小白鲸说道。

"现在你去环礁那里等我们好吗？"哨子说。

"嗯，好的。"小白鲸回答说，"现在我正好有点儿困。"

"我想也是。"莉拉说。

"待会儿见。"哨子说，"别担心。"

他们看着小白鲸朝环礁方向游去。莉拉轻声问哨子："我们怎么才能找到鲸鱼妈妈呢？"

哨子轻声回答道："我不知道。"

然后，他坚定地直视着莉拉的眼睛。

"但我们必须这样做！"哨子说。

3. 援 助

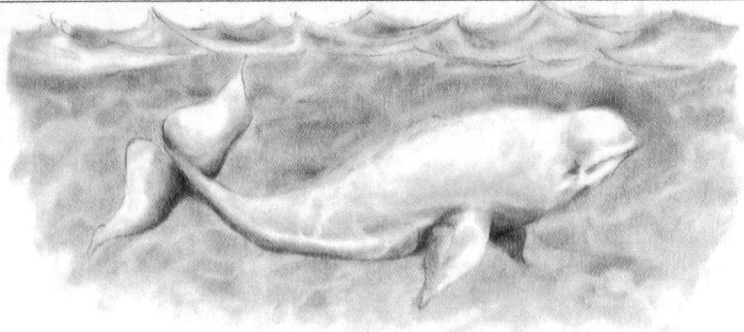

当然啦，莉拉和哨子要做的第一件事，就是去找潘朵拉。海勇擅长制作玩具和修补船只，但遇到问题，还是要靠潘朵拉想出解决方案。

潘朵拉和孩子们站在菜园里，在听完孩子们的讲述之后，她思考了一小会儿。

然后她说："我想到一个办法。"

孩子们早就料到她会有办法。

虽然在过去的很多年里，潘朵拉一直独自生活在灯塔中，但是在这期间，她结识了一些朋友。

他们跟驻守灯塔的潘朵拉截然不同，总是来去匆忙。尽管如此，她仍然记住了一些朋友的名字，有时甚至会请这些海洋邻居帮忙。

有一个曾经帮助过她的邻居是只上了年纪、脾气古怪的鸬鹚，名叫哈克。

　　哈克不喜欢别人。他习惯了孤独，大部分时间都独自待在小岛南边的一个旧木桩上，晾晒他的翅膀。他已经很老了，身上总是湿漉漉的。他最喜欢做的就是连续几个小时地站在那里，伸展开翅膀，感受微风的轻拂。

　　尽管哈克不喜欢任何人，但无论对谁他都会伸出援手。

　　有一次，潘朵拉陷进一处茂密的黑莓树丛中，被刺缠住了。哈克恰巧飞过，停下来帮她从灌木丛中挣脱了出来。自始至终，他一直叽叽咕咕地抱怨潘朵拉把自己搞得"乱七八糟"，并且"浑身是刺"。

　　但不管怎么说，他帮了她的忙，而且看上

去很乐意这么做。

这之后，哈克告诉潘朵拉说，下次再需要他帮忙的话，不管什么时候，只要把灯朝他栖息的那根旧木桩的方向快速闪五下，他就会过来。

自那以后，潘朵拉只找过哈克一次，为的是向他打听去一座樱桃园的路。潘朵拉听说过那个樱桃园，但不知道怎么走。她要去为一只海鹦鹉配制药茶——那只海鹦鹉路过此地时病倒了。潘朵拉知道哈克脾气不好，所以除非确有需要，她不会轻易打扰他。

然而今天，她能想到的最佳求助人选就是哈克。哈克能帮忙找到鲸鱼妈妈。

潘朵拉找到海勇，说明了情况。海勇刚刚把小不点儿放下，让她打个盹儿。

"我去闪灯。"海勇说，"你留在院子里等着哈克。"

海勇爬上四段陡峭的楼梯，然后顺着梯子进入灯室。

他点燃了所有的灯芯，把灯转到西南方向，然后让灯光快速闪动了五下。

不过几分钟，哈克就降落在菜园里。潘朵拉和孩子们正在那里等着他。

"天哪！"哈克抱怨道，"今天风可不小。"

他抖了抖羽毛，清了清喉咙，咳出些……东西，没人能断定那是些什么东西。

莉拉和哨子不觉睁大了眼睛，互相看了看。

潘朵拉却只是冲哈克友好地笑了笑。

"谢谢你过来，哈克。"她说，"我们遇到了一件麻烦事，需要你帮忙。"

"废话少说。"哈克嘟囔道。

潘朵拉向他讲述了事情经过，最后问道："哈克，你能不能飞到海上去寻找那位走失的妈妈？你有本事飞得又快又远。"

"而且，"潘朵拉又巧妙地补充道，"你比任何人都了解这片水域。"

哈克仍然皱着眉头，不过潘朵拉能从他的眼神中看出，她的话令他开心，在他那抱怨个不停的外表下，内心渴望的，实际是他人的赞赏。

他飞快地点了一下头。

"没问题。她叫什么名字？"他问道。

"蜜糖。"哨子和莉拉异口同声地说道。

"你们刚才说她是头白鲸？"

两个孩子点了点头。

"这样的话就容易多了。她雪白的肤色应该跟阳光一样耀眼。"哈克说。

哨子清了清嗓子，向前迈了一步。

"哈克先生，"哨子神情严肃地请求道，"我们能跟你一起去吗，我和莉拉？"

莉拉吃惊地张大了嘴。潘朵拉也是同样的表情。

哈克开始了一连串的动作：先是一阵猛烈的咳嗽，然后是呼呼喘气，接着又吐了一些东西。最后，他紧盯着哨子的眼睛。

"嗯，我觉得没什么不可以。"哈克说。

然后哈克看向潘朵拉。

"只要你同意就行，潘朵拉。"哈克补充道，"也许三双眼睛找起来更快。"

潘朵拉有点儿担心地看着哨子和莉拉。

"要是你们跟哈克一起去的话，一定要牢牢抓紧他。"她说。

孩子们保证说他们会的。

"还有，你们必须在天黑之前回来。"潘朵拉说。

孩子们又一次向她保证。

潘朵拉笑了。她对孩子们充满信心。

随后，孩子们坐在哈克背上，向广阔蔚蓝的大海飞去。

4. 陪 伴

看着哈克和孩子们消失在远处的天空后，潘朵拉转身朝灯塔走去。她爬上台阶，走进塔里，看见海勇在里面。

大狗海勇的脸紧紧地贴在窗玻璃上。

"我刚才看见哨子和莉拉飞过去了，我没看花眼吧？"他问道。

"你没看错。他们要帮哈克一起寻找白鲸妈妈。"潘朵拉回答说。

海勇笑了。

"对这两个孩子来说，这真是一场冒险。"海勇发自内心地喜爱冒险。

"我告诉哈克他必须在天黑之前把孩子们送回家。"潘朵拉说。

"当然了。"海勇回应着，又接着问道，"那个宝宝怎么样了？"

"她在小屋里睡觉。"潘朵拉说。

"不，不，"海勇说，"我指的是另一个宝宝。"

"哦，"潘朵拉笑了，"那个宝宝仍然在环礁那里休息，等着他妈妈。"

"嗯，"海勇说，"我猜他一定觉得有点儿孤独。"

"是的。"潘朵拉说。

"还有点儿害怕。"海勇说。

"没错。"

"我觉得我应该去陪陪他。"海勇说着朝楼下走去。

"你说他叫什么名字来着？"他走到一半，回头喊道。

"塞巴斯汀！"潘朵拉回答道。她听着海勇走下楼梯，走出大门，欣慰地笑了——为自己能拥有如此善良的一位朋友而感到喜悦。

潘朵拉回到小屋，照看小不点儿，并且炖了一些肉。

海勇来到环礁时，小白鲸正在水里来回兜着圈子。

"你好，塞巴斯汀！"海勇喊道。

小白鲸停了下来，脑袋伸出水面四下张望。

"您好！您是哪位？"他用忧伤的声音小声问道。

海勇微笑着向他示意。

"我叫海勇。"海勇说道，"以前是个水手，现在是灯塔和三只小老鼠的守护者。"

"你说的是莉拉和哨子。"塞巴斯汀兴奋地回应道。

"还有他们的妹妹，小不点儿。"海勇说，"对了，莉拉和哨子已经出发去找你妈妈了。"

"太好了，我太想她了。"塞巴斯汀说。

小白鲸看上去随时会哭出来。海勇知道自己必须做点儿什么。

"你喜欢变戏法吗？"他问小白鲸。

"喜欢。"小白鲸眼睛一亮。

"我给你变一个。"海勇说着拿了个倒立。

小白鲸高兴地用尾巴拍打着水面。

"真好玩儿！"他对海勇说。

"你会什么戏法吗？"海勇问道。

小白鲸想了一下。

"我会！"说着，他便潜入水中，消失了好大一会儿工夫。正当海勇开始有些担心，准备潜入水中看一看时，小白鲸冒出了水面，从呼吸孔中喷出一股巨大的水柱。水柱顶端，一只螃蟹吃惊地蹦了起来！

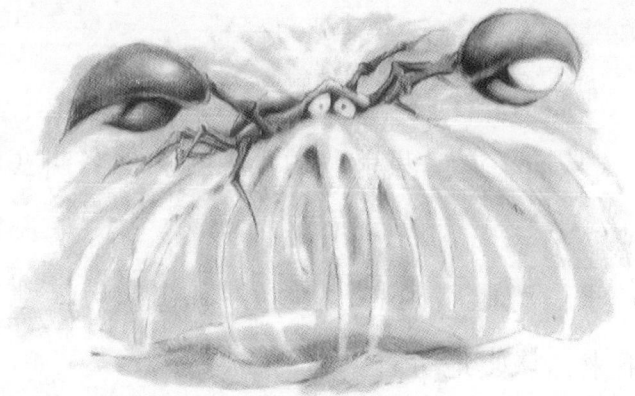

"喂！"螃蟹喊道。

小白鲸停止了喷水。螃蟹叽叽咕咕地抱怨着游回了水中。

海勇笑着鼓起了掌。

"这太棒了！"他说。

小白鲸害羞地笑了。他喜欢这只叫海勇的大狗。

"现在，"海勇说着靠近水边，在一块岩石上坐了下来，"你想听个故事吗？"

"故事？"小白鲸好奇地说，"啊，我想听。"他游到海勇近旁。

"那么，我给你讲一个非常好听的故事。"海勇说。

他向前弯下腰。

"从前，有一只勇敢的小白鲸，他名叫塞巴斯汀……"

小白鲸眼睛闪亮，脸上浮现出微笑。他安静下来，认真地听着。

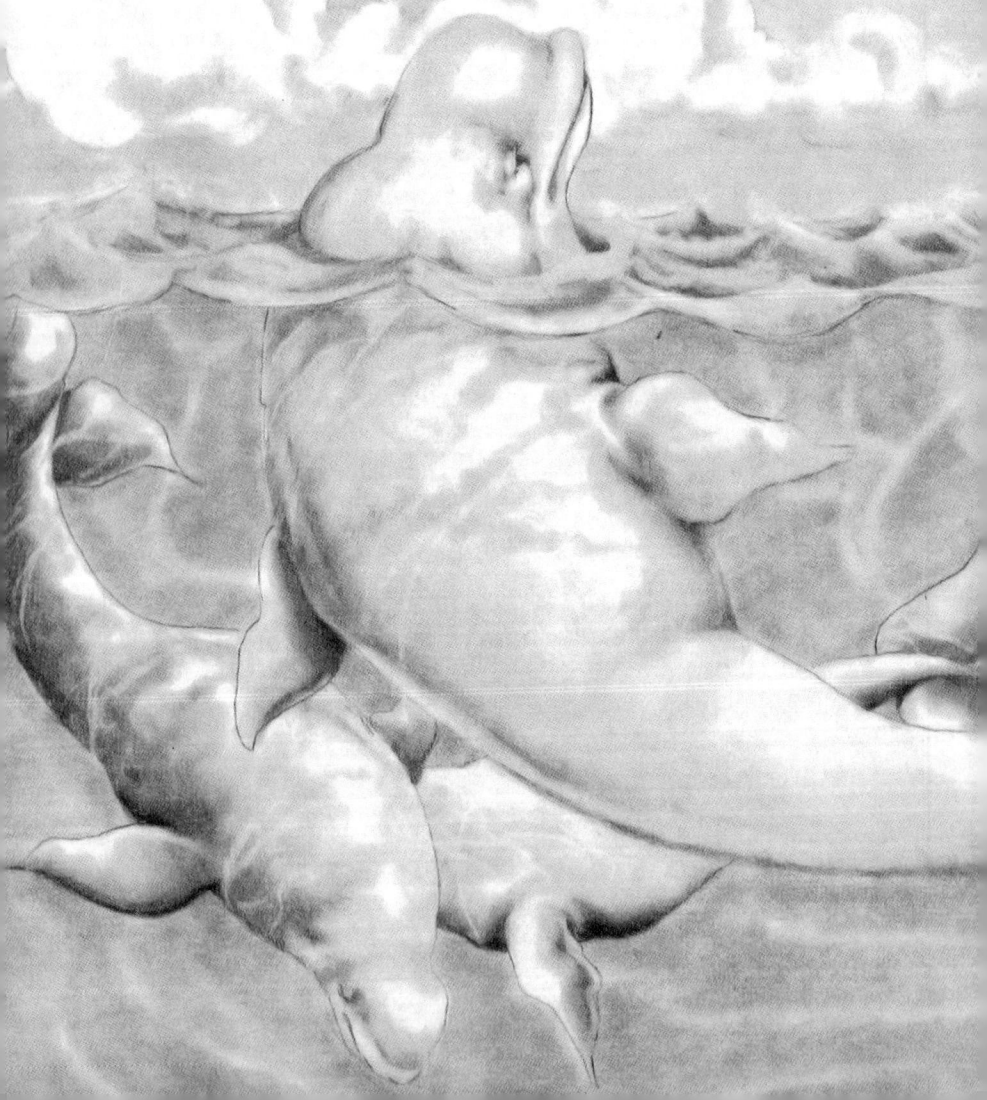

5.鲸鱼妈妈

在海勇给塞巴斯汀讲勇敢的小白鲸的故事时，另外两个孩子表现得同样勇敢，同样经受了非凡的考验。

哨子和莉拉紧紧贴在哈克的背上，在海上不停地搜索着。这很不容易。海洋如此浩瀚，哪怕一头鲸鱼，在广阔的海面上也无非同一个小黑点儿一样。况且，他们是在一只上了年纪的鸬鹚背上，用老鼠的小眼睛去看，就更加困难了。

"天哪，我们怎么能找到她呢？"感觉搜寻了有几个小时之后，莉拉哀叹道。

哨子低头望着一望无际的海面。

"我们会找到的。"他说。

"万一我们找不到呢？"莉拉问。

"我们会找到的。"哨子重复道。

"你们在那里叽叽咕咕说些什么？"哈克喊道。风很大，哈克只能隐约听到背上传来的细小声音。

"莉拉说我们肯定能找到白鲸妈妈！"哨子大声喊道，同时咧嘴冲妹妹笑了一下。莉拉也忍不住笑了。

"你说谁有个哥哥？"哈克大声问道。

哨子只能笑着摇了摇头。

他们三个一起继续搜寻。

一个小时过去了，又一个小时过去了，再一个小时……

两个孩子和哈克在空中逗留的时间越来越长，这只年迈鸟儿的力不从心逐渐显现。他拍打翅膀的速度越来越慢，飞起来摇摇晃晃的。好几次，哈克突然下坠，莉拉几乎确信他们要坠毁了。

"你没事吧？"哨子大声冲哈克喊道。

"你问我今天做了什么？"哈克问他。

哨子和莉拉担忧地互相看了一眼，更紧地

抓住哈克的背。天色越来越暗。天黑之前，他们必须回家。此时，哈克呼哧呼哧地喘着粗气，身子晃晃悠悠的……而他们仍然没有看到鲸鱼妈妈的身影。

"快看！"莉拉突然喊道。

"看哪儿？"哨子问。

"那儿！在那儿！"莉拉用手指着一个地方，坚定地说。

"我什么都没看到。"哨子说。

"我看到了。"莉拉回答。她爬到哈克耳朵边。

"向左转！哈克，"莉拉大声喊道，"左转，朝地平线飞！"

"你用不着这么大声，"哈克抱怨道，"我的耳朵没聋。"

哈克转身朝左边飞去。

"向前，向前飞，他们就在那儿！"

"他们是谁？"哨子一边问，一边努力想看清莉拉看到的。

"鲸群。"莉拉回答道，"整个鲸群。"

她说得没错。当哈克靠近水面时，他们三个都看到了一个庞大白鲸群在游来游去，头顶喷出水来。

"太棒了！"哨子欢呼道。

当他们终于飞到白鲸头顶时，哨子冲其中一头白鲸喊道："我们能落下来吗？"

"你说什么？"白鲸问道。

"我们可以落到你背上吗？"

"请你再说一遍。"

"真能装模作样！"哈克说着便径直落在了白鲸背上。

"喂，干什么！"白鲸抗议道。

"别担心！"哨子从哈克背上爬下来，走到白鲸背上，"我们在找一头名叫蜜糖的白鲸。我们找到了她的宝宝。"

"你们找到了蜜糖的宝宝？"白鲸兴奋地大喊道，"太好了！"

"玛丽莲！"他冲前面的一头白鲸喊道，"他们找到了蜜糖的宝宝！"

"蜜糖的宝宝？"玛丽莲重复道。

"弗雷德！"玛丽莲冲自己前面的白鲸喊道，"他们找到了蜜糖的宝宝。"

就这样，一头白鲸接着另一头，呼喊声在整个白鲸群传递开来，直到蜜糖——塞巴斯汀可怜无助、紧张慌乱、哀伤绝望的妈妈——被找到。

蜜糖游到小老鼠跟前。

"我们所有地方都找遍了！"蜜糖对哨子和莉拉说，"所有地方！"

她的眼中盈满泪水。

"我的孩子没事吧？"她问道。

"他很好！"哨子回答说，"在我们家呢。"

"你们家？"蜜糖问道。

"你很快就能看到了。"哨子说，"跟着我们走就行。快点儿！"

哨子爬回到哈克的背上。

"我们走吧，哈克！"哨子说。

"我们走！"莉拉也爬了上来。

哈克尝试着起飞。他一心想飞起来。他努力拍打着软弱的翅膀，试图飞起来。

但是他做不到。

"我没力气了，孩子们。"哈克喘着粗气疲惫地说，"我这把老骨头不中用了。"

哈克深深地叹了口气。

"你们跟着蜜糖回去吧。我今晚留在这里歇一歇。"

"扔下你回去？"莉拉叫道。

"决不！"哨子说。

"哈克，你是个英雄。"莉拉轻轻拍着哈克衰老的头颅说，"你得跟我们一起回去。老实说，我们决不会丢下你走的。"

哈克皱起眉头（其实他发自内心地感到高兴）。

"我很乐意带你们大家一起走。"蜜糖说。

哈克仍然皱着眉头。

"求求你，哈克。"莉拉说。

"先生，"蜜糖说道，"我急于见到我的孩子，所以我请您答应我的请求。您已经履行了您高尚的职责。"

哈克打心眼儿里喜欢这个词——高尚。

"好吧，好吧。"他嘟囔着在蜜糖的背上坐了下来，"我只是希望不会被其他鸟看到。"

6.永远的朋友

潘朵拉很明智地让灯塔里的灯一直亮着，以防哈克和孩子们没能像他们答应的那样，在天黑前赶回来。事实上，正是借助于灯光，蜜糖才能准确无误地找到那个海岸和环礁——她的小宝贝正在那里等着她。

当蜜糖游近环礁时，她和她背上的乘客看到了动人的一幕：潘朵拉和海勇坐在礁石上，他们正在用大勺子喂小白鲸吃软烂暖和的炖菜，小不点儿则安静地坐在海勇帽子上。

"塞巴斯汀！"鲸鱼妈妈呼唤道。

小白鲸转过头。

"妈妈！"他大声喊道，胡萝卜粒从嘴巴边掉了下来。

啊，多么令人开心的团聚啊！哈克从蜜糖背上飞了下来，把小老鼠们安全地放在岸上。两只小老鼠受到了一次又一次的热烈拥抱。幸福的白鲸妈妈和小白鲸绕着圈子游来游去，脑袋轻轻顶在一起，身体紧紧依偎在一起，歌唱着，欢笑着。

　　等该说的话都说完，终于到了要分别的时候，哨子问小白鲸塞巴斯汀："你会回来看我们吗？"

　　"我会常常回来看你们的。"塞巴斯汀回答说，"我永远是你们的朋友。"

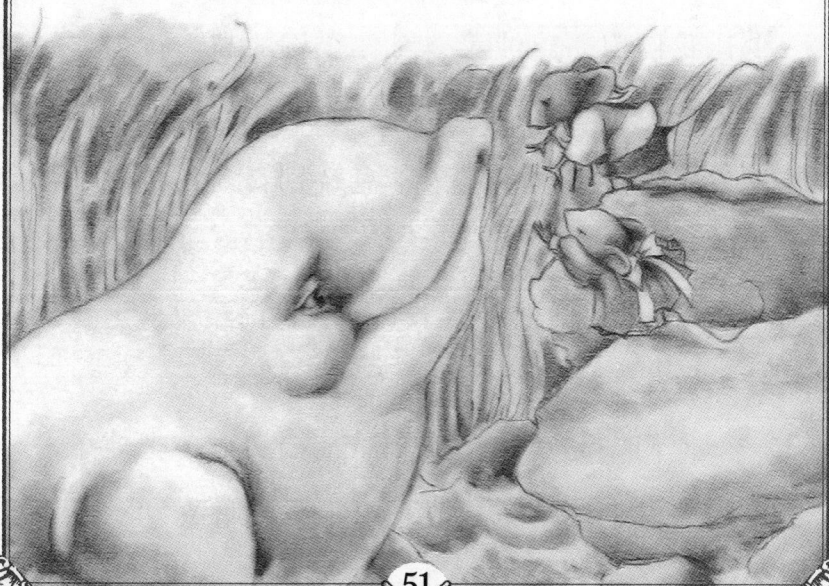

就这样，白鲸妈妈和小白鲸满怀感激地游走了，他们要回到白鲸群中。

夜幕已经降临。两只小老鼠突然感到非常疲惫。

"潘朵拉，还有炖菜吗？"哨子问。

"还有很多，"潘朵拉回答说，"足够每个人吃的，也包括你，哈克，我们的好朋友。"

年迈的哈克咳嗽起来，羽毛一个劲儿地抖动。

"不必麻烦。"哈克说。

"哈克，一点儿也不麻烦。"海勇说，"至少让我们用一碗炖菜，对你今天的高尚行为略表敬意。"

又是这个词，这个哈克特别喜欢的词——高尚。

"哈克，请跟我们来。"莉拉说着拉住这只年迈鸟儿的翅膀。

他们一起走回小屋。潘朵拉和海勇把炖菜舀到大海碗中，满意地看着年迈的哈克和孩子们吃啊吃啊吃啊。

吃过晚饭，哈克坐在海勇最喜欢的椅子上，好在回家之前歇一歇翅膀。

可是，这只老鸬鹚睡着了，第二天早晨之前，他不会醒过来。

三只小老鼠乖巧地钻进壁炉前温暖的袜子床里。潘朵拉还没来得及亲吻他们以及跟他们道晚安，他们就睡着了。

屋外，在无边无际黑黢黢的大海中，一位妈妈和她的孩子重新团聚在一起。他们很快就将回到他们的大家庭中，被欢乐的呼喊声包围。那个大家庭永远欢迎走失的成员回家。

对每个人来说，这都是足够惊险刺激的一天。

1. The Family

In a lonely lighthouse there lived a family of animals who were, in fact, not lonely at all.

Their lighthouse stood on top of a cliff of sharp rocks beside the sea. And it looked as if it were the most forlorn and empty place in the world, standing there all alone.

But if one drew closer to this lighthouse, everything about it changed.

For there were blue petunias growing in window boxes at the little cottage next door.

In the yard sunflowers lined a lovely picket fence and tomatoes and carrots grew in the garden.

At the base of the lighthouse was a handmade wooden wagon filled with toys, and the toys themselves were hand-made: penguins that wobbled, pelicans with large beaks that opened and closed, crabs with movable, clicking legs.

If one drew even closer to the front door of the keeper's cottage, the smell of fresh-baked bread or berry dumplings floated out onto the wind.

And, looking inside this open door, there one would find the happiest family in the world.

They were: Pandora, the cat; Seabold, the dog; and three mouse children—Whistler, Lila, and their baby sister, Tiny.

They had lived here together for less than a year. But already they had made it a home.

On this particular summer day, Whistler and Lila were preparing for a shell-gathering trip along the beach. Whistler had a project.

"We are going to collect broken clamshells," he told Pandora, the cat, as she refilled his cup with warm ginger tea. "And then I am going to build a birdhouse and decorate it with the shells and put it on a post in the garden."

"Lovely!" Pandora purred. "It will have the feeling of the sea and the birds will be happy."

"It was my idea," said Whistler's sister Lila.

"It's true," said Whistler. "Lila thought of it. I'm simply carrying it out."

"Wonderful," Pandora said.

"But I'll help collect the shells," said Lila. "Then I have to finish sewing an apron for my doll."

Lila held up a small wooden mouse doll. It had a tiny blue bonnet, large painted eyes, and a simple flowered dress. It looked a bit like Lila herself.

"I do love summertime, don't you?" Pandora purred happily, slicing another piece of brown bread for Whistler.

"Oh yes," said Lila. Whistler nodded vigorously.

"And," said Lila, "I love summertime better here than any other place in the world."

Hearing this warmed Pandora's heart. Some days she could not quite believe she had been blessed with this little family. For she had first lived all alone at the lighthouse. For four long years she had baked bread for none but herself, poured tea for no one else, and kept the great lamp shining without the help of another.

But all that changed when a dog named Seabold and his broken boat washed ashore one day. For Seabold stayed on with Pandora while his injured leg mended, through fall, then winter, then into spring. As he repaired his beloved boat, Seabold thought surely he would return to the ocean and again sail the wide world.

But then one day they found the children—orphans—floating in a crate and lost, and Pandora and Seabold took them in. They tended to these little ones, cared and cooked for them, tucked them in each evening and welcomed them awake in morning.

And, of course, in time, something very important changed: their hearts. For the three mouse children made of this cottage and its solitary lighthouse a real home. With stories to tell. Bread to bake. Flowers to grow. Games to play.

And Seabold, who had thought he would always live a solitary life, could not leave. For he was a family dog now, and he was needed.

As Whistler and Lila finished their bread and tea this summer morning, Seabold took Tiny to the lagoon to look at the giant sun starfish. These were quite amazing creatures, for they were enormous and had twenty—Seabold counted—twenty legs! They rested in the shallow water or on the cold wet rocks and thought their starfish thoughts. Tiny watched them from the roll of Seabold's soft cap, where she loved to ride, and gurgled happily.

Seabold smiled. He was quite attached to Tiny.

On their way back to the cottage, they passed Whistler and Lila heading for the shore with twine bags in their small paws.

"Lovely morning, children!" said Seabold. "And how are you this day?"

The brother and sister told him of their plans.

"Splendid!" said Seabold. "I must clean the lanterns in the lighthouse or I'd join you myself. But have a wonderful time," he added. "And keep a sharp eye for adventures!"

Seabold always said this to the children as they went off anywhere. It was no wonder that he chose the name *Adventure* for his dear boat.

Still, most days at the lighthouse were simple, quiet sea days, with happy times but no real adventures.

This day, though, would be a lucky one.

This day would have an adventure.

2. The Whale

Whistler and Lila were walking along the rocky shore, happily collecting shells, when from out in the water came a long, sad cry.

"What's that?" asked Lila, stopping and looking across the sea.

She and Whistler stood very still and listened.

There it was again. The saddest, loneliest cry they had ever heard.

Whistler scrambled up a tall stick. Lila followed.

"*Who's there?*" called Whistler as loudly as he could (and a small mouse voice is not very loud).

"*Who's there?*" Lila called after him.

Most fortunately, most luckily, most wonderful for all, the creature who was crying had *very* good ears.

Up from the water popped a shiny white head.

"*Me!*" the creature called, and began to cry.

" My goodness!" said Lila. "It's a baby whale!"

And indeed it was. A baby beluga whale, in fact. And, oh, how it could cry.

"We'll be right there!" shouted Whistler. "Don't move!"

And within minutes the two children had run for their small boat (built for them by Seabold) and were rowing out to the whale.

When they finally reached him, the baby beluga was quite exhausted. Too exhausted even to cry anymore. He simply looked at them with frantic, frightened eyes.

"I've lost my mother," he whimpered.

"Oh, dear!" said Lila in distress. Being an orphan, Lila was very sensitive to babies with lost mothers.

"Where did you lose her?" asked Whistler.

The beluga looked as if he might start crying again. But he didn't.

"Somewhere," he said. "We were swimming and a big pod of humpbacks came through, and there were so many, and I saw a baby I thought I could play with and I followed him and then . . . and then . . ."

The baby whale sobbed.

"Then the humpbacks swam away all of a sudden and I was by myself."

"Oh, *dear*," said Lila.

The little whale floated silently. He was looking most tragic. The two mouse children gazed at him with deepest sympathy.

Suddenly Whistler declared, "*We* will find your mother!"

Lila looked at him in surprise.

The beluga's eyes brightened.

"Really?" he said. " You can find her?"

"Definitely. We are experts at finding lost mothers," Whistler fibbed.

Lila looked at him in even greater surprise.

"Here's what I want you to do," Whistler said to the baby. "Oh, by the way—what is your name?"

"Sebastian," said the whale. Whistler introduced himself and Lila.

"Very happy to meet you," said the well-mannered, tear-soaked beluga.

Whistler resumed. "Here's what I want you to do," he said. " Do you see that lagoon over there?"

The baby nodded his head.

"I want you to go over there and rest," said Whistler. "It's quite nice, the water is warm, and sometimes an otter comes along with a good story."

The whale nodded again.

"All right," he said.

"What is your mother's name?" Whistler asked.

"Mama," said the whale.

" No, no," said Lila. "He means her *real* name."

"Oh," said the baby. "Everybody calls her Honey."

"Honey?" repeated Lila. "What a nice name."

"She's a nice mama," said the beluga.

"Now you go over to the lagoon and wait for us, all right?" said Whistler.

"All right," answered Sebastian. "I'm a little sleepy anyway."

"Of course you are," said Lila.

"See you soon," said Whistler. "Don't worry."

As they watched the baby beluga swim toward the lagoon, Lila whispered to Whistler, "And just how are we going to find that mama whale?"

Whistler whispered back, "I have *no* idea."

Then he looked squarely at Lila.

"But we are going to *do* it!"

3. Some Help

Of course, the first thing Lila and Whistler did was to find Pandora. Seabold was very good at making toys and fixing boats. But it was Pandora who could always figure things out.

And after she heard the children's story as they all stood together in the vegetable garden, Pandora took a few moments to think.

Then she said, "I have an idea."

The children knew she would.

Now, though Pandora had lived many years all by herself at the lighthouse, she had, in that time, made some acquaintances.

They were creatures very different from her, creatures always on the move, but she had learned a few names and had, from time to time, even called on these ocean neighbors for help.

And one neighbor she had relied on before was a cranky old bird—a cormorant named Huck.

Huck didn't like anybody. He kept to himself and spent most of his time on top of a piling on the south side of the island, airing out his wings. He was a soggy old bird, and he loved nothing better than to spread out his wings and stand for hours feeling the breeze.

But even though Huck liked no one, he would *help anyone.*

And once, when Pandora had fallen into a large bramble bush and was all caught up in thorns, Huck—who just happened to be flying by—stopped and helped her pick her way out. He grumbled the whole time about what a "mucky muddle"and a "sticky stickle" she'd gotten herself into.

But he did help her and seemed pleased to do it.

Afterward, Huck told Pandora if she ever needed him again, to flash the great lamp five times—quickly—in the direction of the old piling he stood on. And he'd be by.

Since that time Pandora had called on him only once more, to ask directions to a cherry orchard she'd heard about but didn't know how to find. She had needed to make a medicinal tea for a sick puffin passing through. But she was careful not to bother Huck unnecessarily. She knew he was crotchety.

This day, though, Huck was her best idea. Huck would help find the mother whale.

Pandora found Seabold, who had laid Tiny down for a nap, and explained the situation.

"I'll go flash the lamp," Seabold said. "You stay in the yard and watch for Huck."

Seabold climbed the four steep flights of stairs and then the ladder into the lantern room. He lit all the wicks and turned the great lamp southeast. Then he flashed the light five quick times.

Within minutes Huck was landing in the yard where Pandora and the children stood waiting.

"Criminy," Huck complained. "That's some wind today."

He shook out his feathers and cleared his throat and coughed up a bit of . . . *something*. No one could be sure what.

Lila and Whistler looked at each other with wide eyes.

But Pandora merely smiled kindly at the cormorant.

"Thank you for coming, Huck," she said. "We have a problem and we need your help."

"Well, don't dillydally," grumbled Huck.

And Pandora explained. When she concluded her story she asked, "Huck, do you think you might fly over the sea and look for this missing mother? You will be able to travel so fast and so far."

"And," Pandora added wisely, "you know the waters better than anyone."

Huck was still frowning, but she could see in his eyes that he was pleased. Underneath all the growling, Huck really just wanted to be appreciated.

He gave a quick nod of his head.

"I can do that," he said. "What's her name?"

"*Honey,*" Whistler and Lila said together.

"And you say she's a beluga?" he asked.

The children nodded their heads.

"That helps," said Huck, "her being all white. She'll shine like a light."

Then Whistler cleared his throat and stepped forward.

"Mr. Huck," he said with a serious face, "may we go with you, Lila and me?"

Lila's mouth dropped open in surprise. As did Pandora's.

Huck set off into a great deal of coughing and hacking and spitting. Finally he looked squarely at Whistler.

"Well, I don't see why not," he said.

Then he looked toward Pandora.

"As long as it's all right with you, Pandora," he added. "I figure three sets of eyes will get the job done faster."

Pandora looked at Whistler and Lila with a bit of worry on her face.

"If you go with Huck, you must hold on tight," she said.

The children promised they would.

"And you must be home before nightfall," said Pandora.

The children promised again.

Pandora smiled. She had every confidence in them.

And soon, Lila and Whistler were riding the back of a cormorant, out across the wide blue sea.

4. Some Company

When Huck and the children had disappeared into the faraway sky, Pandora turned back toward the lighthouse and climbed the stairs to find Seabold in the tower.

The dog's face was pressed close to the window.

"Did I just see Whistler and Lila fly by?" he asked.

"You did," said Pandora. "They are going to help Huck find the mother."

Seabold smiled.

"What an adventure for two children," he said. Seabold

truly loved adventure.

"I told Huck he must have them home by nightfall," said Pandora.

"Of course," answered Seabold. "And what of the baby?" he asked.

"She's asleep in the cottage," said Pandora.

" No, no," said Seabold. "The *other* baby."

" Oh," Pandora smiled. "The other baby is still resting in the lagoon, waiting for his mother."

"Hmmm," said Seabold. "I expect he must be feeling a little lonely."

"Yes," said Pandora.

"And a little afraid," added Seabold.

"Yes."

"I think I shall go keep him company," said Seabold, starting for the stairs.

"What did you say his name was?" he called halfway down.

"Sebastian!" answered Pandora. She listened as Seabold descended to the bottom and went out the door. And she smiled in deep satisfaction, to have a friend so kind.

Pandora then returned to the cottage to make a stew and to watch over Tiny.

When Seabold reached the lagoon, the baby whale was swimming in circles.

"Hello, Sebastian!" called Seabold.

The whale stopped and put his head out of the water to look.

"Hello," he answered in a small sad voice. "Who are you?"

The dog smiled and saluted.

"I am Seabold," he said. "Once a sailor of the sea, now the keeper of a lighthouse and three small mice."

"Lila and Whistler!" said Sebastian, perking up.

"And their baby sister, Tiny," said Seabold. "And, indeed, Lila and Whistler are off to find your mother."

"Oh, good," said Sebastian. "For I miss her so much."

The small whale looked as if he might cry at any moment. Seabold could see that he must do something.

"Do you like tricks?" he asked the whale.

Sebastian brightened.

"Yes!" he said.

"I have a trick," said Seabold, and he stood on his head.

The little whale thumped his tail on the water with delight.

"That was very good!" he told Seabold.

"And do *you* have a trick?" asked the dog.

The whale thought a moment.

"Yes!" he said. And he dove under the water. He was gone several moments, and just as Seabold was beginning to worry and to think of diving in, the baby surfaced. He gave a big full spray of water from his spout and there, on top, bounced a very surprised crab.

"Hey!" said the crab.

Sebastian stopped spraying, and the crab, mumbling and griping, swam back under.

Seabold laughed and clapped his paws.

"That was a good one!" he said.

Sebastian smiled shyly. He liked this dog Seabold.

"And now," said Seabold, drawing nearer the edge of the water to settle upon a rock, "would you like to hear a story?"

"A story?" asked Sebastian. "Oh yes!" He swam very

near.

"Then I shall tell you a wonderful story," said Seabold.

He leaned forward.

"Once upon a time there was a brave baby beluga named Sebastian. . . "

The little whale's eyes shone and a smile spread across his face.

He grew very quiet and listened.

5. The Mother

While Seabold was telling Sebastian all about the brave baby beluga, two other children were also being very brave. And also not having much luck.

Whistler and Lila, holding tight to Huck's back, were searching and searching the sea. And this was not easy. The ocean is vast, and even a whale will be but a speck in its waters. And if you are searching through tiny mouse eyes from the back of an old cormorant, your job will be especially hard.

"Oh, dear," said Lila after they had searched for what seemed several hours, "how will we ever find her?"

Whistler peered down toward the miles and miles of open sea.

"We will," he said.

"But what if we *don't?*" asked Lila.

"We *will*," said Whistler.

"What's all that yacking back there?" yelled Huck. It was so windy Huck could barely hear the small voices on his back.

"Lila says she's *sure* we will find the mother!" yelled Whistler, grinning at his sister. Lila could not help grinning back.

"*Who's* got a brother?" yelled Huck.

Whistler just laughed and shook his head.

And they all kept searching.

Another hour passed. And another. And yet another.

And as long as the two children and the old bird stayed

in the air longer and longer, the cormorant's age began to show. His flapping slowed. His flying wobbled. And sometimes he lost altitude and Lila was sure they were about to crash.

"Are you okay?" Whistler would yell.

"Did *what* today?" Huck would yell back.

Whistler and Lila exchanged worried looks and held tighter to the old bird's back. The day was growing darker. They had to be home by night. And there still was no mother, and now with Huck wheezing and wobbling and . . .

"Look!" yelled Lila.

"Where?" asked Whistler.

"Out there," Lila pointed. *"Way out there,"* she said firmly.

"I don't see anything," said Whistler.

"I do," said Lila. She crawled closer to Huck's ear.

"Turn left, Huck," she shouted. "Left toward the horizon!"

"You don't have to yell," complained the bird. "I can hear just fine."

He turned left and flew.

"Keep going, keep going," said Lila. "They're out there."

"Who?" asked Whistler, trying hard to see what Lila saw.

"The whole pod," said Lila. "The *whole pod* of belugas!"

And sure enough, as Huck covered the water, all three began to see a marvelous pod of white whales swimming and spouting up ahead.

"Hooray!" shouted Whistler.

When they were finally above the whales, Whistler called to one.

"May we land?" he called.

"Excuse me?" the whale replied.

"May we land on your back?" Whistler called.

"Pardon me?" said the whale.

"Oh, *posh*," said Huck, and he simply did it. He landed on the whale's back.

"Hey!" said the whale.

"Don't worry," said Whistler, climbing off Huck's

back and onto the whale's. "We re just looking for a beluga named Honey. We found her baby."

"You found Honey's baby?" cried the whale. "Oh, joy!"

"Marilyn!" the beluga called to the whale in front of him. "They've found Honey's baby!"

"Honey's baby?" said Marilyn.

"Freddie!" she called to the beluga in front of her. "They've found Honey's baby!"

And so the calling went, through the pod, one whale to the next, until Honey—Sebastian's poor, frantic, unhappy mama—was found.

She swam to the mouse children.

"We've been searching everywhere!" Honey told Whistler and Lila. *"Everywhere!"*

Her eyes filled up with tears.

"Is my baby all right?" she asked.

"He's great!" said Whistler. "He's at our house!"

"Your *house*?" asked Honey.

"You'll see," said Whistler. "Just follow us. Hurry!"

He climbed back up on Huck.

"Let's go, Huck!" said Whistler.

"Let's go!" said Lila, climbing up.

And Huck tried to go. He wanted to go. He flapped his feeble wings and worked to go.

But he just couldn't.

"I'm all out of gas, kids," Huck said with a tired old wheeze. "These old bones just aren't going to make it."

He gave a heavy sigh.

"You go on and ride back with Honey. I'll stay out here tonight and rest up."

"Go back without you?" cried Lila.

"Never!" said Whistler.

"You're the *hero*, Huck," said Lila, patting his old head. "You have to come back with us. In fact, we won't leave without you."

Huck frowned. (Though deep down he was happy.)

"I will gladly give *all* of you a ride," said Honey.

Huck continued to frown.

"*Please*, Huck," said Lila.

"Sir," said Honey, "I am very anxious to see my baby, so I must ask you, *please*. You have done your noble duty."

Huck liked that word—*noble*—very much.

"All right, all right," he grumbled, settling down on Honey's back. "I just hope no pelicans see me."

"We'll tell them you're a hero, Huck," said Whistler.

"*Our* hero," added Lila.

Huck coughed and hacked and tried his very best not to smile.

But he did anyway. Just a little.

Then they all journeyed home on the back of a whale.

6. A Friend Forever

Pandora was wise enough to keep the lamp burning in the lighthouse, just in case Huck and the children were unable to keep their promise to be home before dark. And indeed it was the light that helped Honey find her way to the correct shore and to the lagoon where her little one waited.

When the mother whale swam nearer the lagoon, she and her passengers saw a wonderful sight. Pandora and Seabold were sitting on top of a rock—Tiny perched in Seabold's cap—and they were feeding the baby whale big spoonfuls of vegetable stew.

"Sebastian!" called the mother beluga.

The little whale's head turned.

"Mama!" he cried, bits of carrot falling from his mouth.

Oh, it was a joyous reunion. Huck flew off the whale's back and deposited the mice children safely on shore, where they were hugged tight again and again. And the happy beluga mother and son swam around and around, nudging heads close, nestling their bodies together, clicking and singing and laughing.

When all the hellos were over and the time had finally come for good-byes, Whistler asked baby Sebastian, "Will you ever come back to see us?"

"I will always come back to see you," answered Sebastian. "I am your friend forever."

And with that, and their deepest thanks, mother whale

and baby swam off to join their pod.

It was night now, and suddenly the mice children felt so very weary.

"Pandora, is there any more stew?" asked Whistler.

"Plenty more," answered Pandora. "Plenty for everyone. Including you, our good friend, Huck."

The old bird coughed and shook his feathers.

"No need to bother," he said.

"It's no bother, Huck," said Seabold. "Why, a bowl of stew is the least we can do for your noble effort today."

There was that word again, that word that Huck liked so much: noble.

"Please come with us, Huck," said Lila, taking the old bird's wing.

So they all walked back to the cottage, where Pandora and Seabold ladled out big thick bowls of stew and watched with pleasure as the old bird and the children ate and ate and ate.

After supper, Huck was given Seabold's favorite chair, to rest his wings before going home.

But the old cormorant fell asleep and would not wake

until morning.

The three mouse children, lovingly tucked into their warm sock-bed by the fire, were also asleep before Pandora could even kiss them good night.

And out in the vast dark waters of the ocean, a mother and a baby were a family again. Soon they would join their larger family, amid those happy calls with which lost ones are always welcomed home.

For everyone, it had been *quite* an adventurous day.

图书在版编目（CIP）数据

灯塔之家. 小鲸鱼塞巴斯汀 /（美）辛西娅·劳伦特
著 ；（美）普莱斯顿·马克丹尼斯绘 ；栾述蓉译. — 南
昌 ： 二十一世纪出版社集团，2023.4
　 ISBN 978-7-5568-6915-2

　 I. ①灯… II. ①辛… ②普… ③栾… III. ①儿童故
事－图画故事－美国－现代 IV. ①I712.85

中国版本图书馆CIP数据核字 (2022) 第195957号

THE LIGHTHOUSE FAMILY: THE WHALE
Simplified Chinese translation copyright © 2023 by TB Publishing Limited
Original English language edition:
Text copyright © 2003 by Cynthia Rylant
Illustrations copyright © 2003 by Preston McDaniels
Published by arrangement with Beach Lane Books,
an imprint of Simon & Schuster Children's Publishing Division.
All rights reserved.

版权合同登记号：14-2022-0064

灯塔之家 小鲸鱼塞巴斯汀
DENGTA ZHI JIA　XIAO JINGYU SAIBASITING
[美]辛西娅·劳伦特／著　[美]普莱斯顿·马克丹尼斯／绘　栾述蓉／译

出 版 人　刘凯军
项目策划　奇想国童书
责任编辑　刘晨露子
特约编辑　郑应湘　孙金蕾
装帧设计　田丽丹
出版发行　二十一世纪出版社集团
　　　　　（江西省南昌市子安路75号 330025）
网　　址　www.21cccc.com
经　　销　全国新华书店
印　　刷　固安兰星球彩色印刷有限公司
版　　次　2023年4月第1版
印　　次　2023年4月第1次印刷
开　　本　710 mm × 1000 mm　1/16
印　　张　5.75
字　　数　23千字
书　　号　ISBN 978-7-5568-6915-2
定　　价　198.00元（全8册）

传世经典桥梁书

灯塔之家

3

雄鹰斯坦利

[美] 辛西娅·劳伦特 著

[美] 普莱斯顿·马克丹尼斯 绘 栾述蓉 译

二十一世纪出版社集团
21st Century Publishing Group

目 录

1. 秋　天

在蔚蓝的大海边，耸立着一座高高的悬崖，悬崖之巅屹立着一座孤零零的灯塔。灯塔中住着一户人家。

他们是猫咪潘朵拉、大狗海勇，还有他们的三个老鼠孩子：哨子、莉拉和小不点儿。

这个家庭的成员们不是生来就在一起的。他们曾经四散八方，做梦都想不到有一天能够找到彼此。

在过去的很多年里，潘朵拉一直独自生活在灯塔中。她忍受着孤独的折磨，守护着灯塔，让明灯闪耀，尽可能多地拯救生命。

海勇曾经是个水手，驾驶着他的小船"探险号"遨游四海。

三个孩子——哨子、莉拉和小不点儿，以前住在一所孤儿院里，直到一天夜晚，他们逃了出来，逃到了海上。

一天，海勇被风暴刮到了岸上，潘朵拉发现了他。再后来，潘朵拉和海勇一起，发现了在海里迷失方向、随波逐流的孩子们。

就这样，这几个流浪者聚到了一起，组成了一个家庭。于是，就有了灯塔之家。

此时正是金秋时节。孩子们和潘朵拉、海勇一起度过了一个美好的夏天。在漫长的夏日里，孩子们采集了很多玫瑰花瓣和薰衣草。眼下，潘朵拉每天早晨都在厨房里忙着做玫瑰和薰衣草果冻，留着冬天吃。

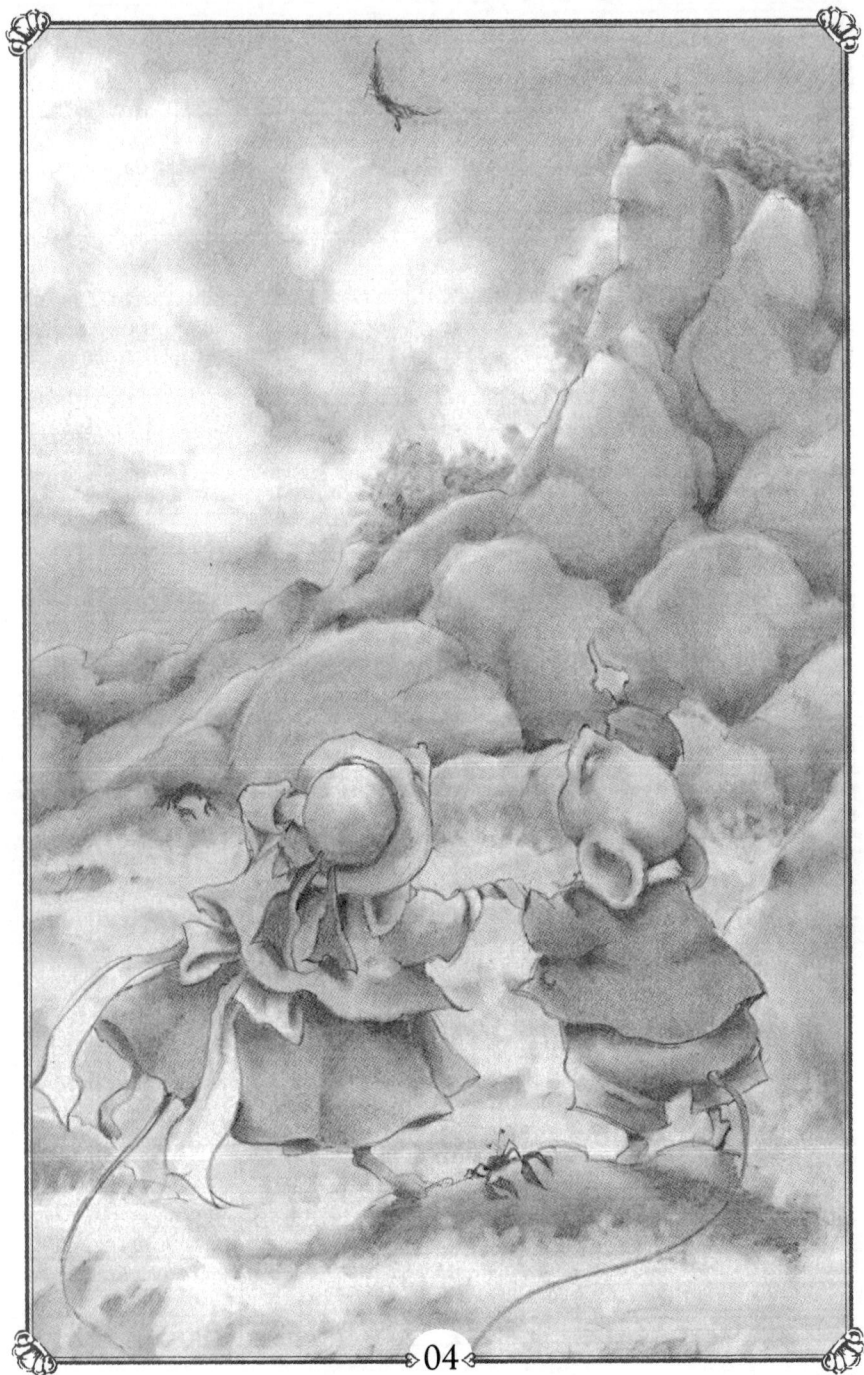

这些日子，户外秋高气爽，碧空万里。海勇带着舒舒服服地蜷缩在他羊毛帽子的卷边里的小不点儿一起，在秋天的菜园里忙个不停。海勇栽种洋葱，把大豆盖好，采收胡萝卜和土豆并冷藏储存，同时播下豌豆种子。小不点儿在旁边看着海勇的一举一动，满心欢喜。她非常依恋海勇。

而两个大孩子——哨子和莉拉——则把美好的清晨时光花在探索岩石海岸上。退潮时，他们爬上湿滑的礁石，小心翼翼地避免踩上藤壶或是打扰到住在石缝里的小螃蟹。如果他俩中有谁不小心惊动了一只躲藏的海鞘，海鞘就会出其不意地喷他一身水。

有时，一只白头鹰会离开他在岸边森林一棵杉树顶上的巢穴，越过孩子们的头顶，一飞冲天。每当这时，哨子和莉拉就会使劲向后仰着脖子，看着他展翅翱翔。

"你觉得他叫什么名字？"这天早晨哨子问莉拉。

"我想，一定是个让人印象深刻的名字。"莉拉回答，"就像他自己一样。"

　　"也许他叫希金·博萨姆。"哨子说。

　　"希金·博萨姆？"莉拉问道，"这是个什么名字？"

　　"我有一次在一本书上看到过的。"哨子说，"感觉好像是个大人物的名字。"

　　莉拉看着白头鹰越飞越远，消失在云层之中。

"也许吧，"她说，"也许他真的叫希金·博萨姆。"

哨子望着白头鹰刚刚从里面飞出的那片高大茂密的森林，叹了口气。

"我真希望潘朵拉能允许我们去那片森林里看看。"

"她担心我们会迷路。"莉拉说着捡起一棵海白菜准备带回家。

哨子和莉拉静静地望向对面——那片蓊郁的森林。

"我猜我们可能会迷路。"哨子说。

"是的，"莉拉说，"很可能。"

他们站在那里，目不转睛地望着苍翠幽深的森林。他俩都渴望到森林中去。

2. 办 法

对于潘朵拉和海勇来说，随着秋天的到来，看守灯塔的任务再次变得繁重起来。夏天几个月的好天气让他们能够稍事休息，而现在，雨季来临，雾季也已开始，暴风雨随时可能降临。

因此，海勇每天晚上都会从床上爬起来好几次去检查塔灯，确保灯火一直燃烧，玻璃罩足够透亮。潘朵拉则每天早晚都要给机械装置上好发条，以确保巨大的透镜能够自动旋转，发送出固定的灯光信号：两秒明，六秒暗。灯塔从来没有出过问题，可海勇还是不放心，怕灯火会熄灭。所以他干脆一整夜都守着灯火，直到快天亮时，他才熄灭灯火，拉上灯室窗帘，下楼和全家人一起吃早饭。

现在这个时候，早晨已经很冷，需要生火取暖了。厨房炉火带来的浓浓暖意让家里的每一位都感到幸福。他们围坐在潘朵拉的餐桌前吃着山核桃粥、樱桃和热乎乎的枫糖浆。

海勇像往常一样双手捧起小不点儿，把她放在自己的蛋杯中。那是餐桌上小不点儿最喜欢坐的位置。

"海勇，我们可以去森林吗？"哨子问道。

莉拉惊讶地看着哨子。她没想到他会提出这个问题，至少没想到他会问得这么直接。

海勇微笑着看了看潘朵拉。

"潘朵拉担心你们会迷路，"海勇说道，"我也是。"

潘朵拉严肃地点了点头。

"那么，"哨子并没有放弃，"该怎么确保不会迷路呢？你在海上航行时是怎么避免迷失方向的？"

海勇给小不点儿喂了一小勺粥。

"我有一个罗经盆。"海勇回答说。

“罗经盆是什么东西？”莉拉问道。

“罗经盆能给水手指示正确的方向。”海勇解释道，“人们在海上用罗经盆，在陆地上用指南针。”

哨子看了看莉拉。莉拉望向潘朵拉。

“潘朵拉，我们能学着使用指南针吗？”莉拉问道。

就这样，孩子们找到了去森林的办法。

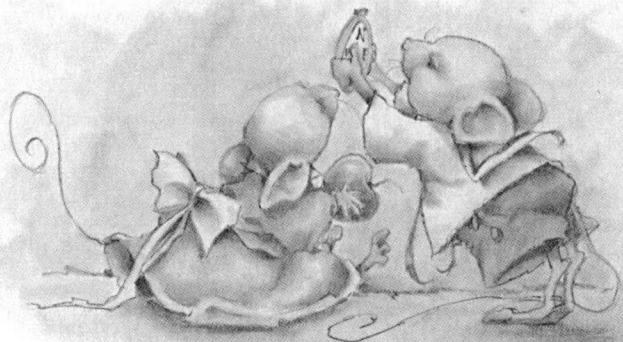

3.森　林

这一天，天气格外晴朗。哨子和莉拉准备到森林中去。俯视大海的峭壁之上开满了红色、橙色和粉色的野花，有成千上万朵，潘朵拉把它们叫作"大自然的画笔"。天空像纯净的蓝宝石一样，柔和的微风清新而凉爽。

潘朵拉帮莉拉穿好毛衣，戴好软帽。海勇站在一边，提醒哨子所有注意事项：

"注意看指南针。

"你们两个不要分开。

"太阳在头顶正上方时回家，正好赶上吃午饭。潘朵拉准备做水果派。"

"水果派！"哨子说，"那我们闻着味儿就能找到回家的路了。"

"闻着味儿也要看指南针。"海勇说。

莉拉一边整理软帽一边看着海勇。

"海勇，我们会非常小心的。"她说，"而且我们已经可以熟练地使用指南针了。"

"你们的确学会使用指南针了。"海勇说，"我相信你们能从这里一直走去北极。"

"那边有我的几个朋友，你们可以去拜访一下。"潘朵拉微笑着说，"其中一个是会唱歌的海象。"

"真的吗？"哨子问。

"你怎么会认识海象呢？"莉拉很好奇。

"哦，他刚巧路过这里。"潘朵拉回答说，"正赶上他喉咙痛。"

"你帮了他？"莉拉问道。

"我让他喝了杯玫瑰根茶，他的声音就像银铃那样动听了。"潘朵拉说道。

"嗯，我们不会走到北极那么远。"哨子说，"至少今天不会。"

潘朵拉再次笑起来。"我希望不会。"她说，"无论如何都该回家吃水果派。"

"没错。"莉拉说。

海勇递给两个孩子他们的麻绳包，以及一个核桃壳做的装满水的水壶。

"指南针。"他提醒两个孩子。

"带上了。"哨子回答。

两个孩子各自在小不点儿柔软的小脑袋上亲了一口，便走出了大门。

"我们到了森林之后，我想去找仙女环。"在沿着悬崖往森林走的路上，莉拉对哨子说道。

"仙女环是什么东西？"哨子问道。

"是树底下蘑菇组成的圆环，"莉拉解释说，"潘朵拉有一次告诉我的。她小时候采了这些蘑菇给她妈妈，她妈妈用它们做了很美味的汤。"

"我只想看甲虫。"哨子说。

"好恶心。"莉拉说。

孩子们离幽暗的森林越来越近。每走近一步，树木都似乎变得更高大。铁杉、雪松、云杉、冷杉密密匝匝地排列着，全都高耸入云，遮天

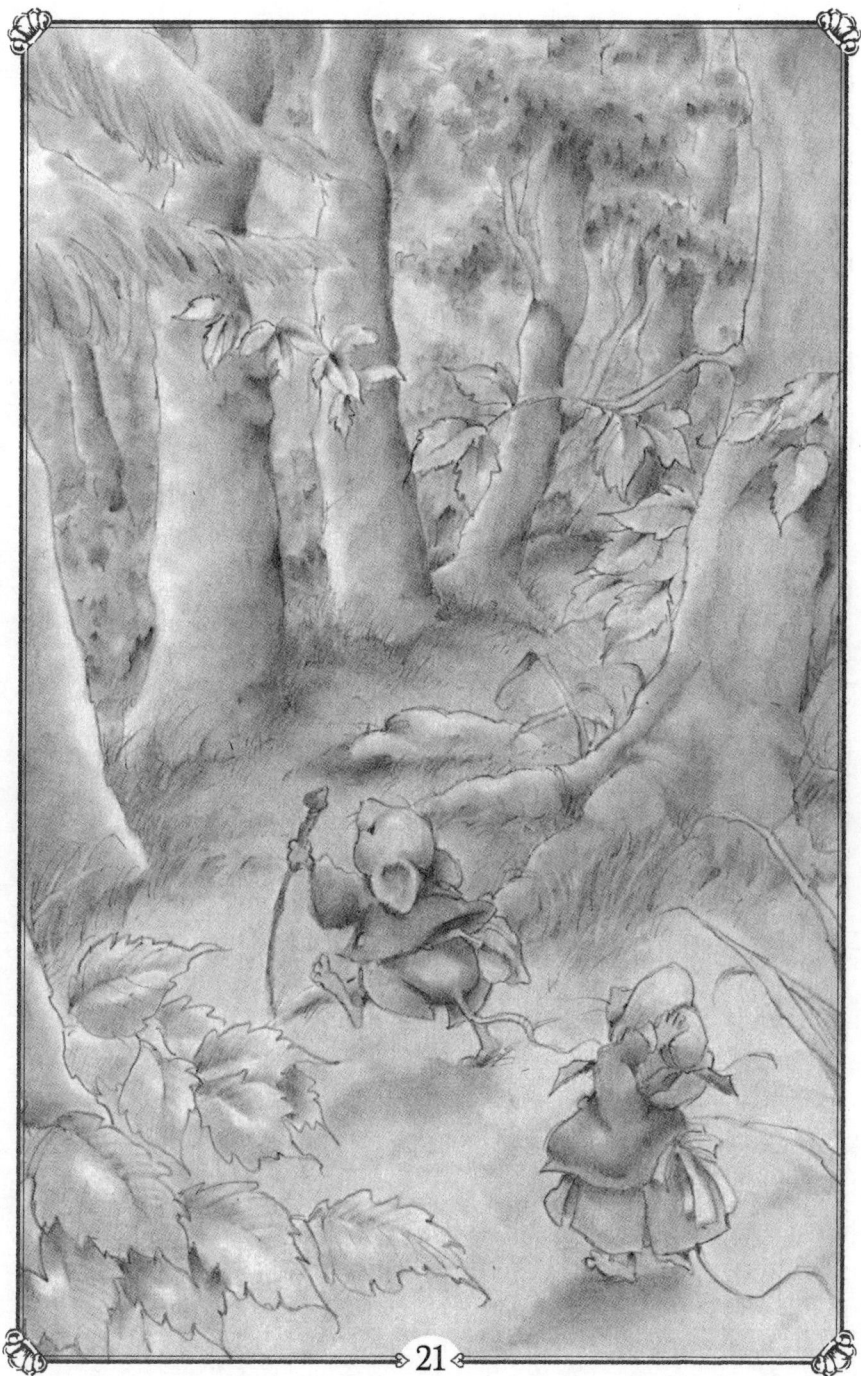

蔽日。

哨子查看了一下指南针，他和莉拉回头朝家的方向望了一眼。

"我知道我们的位置。"哨子说。

"我也知道。"莉拉说，"我能看到那边的灯塔。"

"嗯，要是有雾的话，指南针可以给我们指示方向。"哨子说。

"我能不能回家吃水果派就全指望它了。"莉拉说道。

两个孩子回头朝家的方向看了最后一眼，转过身，走进了森林。

"这里这么冷啊。"莉拉说，"不过我喜欢。"

哨子抬头看了看挂满苔藓的树枝，那些苔藓好像长长的灰胡子一样。

"这些树看上去很老了。"他说。

"而且充满智慧。"莉拉应道。

两个孩子继续往前走。地上到处都被巨蕨和长满苔藓的圆木所覆盖。哨子爬进一根

圆木里。

"这里有一股好闻的绿色的味道。"他说。

莉拉也跟着进去了。

"这里特别适合玩过家家游戏。"她说。

"还可以玩海盗游戏。"哨子说，"这里感觉像一艘船。"

他们继续向森林深处走去。森林里静悄悄的，跟海边截然不同。海边总是充斥着海浪的喧嚣和海鸥的鸣叫声，森林却是静默的。它似乎在侧耳倾听两只带着核桃壳水壶和指南针的小老鼠细声细气的交谈声。

"快看！"莉拉叫起来，"仙女环！"

果真，在一棵高大的冷杉脚下，在绿色的苔藓上，长着一圈软乎乎、胖嘟嘟的蘑菇。

"它们真美。"莉拉说。

"是的。"哨子表示赞同。

在潮湿、阴冷的苔藓的衬托下，仙女环闪闪发亮。

"我真不忍心摘它们。"莉拉说。

"我也不忍心。它们太完美了。"哨子回答。

"我们还是不要摘了。"莉拉说，"改带越橘回去好了。"

"说得对。"哨子回答，"那我们看看指南针，开始往回走吧。"

他把手伸进一个衣服口袋。然后，又换成另一个口袋。接着，又去摸第一个口袋，又换成第二个口袋。

"莉拉……"他嗫嚅着开口。

他的妹妹看着他说："啊，不会吧？"

4. 迷 路

哨子说："我确信我们能找到回家的路。"

他们朝着哨子感觉是家的方向走。

"毕竟我们也没走多远。"他补充道。

"我有种预感，我们可能赶不上吃水果派了。"莉拉回答。

"我怎么会把指南针弄丢了呢？怎么可能呢？"哨子自责地嘀咕着。

"东西很容易被弄丢。"莉拉说，"我经常丢东西。"

哨子站住脚，仔细地听了一会儿森林里的动静。

"怎么了？我们要掉头吗？"

"不用，"哨子回答说，"我觉得没问题。我相信这条路是对的，起码我感觉是这样。"

"不管怎么说，"哨子补充道，"海勇会对我很失望。"

"海勇从来不会对我们失望。"莉拉说。

她说得没错。海勇明白：错误在所难免。

"唉，真希望我没有弄丢他的指南针。"哨子说。

他又一次停了下来。

"等等！"他说。

"怎么啦？"莉拉也站住了。

"稍等。"哨子回答。他在侧耳倾听。

"会有人来帮助我们吗？"莉拉问道。

"嘘，别说话。"哨子说。

两只小老鼠一声不吭、一动不动地站定在那里。

"是海浪的声音！"哨子叫道，"我们靠近海边了。"

两个孩子顺着浪涛起伏的微弱声音急匆匆穿过森林。

"我们现在离海边更近了。我听到海鸥的叫声了。"莉拉说。

"没错！"哨子激动地说，"快点儿！"

孩子们看到前方森林的边缘有亮光，看到了蓝色的地平线。他们拼命地向前跑去，把幽深黑暗的森林抛在身后。

"我们出来了。"哨子脚踩在一处峭壁的石头上喊道。

"万岁！"莉拉欢呼道。他们眼前是蔚蓝而美丽的大海。

"可是灯塔在哪个方向呢？"莉拉问道。她极目朝海岸的一个方向望去，然后又朝另一个方向张望，但是，看不到灯塔。

"我们该走哪条路呢？"她问。

"或许我可以帮忙。"他们身后，一个声音响起。

孩子们转过身。

是希金·博萨姆！他衔着指南针！

5. 斯坦利

"**我**看见它从你的口袋里掉出来了。"白头鹰说着把指南针递给哨子。

"真是没想到!"哨子说,"谢谢你!"

"什么都逃不过我的眼睛。"

"我相信你说的话。"莉拉说,"我叫莉拉,这是我哥哥哨子。"

"很高兴认识你们。"白头鹰说,"我叫斯坦利。"

"斯坦利?"哨子疑惑地反问道。

"你确定吗?"莉拉问道。

白头鹰低头看了他们一眼。

"我从生下来就叫斯坦利。"

"我们还以为你叫希金·博萨姆呢。"莉拉说。她跟白头鹰解释了原因。

"原来是这样。"白头鹰说，"嗯，那个名字挺不错的，只不过不是我的名字。"

"倒也没关系。"哨子说，"斯坦利叫起来更亲切。"

"为什么你等到现在才把指南针还给我们？"莉拉问道。

"因为我想让你们有机会自己寻找解决问题的办法。你们做得很棒！"斯坦利说。

"谢谢你！"哨子骄傲地回答。他很高兴斯坦利给了他们这个机会。

"直觉至关重要。"斯坦利说。

"没错。"哨子回答。

"但我看现在你们的直觉无法告诉你们该走哪条路。"斯坦利说。

"我的直觉只告诉了我一件事，那就是我饿了。"莉拉回答。

"好吧，那就跟我来吧。"斯坦利说。

"我们去哪儿？"哨子说。

"去我家。"斯坦利回答道。眨眼间，他捧起两个孩子，把他们放进他的前胸口袋，带着他们飞到了森林中最高的一棵大树的树梢。

"太惊人了！"哨子在斯坦利的巢中大声喊道。

"不可思议！"莉拉说道。

两只小老鼠从来没有爬上过任何一棵树，然而此时此刻，他们坐在整个森林中最高的一棵树上，视线所及全是冷杉和雪松尖尖的树梢。

"我没想到森林的面积这么大。"哨子说。

"它像大海一样，"莉拉说，"无边无际。"

哨子和莉拉互相看了一眼。

"我们刚才有可能会迷路。"莉拉说。

"很可能。"哨子表示赞同。

"但是你们没有。"斯坦利说。

"谢谢你一直看顾着我们。"哨子对斯坦利说。

"是的，谢谢你。"莉拉说。

“小事一桩，不值一提。”斯坦利说，“我去给你们拿盘松子。”

“太好了！”莉拉欢呼道。

“斯坦利，你喜欢水果派吗？”哨子问。

“是的，非常喜欢。”斯坦利回答。

哨子笑起来：“那么用我的指南针，我们将很快给你找到一些水果派。”

6.星 空

斯坦利陪着孩子们走回灯塔之家。

"斯坦利，你真是太好心了，陪着我们走回灯塔。"哨子说，"我们知道要是以你自己的方式，会快很多。"

"嗯，我想看看你们是否能够好好地利用指南针。"斯坦利回答说，"显然，你们用得很好。"说着，他指向了前方。

"灯塔！"莉拉叫起来，"到家了！"

"什么味道这么好闻？"斯坦利问道。

"我告诉过你。"哨子咧嘴笑着说。

两只小老鼠走到通向灯塔的小路时，正好

是水果派出炉的时间。高大威武的斯坦利跟在他们后面。海勇从厨房门口探头看见了他们，对潘朵拉说："我想，孩子们经历了一场奇遇。"

午饭吃的是李子和山楂水果派，美味极了。海勇和斯坦利有很多共同话题，他们都是经验颇丰的海上旅行者。当然啦，孩子们也需要讲讲他们的森林之旅。

"我很高兴你们没有碰那个仙女环。"潘朵拉说，"我觉得它给你们带来了好运，让你们在失去指南针的情况下，也走出了森林。"

"是的。"莉拉回答，"一定是因为那个仙女环。"

"我觉得是多亏了我的鼻子。"哨子说。

"你的鼻子？"潘朵拉不太明白。

"我觉得我是闻着味道找到了正确的方向。"哨子回答。

"没错。"海勇说，"我航海时一直是这么做的。"

"我还以为你靠的是罗经盆。"莉拉说道。

"罗经盆只不过验证了我的直觉，"海勇回答，"而直觉是至关重要的。"

"说得对。"斯坦利庄严地点了点头，随即又拿起一个水果派，大口吃起来。

在午餐的交谈中，一家人得知斯坦利还是个业余的天文学家。说起这个时，斯坦利从口袋里掏出一个破旧的本子。

"这是我的星空日志，记录了我所有的观察。"斯坦利解释说。

"太棒了！"哨子叫道，"能给我们看看吗？"

斯坦利把笔记本平铺开，两个大孩子站在他的肩头，小不点儿爬到他的头顶，孩子们和他一起看他绘制的星空图。

"这是小犬座。这颗是天狼星。"斯坦利介绍说。

"我没想到天上有这么多狗。"海勇说。

"这个是我最喜欢的星座，"斯坦利微笑着说，"天鹰座。"

"看上去真的像只鹰。"莉拉说。

"或许你会喜欢从我们灯塔的栈道上观看星空。"潘朵拉对斯坦利说。

"啊，太好了。"哨子高兴地叫起来，"你可以把所有的星座指给我们看。"

"可以吗？求你了。"莉拉恳求道。

于是，这天晚上，全家人跟斯坦利一起聚集在灯塔的栈道上。斯坦利把星星指给他们看。哨子一边听一边记笔记，制作了自己的星空日志。斯坦利指出了北斗七星、金牛星和七姐妹星。他还指给灯塔一家看月亮在夜空中运行的轨迹。

"有很多次我都是跟着月亮走。"海勇说话的口气中充满了作为一个优秀水手的骄傲。

观察星空之后，潘朵拉给每个人端来了茶。这之后，斯坦利准备回家了。

"记得观看流星。"斯坦利提醒孩子们说，"对着每颗流星许下心愿。"

"斯坦利，谢谢你。谢谢你为我们做的每一件事。"海勇说。

斯坦利离去之后，哨子和莉拉回到栈道上，又观察了一小时的星空。

就在那一小时内，他们看见了十六颗流星，每个人都许下了十六个美好的心愿。

The LIGHTHOUSE FAMILY

THE EAGLE

1. Fall

On a cliff far above the blue waters of the ocean there stood a solitary lighthouse, and in this lighthouse lived a family.

They were: Pandora, the cat; Seabold, the dog; and Whistler, Lila, and Tiny, three mouse children.

This family had not always been together. They once were scattered far and wide, and none had ever guessed they would find one another one day.

For many years Pandora had lived all alone at the lighthouse, bearing her loneliness so she might save others by keeping the light burning.

Seabold had been a sailor, steering his little boat *Adventure* across the waters of the world.

And the three children—Whistler, Lila, and Tiny—had lived within the walls of an orphanage, until the night they escaped to the sea.

But one day Seabold washed ashore in a storm and

Pandora found him. Then Pandora and Seabold, in turn, found the children, lost and adrift in the ocean.

Thus these wanderers came together, made a home, and thereafter they were the lighthouse family.

Now it was fall. The children and Pandora and Seabold had enjoyed a lovely summer.

Through the long days the children had collected rose petals and lavender, and now Pandora was kept busy each morning in the kitchen, making rose petal and lavender jellies for the winter table.

Outside on these crisp, blue days, Seabold—with Tiny tucked snug in the roll of his wool cap—tended the fall garden. He planted onions, covered the beans, harvested the carrots and potatoes for cold storage, and sowed peas. Tiny watched his every move, full of delight. Tiny was very attached to Seabold.

And on these splendid mornings Whistler and Lila, the oldest children, explored the rocky shore. At low tide they climbed over the slippery stones, careful not to step on the barnacles or disturb the small crabs living in the crevices. If one of them disturbed a sea squirt who was hiding, the mice got a surprise shower!

Sometimes a bald eagle left his nest at the top of a fir tree in the woods beyond the shore and soared grandly above the children. Whistler and Lila arched back their heads and watched him glide.

"What do you think his name is?" Whistler asked Lila this morning.

"Something impressive, I expect," Lila said. "Like him."

"Perhaps 'Higginbotham'," said Whistler.

"'Higginbotham'?" asked Lila. "What sort of name is that?"

"I saw it in a book once," said Whistler. "It seems an important name."

Lila watched as the eagle flew farther and farther, disappearing into the clouds.

"Maybe so," she said. "Maybe that's Higginbotham."

Whistler looked toward the thick, tall trees from which the eagle had flown. He sighed.

"I wish Pandora would allow us to explore the woods," he said.

"She's afraid we might become lost," said Lila, picking

up a sea lettuce to take home.

Whistler and Lila looked silently across the shore toward the dark forest.

"I suppose we might get lost," said Whistler.

"Yes," said Lila. "We might."

They stood gazing at the deep, green woods. Both wanted very much to go there.

2. A Way

With the fall, lighthouse keeping had again become serious work for Pandora and Seabold. The few summer months of fair weather had allowed them some rest from their duties. But now the rains were coming back, fog season had begun, and there was always the chance of a storm.

Thus Seabold rose up from his bed several times during the night to check the light and make sure the flame still burned and the glass remained clear. Pandora wound the mechanism that rotated the giant lens each morning and night so that the light beamed out its constant signal: two seconds on, six seconds eclipse. It had never failed. But Seabold worried about the flame.

So he tended the lamp through the night. Then, just before daybreak, he snuffed out the flame, closed the curtains, and joined the family for breakfast.

Mornings were chilly enough now for a fire, and the deep warmth of the kitchen stove made everyone happy. They all sat together at Pandora's table for a porridge of hickory nuts, cherries, and warm maple syrup.

Seabold scooped up Tiny and put her in his eggcup, as always. It was Tiny's favorite place at the table.

"Seabold, may we go into the forest?" asked Whistler.

Lila looked at Whistler in surprise. She hadn't known he was going to ask this. At least not so directly!

Seabold looked toward Pandora and smiled.

"Pandora worries you will become lost," said Seabold. "And so do I."

Pandora gravely nodded her head.

"Well then," Whistler began, "how does someone make sure he doesn't get lost? How did you sail the ocean without becoming lost?"

Seabold offered Tiny a small spoonful of porridge.

"I had a binnacle," said Seabold.

"What is a binnacle?" asked Lila.

"A binnacle points a sailor in the right direction," said Seabold. "On water, one uses a binnacle. On land, one uses a compass."

Whistler looked at Lila. Lila looked at Pandora.

"Pandora, may we learn to use a compass?" asked Lila.

And that was how the children found a way to the forest.

3. The Forest

The day that Whistler and Lila prepared for their journey into the trees was a beautiful one. The bluffs above the waves were covered with what Pandora called "paintbrush"—hundreds of wildflowers in reds, oranges, and pinks. The sky was sapphire blue. The soft winds were cool and clean.

Pandora helped Lila with her sweater and bonnet while Seabold stood nearby and reminded Whistler of all the rules:

"Watch the compass.

"Never separate.

"And come home when the sun is directly overhead. It will be time for lunch and Pandora is baking tarts."

"Tarts!" said Whistler. "We shall *sniff* our way back home!"

"Sniff and watch the compass," said Seabold.

Lila looked at Seabold as she straightened her bonnet.

"We will be very careful, Seabold," she said. "We are very good with the compass now."

"That you are," said Seabold. "I do believe you could find your way to the North Pole from here."

"I have a few friends there you might visit," Pandora said with a smile. "Among them a walrus who sings."

"Really?" asked Whistler.

"How did you meet a walrus?" asked Lila.

"Oh, he was just passing through," said Pandora. "And he had a sore throat."

"Did you help him?" asked Lila.

"A cup of roseroot tea and he was singing like a bell," said Pandora.

"Well, we aren't going as far as the North Pole," said Whistler. "At least not today."

Pandora smiled again.

"I should hope not," she said. "One should always come home for tarts."

"Yes," said Lila.

Seabold handed the children their twine bags and a walnut flask filled with water.

"The compass," reminded Seabold.

"Right-o," said Whistler.

And with a kiss from each on Tiny's soft head, the two children stepped out the door.

"I think that once we are in the forest, we should search for a fairy ring," Lila said to Whistler as they walked along the cliff toward the woods.

"What is a fairy ring?" asked Whistler.

"It's a circle of mushrooms under a tree," said Lila. "Once, Pandora told me that when she was little, she collected them for her mother. Her mother cooked them into a nice soup."

"I'm just hoping to look at bugs," said Whistler.

"Ugh," said Lila.

As the children drew nearer to the dark forest, the trees seemed to grow taller and taller with each step. Hemlock, cedar, spruce, and fir—all rose up to the sky in tight rank, blocking out the sunlight.

Whistler checked the compass as he and Lila looked behind them toward home.

"I know where we are," said Whistler.

"So do I," said Lila. "I can see the lighthouse right over there."

"Well," said Whistler, "in a fog the compass would have guided us."

"I am counting on it," said Lila, "for I can already taste those tarts."

Looking back toward home one last time, the two children turned and walked into the woods.

"It's so chilly in here," Lila said, "but I like it."

Whistler looked up at the branches hung with lichens like long, gray beards.

"The trees feel old," he said.

"And wise," answered Lila.

The children walked farther. Everywhere giant ferns and mossy logs covered the forest floor. Whistler stepped inside one of the logs.

"There's a good, green smell in here," he said.

Lila stepped in too.

"This would be perfect for playing house," she said.

"Even pirates," said Whistler. "It feels like a ship."

The children walked even farther. The forest was so

quiet. It was different from the seashore, which was always noisy with the beating of waves and the calling of gulls. The forest was still. It seemed to be listening to the soft voices of two little mice carrying a walnut flask and a compass.

"Look!" said Lila. "A fairy ring!"

Indeed, at the foot of a tall fir, in a bed of green moss, lay a circle of soft, heavy mushrooms.

"They're beautiful," said Lila.

"I know," said Whistler.

The fairy ring glistened in the cool, damp moss.

"I almost don't want to pick them," said Lila.

"Neither do I," said Whistler. "They're perfect."

"Let's leave them," Lila said. "We'll bring home huckleberries instead."

"Right," answered Whistler. "We'll check the compass now and start turning back."

He reached into a pocket. Then he reached into another pocket. He went back to the first pocket. Then he went back to the second.

"Lila . . . ," Whistler began.

His sister looked at him.

"Oh no," she said.

4. Which Way?

"I'm sure we'll find our way back," said Whistler as they walked in the direction he thought would take them home.

"After all, we've hardly traveled far," he added.

"I have a feeling we'll miss the tarts," said Lila.

"How could I have lost the compass?" asked Whistler. "How?"

"It's easy to lose things," said Lila. "I do it all the time."

Whistler stopped. He listened to the forest a moment.

"What is it?" asked Lila. "Should we turn the other way?"

"No," said Whistler, "I don't think so. I believe this is

the right way. I just feel it somehow.

"Anyway," he continued, "Seabold will be so disappointed in me."

"Seabold is never disappointed in us," said Lila.

It was true. Seabold understood mistakes.

"Well, I do wish I hadn't lost his compass," said Whistler.

Whistler stopped again.

"Wait," he said.

"What?" asked Lila. She stopped too.

"Just wait," said Whistler. He listened.

"Is someone coming to help us?" asked Lila.

"Shhh," said Whistler.

The two mice remained very still and quiet.

"It's the surf!" cried Whistler. "We're near the surf!"

The children hurried through the forest, following the faint sounds of the ocean's ebb and flow.

"We're getting closer," said Lila. "I hear gulls."

"Yes!" said Whistler. "Hurry!"

Ahead the children saw a light glowing against the forest's edge. They saw a blue horizon. And they ran as fast as they could, away from the thick darkness of trees.

"We're out!" said Whistler, stepping out onto a rocky bluff.

"Hooray!" said Lila. The ocean was blue and beautiful below them.

"But which way is the lighthouse?" asked Lila. She looked far down the shore in one direction, then far down the shore in another. There was no lighthouse.

"Which way do we go?" she asked.

"Perhaps I can help," said a voice behind them.

The children turned around.

It was Higginbotham. And he had the compass.

5. Stanley

"I saw it fall out of your pocket," said the eagle, handing the compass to Whistler.

"Amazing!" said Whistler. "Thank you!"

"I see everything," said the eagle.

"I'm sure you do," said Lila. "My name is Lila, and this is my brother, Whistler."

"Pleased to meet you," said the eagle. "I'm Stanley."

"Stanley?" asked Whistler.

"Are you sure?" asked Lila.

The eagle peered down his beak.

"I have been Stanley all my life," he said.

"We thought you were Higginbotham," said Lila. She explained why.

"Oh," said the eagle. "Well, it's a fine name. It's just not mine."

"That's all right," said Whistler. "Stanley is friendlier."

"Why did you not return the compass until now?"

asked Lila.

"I wanted to give you a chance to help yourselves," said Stanley. "You did a fine job."

"Thank you!" Whistler said proudly. He was glad Stanley had given them that chance.

"Instinct is everything," said Stanley.

"Exactly," said Whistler.

"But your instinct isn't telling you which way to go now, I see," said Stanley.

"My instinct is telling me only that I'm hungry," said Lila.

"Yes," said Stanley. "Come along then."

"Where are we going?" asked Whistler.

"To my home," said the eagle. And in an instant he scooped up both children, placed them in his vest pocket, and flew them to the top of the tallest tree in the forest.

"Astounding!" cried Whistler from Stanley's nest.

"Astonishing!" said Lila.

Neither of the mice had ever climbed a tree. And here they were, in the tallest tree of all, looking out across the sharp peaks of firs and cedars that stretched away from them as far as they could see.

"I didn't know a forest stretches so far," said Whistler.

"It stretches forever," said Lila, "like the ocean."

Whistler and Lila looked at each other.

"We might have become lost," said Lila.

"We might have," said Whistler.

"But you didn't," said Stanley.

"Thank you for watching over us," Whistler said to Stanley.

"Yes, thank you," said Lila.

"No trouble at all," said Stanley. "Let me fix you a plate of pine nuts."

"Wonderful," said Lila.

"Do you like tarts, Stanley?" asked Whistler.

"Oh yes," said the eagle. "Passionately."

Whistler smiled.

"Then with my compass," he said, "we shall soon find you some."

6. The Stars

The eagle walked the children home.

"It's good of you to walk to the lighthouse with us, Stanley," said Whistler. "We know you could get there so much faster on your own."

"Well, I wanted to see you put the compass to good use," said Stanley, "which you surely have," he added, pointing ahead.

"The lighthouse!" cried Lila. "Home!"

"What is that *delicious* smell?" asked Stanley.

"I told you," Whistler said with a grin.

Right on time for tarts, the mice walked up the path to the lighthouse with the tall, imposing eagle in tow. Looking out the kitchen door, Seabold said to Pandora, "I think the children have had an adventure."

The lunch of plum and thorn apple tarts was a wonderful affair. Seabold and Stanley had much to talk about, both being old travelers of the sea. And of course, the children had to describe their journey into the woods.

"I am glad you left the fairy ring behind," said Pandora. "I believe it brought you luck. You did find your way out of the woods without a compass."

"Yes," said Lila, "it must have been the fairy ring."

"I think it was my nose," said Whistler.

"Your nose?" asked Pandora.

"I think I sniffed us in the right direction," said Whistler.

"Oh yes," said Seabold. "I did that all the time when I was sailing."

"I thought you used a binnacle," said Lila.

"The binnacle just confirmed my instincts," answered Seabold. "Instinct is everything."

"Oh yes," said Stanley, nodding his regal head before biting into another tart.

In the course of lunchtime conversation, the family found out that Stanley was also an amateur astronomer. As he spoke of this, he pulled a worn book from his pocket.

"This is my Starry Sky Notebook," said Stanley. "In it I keep all my observations."

"Amazing!" said Whistler. "May we see?"

The eagle spread open the pages of his notebook and with the children standing on his shoulders and Tiny clinging to the top of his head, Stanley showed them his drawings of the stars.

"Here is the constellation Little Dog," said Stanley. "And here is the Dog Star."

"More dogs in the heavens than I ever knew," said Seabold.

"And here is my favorite constellation," said Stanley with a smile. "The Eagle."

"It does look like an eagle!" said Lila.

"Perhaps," Pandora said to Stanley, "you might like to stargaze from the catwalk of our lighthouse."

"Oh yes!" said Whistler. "You could show us all the constellations!"

"Please, could you?" asked Lila.

And so that evening on the catwalk of their lighthouse, the family assembled with the eagle who would show them the stars. Whistler had made his own Starry Sky Notebook and as Stanley spoke, Whistler took notes. Stanley pointed out the Dippers and the great Bull and the Seven Sisters.

He showed the family how the moon follows a path across the night sky.

"I have followed the moon many a time," said Seabold. In his voice was the pride of a sailor who had traveled well.

When the gazing was done, Pandora made tea for everyone, then the eagle set about to return home.

"Don't forget to watch for shooting stars," he reminded the children. "And make a wish on every one."

"Thank you, Stanley," said Seabold. "Thank you for everything."

When the eagle was gone, Whistler and Lila returned to the catwalk to watch the sky for another hour.

In that hour they saw sixteen shooting stars, and they each made sixteen perfect wishes.

图书在版编目（CIP）数据

灯塔之家. 雄鹰斯坦利 /（美）辛西娅·劳伦特著 ；
（美）普莱斯顿·马克丹尼斯绘 ；栾述蓉译. -- 南昌 ：
二十一世纪出版社集团，2023.4
ISBN 978-7-5568-6915-2

I. ①灯… II. ①辛… ②普… ③栾… III. ①儿童故
事－图画故事－美国－现代 IV. ①I712.85

中国版本图书馆CIP数据核字 (2022) 第195958号

THE LIGHTHOUSE FAMILY: THE EAGLE
Simplified Chinese translation copyright © 2023 by TB Publishing Limited
Original English language edition:
Text copyright © 2004 by Cynthia Rylant
Illustrations copyright © 2004 by Preston McDaniels
Published by arrangement with Beach Lane Books,
an imprint of Simon & Schuster Children's Publishing Division.
All rights reserved.

版权合同登记号：14-2022-0064

灯塔之家 雄鹰斯坦利
DENGTA ZHI JIA XIONGYING SITANLI
[美]辛西娅·劳伦特／著 　[美]普莱斯顿·马克丹尼斯／绘 　栾述蓉／译

出 版 人　刘凯军
项目策划　奇想国童书
责任编辑　刘晨露子
特约编辑　郑应湘　孙金蕾
装帧设计　田丽丹
出版发行　二十一世纪出版社集团
　　　　　（江西省南昌市子安路75号 330025）
网　　址　www.21cccc.com
经　　销　全国新华书店
印　　刷　固安兰星球彩色印刷有限公司
版　　次　2023年4月第1版
印　　次　2023年4月第1次印刷
开　　本　710 mm×1000 mm　1/16
印　　张　5.25
字　　数　22千字
书　　号　ISBN 978-7-5568-6915-2
定　　价　198.00元（全8册）

赣版权登字-04-2022-660　　　　版权所有，侵权必究
购买本社图书，如有问题请联系我们：扫描封底二维码进入官方服务号。
服务电话：010-64049180（工作时间可拨打）；服务邮箱：qixiangguo@tbpmedia.com。

传世经典桥梁书

灯塔之家

4

老海龟极光

[美] 辛西娅·劳伦特 著

[美] 普莱斯顿·马克丹尼斯 绘　栾述蓉 译

21 二十一世纪出版社集团
21st Century Publishing Group

献给布鲁斯·T。
——普莱斯顿·马克丹尼斯

项目策划　奇想国童书
责任编辑　刘晨露子
特约编辑　郑应湘　孙金蕾
装帧设计　田丽丹

目 录

1. 大　雾

在大海美丽的碧波上空，一座陡峭的悬崖边上，骄傲地矗立着一座灯塔。灯塔里住着一户人家。

这是一个非同寻常，同时又非常幸福的家庭。曾几何时，这个家庭的成员分散在世界各地，过着截然不同的生活，从没想到将来有一天他们会聚在一起。

猫咪潘朵拉，过去一直独自住在灯塔中，以极大的勇气年复一年地守护着那盏明灯，帮助那些在浓雾和黑暗中航行，或是船只遭逢危险的水手。当水手们远远看见明亮的灯光时，他们会小心翼翼地掉转船头，避开岸边致命的礁石。

大狗海勇，在过去的很多年中，是一位出

色的水手。他有艘名叫"探险号"的船，他为这艘船深感自豪。但是，在一个漆黑的夜晚，海勇被风暴抛到了海里。这原本可能使他的生活转向不幸，没想到他却因祸得福，被冲到了潘朵拉所在的海岸上——他活了下来。潘朵拉发现了海勇，把他带回家。他们都发现对方是一个很好的朋友。

大狗海勇心里清楚他必须回到海上，只待他的伤口愈合、船只修好，他就会继续水手的生活。潘朵拉也清楚这一点：大海是海勇生活的中心。她理解。

但是有一天，他们发现了那几个孩子，一切自此改变。

海勇发现了三只老鼠孤儿——哨子、莉拉和他们的小妹妹小不点儿——在广阔的蓝色海面上的一只木板箱中随波漂浮。这些孩子逃离了身处孤儿院的不测命运，被带进灯塔里，得到了温暖、食物，更重要的是得到了——爱。

海勇没有离开，孩子们也没有离开。他们

有幸找到彼此，便都决定留下来。在这个庇护所——潘朵拉孤独的灯塔里，他们成了一家人。从此，灯塔不再孤独。

转眼，冬天快要到了，白昼变得越来越短，天气也越来越冷。几乎每天早上，岸边都会被潮湿的浓雾所笼罩。从他们位于悬崖高处的小屋窗户望出去，哨子和莉拉能够看到头顶湛蓝的天空，但往下却只能看见好似一条灰毯一般铺展开的浓雾。有时候，他们看见小船的桅杆从雾中探出来，就像雪堆上露出的小枝丫。

在这样的日子里，守护灯塔的工作变得非常重要。海勇经常连续几个小时站在悬崖边，吹响手里的雾角，指引小船靠岸，警示大型帆船远离海岸。莉拉和哨子喜欢在海勇工作的时候陪在他身边。但是在那些狂风天，潘朵拉担心两个孩子会被大风吹下悬崖，便坚持要求他们把自己系在门廊柱子上。这样一来，毫无疑问，孩子们想要玩耍，必须要有足够的创造力才行。同时，还需要十足的耐心，因为他们只能在海勇吹雾

角的间歇才能听清对方说的话。

"我们来假装被海盗捉住了吧。"哨子提议说，"他们把我们绑在桅杆上，逼迫我们告诉他们财宝藏在哪里。"

"我们假装是风筝吧。"莉拉说着，张开双臂，来回转圈。

海勇吹响了雾角，孩子们耐心等待着。

等四周再次安静下来之后，哨子说："啊呀呀呀，今天可真冷。也许我们应该假装正要回家去喝茶。"

"同意！"莉拉拽了拽围巾，哆嗦着说，"我们假装就住在这里，可以跑进屋里取暖。"

"还有一位好心人给我们烤好吃的点心。"哨子说。

"还有甜品。"莉拉补充说。

她看着自己的哥哥。

"我们不必假装这样的故事会发生，实在是太好了，不是吗？"莉拉微笑着问。

哨子正要回答，突然，从他们下方的浓雾中传来一个声音——

"喂，上面有人吗？"

莉拉看了看哨子。

"天哪！"莉拉说。

"那是谁呀，海勇？"哨子叫道。

"你听到了吗？"莉拉也跟着问道。她很想解开身上的绳子，跑到海勇身边，不过她不想让潘朵拉担心。

"谁在那里？"海勇的喊叫声冲进雾层。

他等待着回应，孩子们也等待着有人回应，

但是，一片寂静。

海勇回到孩子们身边，牵起他们的安全绳。

"孩子们，我准备到岸边去看看。"海勇说道，"你们必须回到屋里去，跟潘朵拉待在一起，等我回来。让潘朵拉准备好热茶，刚才那声呼唤听起来颇为神秘，谁知道我会带什么人回来。"

"海勇，我能跟你一起去吗？"哨子问道。

"我也可以去吗？"莉拉问道。

海勇仔细打量了一下他们。

"求你了。"哨子说道，"我们想帮忙。"

海勇笑着拍了拍哨子的肩膀。

"这一点我一清二楚。好吧，那就快点儿跑去跟潘朵拉说一声。"

孩子们急忙跑进厨房，告诉潘朵拉这个消息。潘朵拉正抱着一个面盆，在搅和着什么东西；小不点儿则蜷缩在窗台上的一个灭烛罩中，睡得正香。

"啊，好的。"潘朵拉说，"去吧，海勇可

能需要你们的帮助。"

她举起仍然绑在两个孩子身上的绳子的一端。

"但是一定要确保你们都安全地跟海勇绑在一起。"潘朵拉叮嘱道，"否则要是有强风，后果不堪设想。"

孩子们跑回屋外。在把安全绳的一端绑在海勇的大衣纽扣上之后，他们开始小心翼翼地走下悬崖，去寻找刚才那个可能需要帮助的人。

2. 海 龟

悬崖的坡面既陡又滑。去往海边的路上，孩子们非常庆幸跟海勇绑在了一起，因为他们自己几乎无法站稳。随着高度的降低，雾变得越来越浓。

等他们到达悬崖下，莉拉抓住了海勇的爪子。

莉拉伸手触摸眼前白茫茫的一片。"海勇，我们这是在哪儿？"莉拉问道。

"你怎么了，孩子？我们就在灯塔正下方啊！"海勇说。

"我们该怎样找到回去的路？我连自己的脚都看不见了。"莉拉说道。

海勇扑哧一声笑了。

"你忘了我有一个嗅觉多么灵敏的鼻子。"海勇说，"别担心，我从这里就能闻到我们厨房炉子里燃烧的木柴味。"

"好了，孩子们，我们别说话了，仔细听听。"海勇说。

于是，他们三个静静地站在那里，努力地倾听可能在浓雾中迷了路的人发出的声音。

"喂！有人吗？"一个声音喊道，"有人吗？"

"有人！"海勇大声回应道，"我们在这里！"

海勇领着孩子们小心翼翼地朝东边走去。

"我们来了！"海勇喊道。

"我在这里，"那个声音回答道，"我在这里。"

凭借海勇的大嗓门儿和灵敏的鼻子，他和两个孩子慢慢地向雾中那个迷路者发出的声音靠近。

当他们离那个呼喊"喂"以及"我在这里"的声音更近一些的时候，哨子发现前面有一块巨大而又光滑的"石头"。

　　"我觉得那个呼唤的声音就在那块'石头'后面。"哨子说。

　　他小心翼翼地朝"石头"走过去。

　　突然，"石头"抬起了头。

　　哨子、莉拉，甚至是海勇，都惊讶得跳了起来。

　　只见那块"石头"说："真高兴见到你们。"

"天哪！"哨子叫道，"是只海龟。"

海勇蹲了下来。两个孩子往前走近了几步。他们看到了一张温柔的绿色面庞，还有满含泪水的两只圆圆的眼睛。

"我叫极光。"海龟说道。

"哎呀，天哪。"莉拉说着把手伸进口袋，"您需要条手绢。"

海龟笑了。

"不用了，我没事。"极光解释说，"我们海龟经常流泪，但并不总是因为伤心。"

海勇碰了碰自己的帽檐以示敬意。

"我叫海勇。这是哨子和他的妹妹莉拉。我们是山上那座灯塔的守护者。我们特地前来相助。"

"啊，谢谢你们，真是太感谢了。"极光说，"我听到了你的雾角声。我本来急着往南走，结果被狂风裹挟，一路被吹到了这片大雾中。我现在感觉非常冷。说实话，我根本不该在这儿的。我们海龟不适应北方的海。"

"那您为什么要游到北方来？"哨子问道。

"我觉得这个我们可以稍后再谈。"海勇打断了他，"我们得先想个办法，让极光暖和起来。"

"我们的灯塔里有一个温暖的炉子。"莉拉说。

海勇抬头看了看，叹了口气。

"没错，但是让极光爬上这座陡峭的悬崖，实在太困难了。"

更多的眼泪从极光的眼底涌出。

"现在这些是伤心的眼泪吗？"莉拉问道。

极光点了点头。

"哦，亲爱的。"莉拉说道。

"潘朵拉是解决问题的专家。"海勇说，"她会知道该怎么办。"

"但我们不能把极光单独留在这里。"哨子说。

"一点儿没错。"海勇说，"所以你和莉拉留在这里陪着她，直到我带着潘朵拉回来。"

"好的！"莉拉说，"好主意！"

海勇脱下外套，盖在极光的背上。

"这能让您暖和一点儿。"他说，"孩子们跟外套绑在一起，很牢靠。你们都不会迷失在浓雾中了。我会尽快赶回来，一切都会好起来的。"

哨子注视着极光："有海勇和潘朵拉在，一切都会好起来的。"

"您还需要手绢吗？"莉拉问道。

极光笑了。

"需要，"极光抽搭着说，"谢谢你。"

3. 计 划

在海勇去找潘朵拉的时候，孩子们了解到极光为何会长途跋涉，来到北方。

"我想去看北极光。"极光说。

"北极光？"哨子问道。

"是的。"极光回答说，"事实上，我的全名就是北极光。我妈妈小的时候，有人跟她提起过北极光。于是，她梦想着有朝一日能亲眼一见。但是我们海龟注定要生活在温暖的水域，所以她不敢冒险到北方来。"

极光露出了一个自豪的微笑。

"于是，她给她的第一个孩子起名为'极光'。

在我漫长的一生中，我发誓一定要亲眼看到北极光——我名字的由来。"

"那您看到了吗？"莉拉问道。

"噢，是的，"极光说，"我看到了。"

"北极光是什么样？"哨子问道。

极光注视着两个孩子，温柔的大眼睛中再一次蓄满了泪水。

"它比我见到的任何日出或日落都要美，比月亮和星星还要美，也比珊瑚礁更美。"

"真的吗？"莉拉问道。

极光点点头。

"粉色、蓝色和绿色的光布满了黑暗的天空，像水一般涌动着，波光荡漾，泛着涟漪，只不过它们是光。"

"要是能看到这种景象，我愿意付出任何代价。"哨子感叹说。

"我花了一百年的时间，终于看到了。"极光说，"有一天，你肯定也会见到的。"

"一百年？"莉拉吃惊地反问道。

"从我出生那天算起。"极光回答道。

"我的天哪，您一定见识过很多事情。"莉拉说。

"是的，但没有比北极光更美的了。"极光回答说。

"您还觉得冷吗？"哨子问道，"也许您应该缩进壳里取暖。"

"我们海龟没法儿像陆龟那样整个儿缩进壳里。"极光说，"不管发生什么事，我们必须昂首面对。"

"嗯，救援很快就来了。"莉拉说。

"喂！"海勇的声音从雾中传来。

"您看，是吧？"莉拉对极光说。

"海勇，我们在这里。"哨子喊道。

"小心，小心。注意脚下。"海勇耐心的声音从雾中传来。随后，海勇和潘朵拉从雾中出现，潘朵拉随身携带着小桶。

"潘朵拉，这是我们的朋友极光。"哨子介绍道。

潘朵拉放下手里的桶，对着海龟微笑。

"极光，很高兴见到您。我为您的遭遇感到难过。"

"谢谢你。"极光说，"其实在这里，我觉得很开心，因为我认识了这么棒的朋友。"

海勇笑着指了指自己的毛线帽子。

"这里还有一个。我们把小不点儿也带来了。"

极光抬头看了看老鼠宝宝。她正舒舒服服地待在海勇的帽檐里，头上戴着一只小袜子。

"啊，好可爱的宝宝。"极光说。

"我们得先让您暖和起来。我有办法帮您回家，但首先，我们得让您暖和起来。"潘朵拉说着跪下来，打开她带来的桶的盖子，用戴着手套的爪子拿出一块光滑的石头。

"海勇和我用炉子把这些石头烤热了。"

潘朵拉说，"它们的热量能一直保持到早晨，然后我们会再带新的来。"

接着，她转身对着哨子和莉拉。

"孩子们，你们能把这些石头放在极光的壳周围，帮她取暖吗？"

"当然啦。"哨子回答。

两个孩子围着极光的壳，仔仔细细地把这些烤过的石头摆成一圈。潘朵拉则从口袋里掏出用热毛巾包裹着的散发着热气的橡子松饼和一罐甜菜罐头。

"我想您可能饿了。"潘朵拉说。

"哦，是的，"极光说，"非常感谢。"

当大家分吃松饼和甜菜罐头，享受烤过的石头

散发出的温暖时，潘朵拉开始说起她的计划。

"在这个时节，鹈鹕随时会路过这里。"潘朵拉说，"我查看了我的工作日志，他们即将踏上南下的旅程。"

"我跟许多鹈鹕都很熟悉，"潘朵拉继续说道，"因为他们有时会在灯塔的屋顶上休息。我甚至还帮好几只鹈鹕治疗过翅膀，我相信他们一定会乐意帮我的忙。"

潘朵拉看了看孩子们，又看了看极光，笑了笑说："听着，我的计划是这样的。"

大家一起全神贯注地听着潘朵拉的计划。当她说完后，大家异口同声地欢呼道："太棒了！"

4.鹈鹕

在接下来的几天里，哨子和莉拉多次下山到岸边照顾极光。潘朵拉和海勇需要看护灯塔和小不点儿，所以这两个孩子承担了帮助海龟的重要职责。他们用麻织袋给她带来热乎乎的食物，包括烤野土豆（"太好吃了！"极光评价道）和炒荨麻（"味道好极了！"极光又评价道）。孩子们给她讲他们的故事，她听得津津有味。而当海勇带着更多的热石头过来时，所有人都更加开心。

等到第三天早晨，终于，一只鹈鹕独自掠过水面。当时，孩子们正跟潘朵拉和海勇在厨房吃早餐，莉拉看见了这只鸟。

"是鹈鹕！他们来了！"莉拉喊道。

所有人都跑到了外面。他们看到，远远地，有十几只大鸟朝灯塔的方向飞来。

"挥舞起你们的围裙，孩子们，使劲地挥！"潘朵拉命令道。她提前给了每个人一条围裙，让他们挥舞起来，示意鹈鹕降落。

"我希望他们不要误会这是我平时穿的。"海勇边说边挥舞着手里的围裙。

"我也不穿围裙啊。"哨子说。

鹈鹕一只接一只地开始降落。当他们全都落下来之后，总共有十五只。

"你好啊，潘朵拉。"其中一只鹈鹕说。他那巨大的喉囊张开后是如此宽大，让莉拉紧张得直往后退。

"你好，奥古斯都！"潘朵拉说，"很高兴再次见到你。你们在极地的夏天过得还愉快吧？"

"好极了。"鹈鹕说。

"是吗，太好了。"潘朵拉说，"奥古斯都，

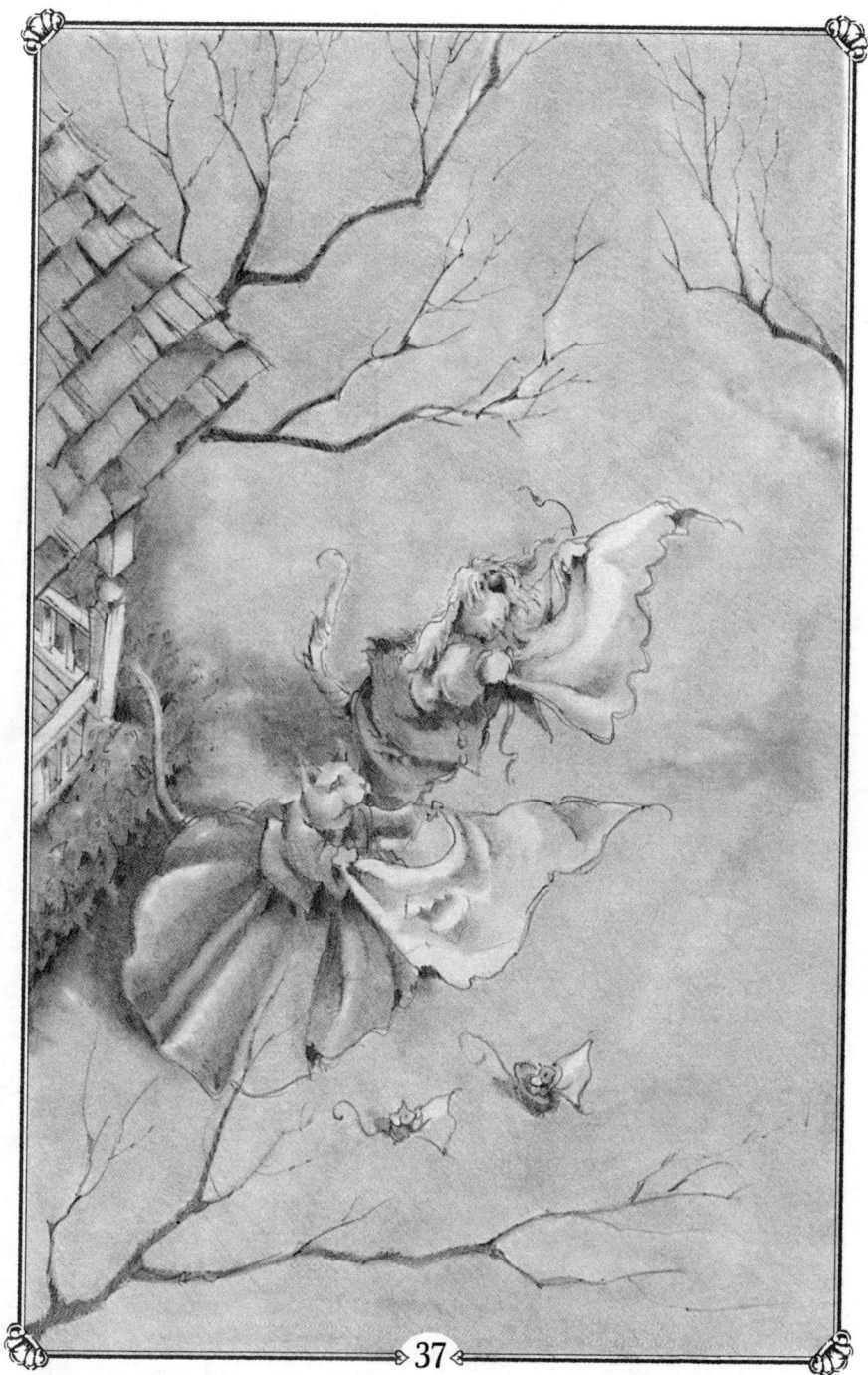

我需要你的帮助。请允许我先介绍一下我的家人，然后再来解释事情的原委。"

潘朵拉把孩子们和海勇介绍给奥古斯都和其他鹈鹕。

"潘朵拉，你拥有了一个小家庭，我真为你感到高兴。"奥古斯都说，"看得出你现在很幸福。"

"谢谢你，奥古斯都。"潘朵拉回答说。

"那么我能为你做些什么呢？"鹈鹕问。

潘朵拉向他说明了情况。她告诉鹈鹕极光是如何被困在了大雾中，并且说因为现在海水太冷

了，极光无法继续往南游。这只海龟需要回家，可是她无法游回去。

"但是如果不游泳的话，她怎样才能渡过大洋？"奥古斯都问。

潘朵拉看着他，平静地回答说："为什么一定要游泳呢？当然是，飞过去了。"

就这样，没过多久，一只百岁的海龟就被六只身强力壮的鹈鹕围了起来。帆船绳子一头衔在鹈鹕嘴里，另一头则缠绕在极光的龟壳上，就像渔网袋的把手一样。

"您不必担心。"潘朵拉轻声对极光说，"据我所知，鹈鹕的翅膀是大多数鸟儿中最长的。他们的翅膀就像最高的船只的帆，能够借助风力飞行，您也会飞起来。"

"您明天就能到家了，"海勇说，"我估计。"

极光勇敢地看着他俩，还有站在他们身边的哨子和莉拉，以及在海勇帽子卷边里的宝宝小不点儿。

"我不害怕。"她说，"我已经看到了北极光。"

莉拉从裙子的口袋里掏出一个东西。

"哨子和我给您做了这个，极光，要记得我们呀。"

她说着抬起海龟的前鳍，把一条贝壳手链套到上面。手链中间部位那个最大的贝壳，闪烁着粉色、蓝色和绿色的光芒。

"这是我在一场暴风雨后找到的鲍鱼壳。"哨子说，"它闪耀着跟北极光一样的光芒。"

大颗滚圆的泪珠从海龟的眼睛里滑落。

"啊，亲爱的。"莉拉说着掏出她的手帕。

"我永远不会忘记你们，"极光说，"不会

忘记你们中的任何一个。"

"一帆风顺，极光。"海勇说。

"祝你好运。"潘朵拉说。

奥古斯都一声令下，六只强壮的鹈鹕张开长长的翅膀，迎着风，带着海龟飞了起来。

"再见！再见！"灯塔之家的全体成员喊道。

"再见啦！"极光叫道。

灯塔一家默默地注视着海龟消失在蓝色的地平线上。

莉拉的眼睛湿润了。

"哦，宝贝。"潘朵拉掏出手帕。

"做得好。"海勇拍了拍哨子的肩膀说，"做得很好。"

在返回灯塔的路上，哨子问海勇，会不会有那么一天，他们也能驾船北上，去看北极光。

大狗海勇回答道："当然可以。绝对没问题。"

The

LIGHTHOUSE FAMILY

THE TURTLE

1. Fog

At the edge of a rocky cliff, high above the beautiful waves of a blue-green sea, there stood a proud lighthouse, and in this lighthouse there lived a family.

This was an unusual family, but a very happy one. At one time they had all been scattered about the world, living very different lives, never knowing that the future would one day bring them together.

There was Pandora, the cat, who had lived all alone at the lighthouse. Bravely she tended the great lamp year after year to help those who sailed the seas in fog and darkness and who might be in danger of shipwreck. Seeing the bright beacon across the water, sailors carefully turned their ships away from the deadly rocks of the shore.

Seabold, the dog, was for many years a sailor himself and a very fine one. He was quite proud of the boat he called *Adventure*. But one dark night Seabold was tossed into the ocean in a storm, and though this might have been an unlucky turn in the dog's life, it was, in fact, good fortune. For Seabold washed up, alive, on Pandora's shore. Pandora found him, sheltered him, and they found in each other a true friend.

The dog, however, knew that he must return to the sea, to a sailor's life, once he and his boat were mended. Pandora knew this too, for the sea was the very heart of Seabold's life, and she understood.

But then one day they found the children, and everything changed.

Pandora spotted three orphan mice—Whistler, Lila, and their baby sister Tiny—adrift in a crate in the vast blue waters. The children, who had fled an uncertain fate in an orphanage, were carried into the lighthouse, warmed, fed, and, ultimately, loved.

Seabold did not leave. The children did not leave. Having found one another, everyone wanted to stay. So in the sanctuary that was Pandora's lonely lighthouse, they all became a family. And the lighthouse was lonely no more.

Now winter was nearing. The days were shorter and colder, and a thick, damp fog rolled into shore nearly every morning. From their cottage window high on the cliff, Whistler and Lila could see the clear blue sky above them but only a gray cotton blanket of fog below. Sometimes they saw the masts of small boats poking up through the fog like twigs in a snowdrift.

Lighthouse keeping became very important work in these times. Seabold often stood at the edge of the cliff for hours, sounding a foghorn in his hands, guiding small boats in to shore and warning the large schooners away. Lila and Whistler loved to be near Seabold as he worked, but on the windiest days Pandora so worried they might be blown off the cliff that she insisted the children tie themselves to the porch post. This, of course, required the children to be very creative in their play. They also had to be patient, for they could hear each other's voices only between the blasts of Seabold's horn.

"Let's pretend we've been captured by pirates," suggested Whistler. "They've tied us to the masts until we tell them where the treasure is."

"Let's be kites," said Lila, spreading her arms wide and spinning in circles.

Seabold sounded the horn. The children waited.

When all was quiet again, Whistler said, *"Brrrr.* It's so cold today. Maybe we should just pretend we're on our way home for tea."

"Yes!" said Lila, shivering and tucking in her scarf. "Let's pretend we live right here and can run inside and get warm."

"And that someone nice will bake us something toasty," said Whistler.

"And sweet," added Lila.

She looked at her brother.

"Isn't it nice we don't have to pretend *that* story?" Lila asked with a smile.

But just as Whistler was about to answer, they suddenly heard a voice from the thick fog below:

"Hello? Hello up there?"

Lila looked at Whistler.

"Goodness," she said.

"Who is it, Seabold?" called Whistler.

"Did you hear?" called Lila. She wished she could untie herself and run to Seabold's side. But she knew she

49

must mind Pandora.

"*Who goes there?*" Seabold shouted down into the fog bank.

He waited for an answer. The children waited for an answer. None came.

Seabold returned to the children and gathered up the ropes, which had kept them safe.

"I am going down to the shore, children," Seabold said. "You must go inside and wait with Pandora. And have her set hot tea to brewing, for that was a very mysterious call. Who knows what I might bring back."

"May I come with you, Seabold?" asked Whistler.

"And I?" asked Lila.

Seabold carefully studied them.

"Please?" asked Whistler. "We like to help."

Seabold smiled and patted the boy's shoulder.

"Indeed you do," he said. "Run, then. Tell Pandora."

The children hurried into the kitchen to tell Pandora the news. Pandora was mixing up something in a bowl while Tiny slept tucked in a candlesnuffer on the windowsill.

"Oh, yes," said Pandora. "Do go. Seabold may need

your help."

She lifted up the ends of the ropes still attached to the children.

"But see to it that you are safely tied to Seabold," she said. "A strong gust and I dread to think what might happen."

The children ran back outside. Then, with the ends of their safety ropes looped to the buttons of Seabold's coat, they started carefully down the cliff to see who might be helped.

2. The Turtle

The steep sides of the cliff were very slippery. As the children made their way down to the shore they were very glad indeed they were anchored to Seabold, for they could barely hold their footing. As they descended the fog became thicker and thicker.

When they reached the bottom, Lila took Seabold's paw.

"Where are we, Seabold?" asked Lila, reaching out into the eerie whiteness.

"Why, we are just below the lighthouse, child," said Seabold.

"How will we find our way back?" asked Lila. "I can't see even my feet."

Seabold chuckled.

"You forget what a fine nose I have," said the dog. "Don't worry. I can smell the crackling wood of our kitchen stove from here.

"Now, children," said Seabold, "let's be quiet and listen."

The three stood silently, straining to hear anyone who might be lost in the dense mist.

"Hello?" called a voice. *"Hello?"*

"HELLO!" boomed Seabold. "WE ARE HERE!"

Seabold guided the children carefully to the east.

"WE ARE COMING!" shouted Seabold.

"*I'm here!*" answered the voice. "*I'm here!*"

With the help of Seabold's strong voice and fine nose, he and the children made their slow way to the lost voice in the fog.

As they came nearer to the *hellos* and *right* heres being called, Whistler spotted a smooth large rock up ahead.

"I think whoever it is is behind that rock!" he said.

They all stepped carefully toward it.

Suddenly the rock lifted its head.

Whistler, Lila—even Seabold—jumped in surprise!

The rock said, "I am so happy to see you."

"Heavens!" said Whistler. "It's a sea turtle!"

Seabold crouched down. The children stepped in closer. And everyone looked into a gentle green face and round eyes flowing with tears.

"My name is Aurora," said the turtle.

"Oh, dear," said Lila, reaching into her pocket. "You need a hankie."

The turtle smiled.

"No, it's all right," said Aurora. "Sea turtles often cry. But we aren't sad."

Seabold tipped his hat.

"I am Seabold," he said, "and this is Whistler and his sister Lila. We keep the lighthouse on the hill, and we've come to help you."

"Oh, thank you, thank you," said Aurora. "I heard your horn. I was hurrying south when a gale caught me and blew me into this fog. And now I am so very cold. I shouldn't be here at all, really. Sea turtles are not made for these northern waters."

"Why did you swim north?" asked Whistler.

"That story can wait, I think," said Seabold. "First we must find a way to help Aurora keep warm."

"We have a nice stove in the lighthouse," said Lila.

Seabold looked above him and sighed.

"Yes, but that cliff is much too difficult a climb for Aurora," he said.

More tears fell from Aurora's eyes.

"Are those sad tears now?" asked Lila.

Aurora nodded her head.

"Oh dear," said Lila.

"Pandora is our problem solver," said Seabold. "She

will know what to do."

"But we can't leave Aurora here alone," said Whistler.

"Exactly," said Seabold. "And that is why you and Lila will be staying here with her until I return with Pandora."

"Yes!" Lila. "Good idea."

Seabold pulled off his coat and draped it across Aurora's back.

"This will help keep you warm," he said. "And the children are nicely attached to it, so no one will stray in the fog. I'll be back quickly and everything will be just fine."

Whistler looked at Aurora.

"It always is," he said, "with Seabold and Pandora."

"Would you like a hankie now?" asked Lila.

Aurora smiled.

"Yes," she said, sniffling. "Thank you."

3. The Plan

While Seabold was away fetching Pandora, the children learned why Aurora had traveled so far north.

"I wanted to see the northern lights," said Aurora.

"The northern lights?" asked Whistler.

"Yes," said Aurora. "In fact, I was named for them. *Aurora borealis*. Someone told my mother about the lights when she was small, and she dreamed of seeing them one day. But we sea turtles are meant to stay in warm waters, and she was afraid to venture north."

Aurora smiled proudly.

"Instead, she named her first baby Aurora. And all my long life I have promised myself to see the lights for which I was named."

"And did you see them?" asked Lila.

"Oh, yes," said Aurora. "Yes, I did."

"What did they look like?" asked Whistler.

Aurora looked at the children, her large gentle eyes full

of tears.

"They were more beautiful than any sunrise or sunset that I have ever seen. More beautiful than the moon and stars. More beautiful than a coral reef."

"Really?" asked Lila.

Aurora nodded.

"The lights filled up the black sky with pinks and blues and greens, and they moved like water. They rippled and flowed like water. But they were lights."

"I would give anything to see that," said Whistler.

"Though it took me a hundred years, I found them," said Aurora. "You will surely find them too someday."

"A hundred years?" repeated Lila.

"Since the day I was born," answered Aurora.

"Goodness," said Lila. "You've seen many things."

"Yes," said Aurora. "But nothing so beautiful as the northern lights."

"Are you still cold?" asked Whistler. "Maybe you should pull inside your shell for warmth."

"Sea turtles cannot tuck inside their shells like land turtles do," said Aurora. "We must face what comes our way."

"Well, soon *help* will come your way," said Lila.

"HELLO!" called Seabold's voice from the fog.

"See?" said Lila to Aurora.

"Over here, Seabold!" shouted Whistler.

"Carefully, carefully. Watch your step," came Seabold's patient voice through the fog. Then there they were, Seabold and Pandora, carrying buckets, come to help.

"Pandora, this is our friend Aurora," said Whistler.

Pandora set down her bucket and smiled at the turtle.

"I'm so pleased to meet you, Aurora," she said. "And so sorry for your distress."

"Thank you," said Aurora. "But I think I am actually *happy* being here. I am making wonderful friends."

Seabold smiled and pointed to his wool cap.

"And here is another. We brought along Tiny."

Aurora looked up at the small baby mouse, wrapped snugly in the roll of Seabold's cap, wearing a tiny sock on her head.

"Oh," said Aurora, "a beautiful baby."

"We must warm you up," said Pandora. "I have a plan

to get you home, but first we must warm you up."

She knelt down and removed the lid from her bucket. She lifted out a smooth rock with her mittened paws.

"Seabold and I heated these stones in the stove," said Pandora. "They will keep their heat through the morning, then we will bring more."

Pandora turned to Whistler and Lila.

"Children, can you place these all around Aurora's shell, to keep her warm?"

"Certainly!" said Whistler.

As the children carefully encircled Aurora's shell with the toasty stones, Pandora pulled from her pockets hot acorn muffins wrapped in warm towels and a jar of canned beets.

"I thought you might be hungry," said Pandora.

"Oh, yes," said Aurora. "Thank you very much."

As everyone shared the muffins and beets and the warmth of the heated stones, Pandora began to speak of her plan.

"The pelicans will be passing through any day now," said Pandora. "I checked my logbook, and they are due on their journey south.

"I know many of the pelicans by name," Pandora continued, "for they sometimes rest on the roof of the lighthouse. And I have even mended a few wings, a favor I know they would love to repay."

Pandora looked at the children. She looked at Aurora. She smiled.

"Now, this is my plan," she said.

They all listened closely to Pandora's plan. And when she had finished, everyone had the same reaction: "*Brilliant!*"

4. The Pelicans

During the next few days, Whistler and Lila made many trips down to the shore to tend to Aurora. Pandora and Seabold needed to take care of both the lighthouse and Tiny, so the two children had the important duty of helping the turtle. They brought her warm food wrapped up in their twine bags, including baked wild potatoes ("astonishing," said Aurora) and stir-fried nettles ("heavenly," she said). The children told her their stories and she listened to them. And all were made happy when Seabold arrived with more hot stones.

Finally, on the third morning of waiting, a lone pelican flew across the water. The children were having breakfast with Pandora and Seabold in the kitchen when Lila spotted the bird.

"A pelican! They're coming!" she cried.

Everyone ran outside. Off in the distance they could see at least a dozen of the large birds flying in the direction of the lighthouse.

"Flutter your aprons, children! Flutter your aprons!" said Pandora. She had given everybody one of her aprons to wave, to signal the pelicans to land.

"I hope they don't think I wear this," said Seabold, fluttering the apron in his paw.

"Nor I," said Whistler.

One by one the pelicans began to land. When they were finished, there were fifteen in all.

"Greetings, Pandora," said one of the birds. He stretched his giant pouch so wide that Lila nervously backed away.

"Hello, Augustus," said Pandora. "So nice to see you again. Did you have a good summer at the pole?"

"Perfect," said the pelican.

"Oh, good," said Pandora. "I need your help, Augustus. First let me introduce my family, then I'll explain."

Pandora introduced the children and Seabold to Augustus and all of the other pelicans.

"Pandora, I am glad you have this little family now," said Augustus. "I see contentment in you."

"Thank you, Augustus," said Pandora.

"Now, how may I help you?" asked the bird.

Pandora explained the situation. She told the pelicans how Aurora had become stranded in a fog and was unable to complete her journey south, for the waters were now much too cold. The turtle needed to go home, yet she could not swim.

"But how does one travel the ocean if not by swimming?" asked Augustus.

Pandora looked at him and quietly answered. "Why, by flying, of course."

And within a very short time, a one-hundred-year-old sea turtle found herself surrounded by six strong pelicans, sailing rope stretching from their beaks and wrapping around her shell like the handles of a fishnet bag.

"You mustn't worry," Pandora said softly to Aurora. "Pelicans have the longest wings of most birds I know. Their wings are like the sails of the tallest ships, and when the wind catches them, the birds will fly. And so will you."

"You'll be home tomorrow," said Seabold, "by my calculations."

Aurora looked bravely at them both, and at Whistler and Lila who stood by their sides, and at baby Tiny in the roll of Seabold's cap.

"I'm not afraid," said Aurora. "I have seen the northern lights."

Lila pulled something from the pocket of her dress.

"Whistler and I made this for you, Aurora, to remember

us by," said Lila.

She lifted the turtle's front flipper and slid a shell bracelet onto it. The largest shell, in the middle, glowed with pinks and blues and greens.

"That's an abalone shell I found after a storm," said Whistler. "It has the colors of the aurora borealis."

Big round tears dropped from the sea turtle's eyes.

"Oh dear," said Lila, pulling out her hankie.

"I will never forget you," said Aurora. "Any of you."

"*Bon voyage*, Aurora," said Seabold.

"Godspeed," said Pandora.

And with a word from Augustus, the six strong pelicans spread their long, long wings, caught the wind, and lifted the turtle into the air.

"Good-bye! Good-bye!" called the lighthouse family.

"Good-bye!" called Aurora.

And the family watched in silence as the sea turtle disappeared into the blue horizon.

Lila's wide eyes were wet.

"Oh dear," said Pandora, pulling out a hankie.

"Well done," said Seabold, patting Whistler on the

shoulder. "Well done."

On the way back to the lighthouse, Whistler asked Seabold if they might sail north to see the lights one day.

And the dog answered, "Absolutely. Oh yes, absolutely."

图书在版编目（CIP）数据

灯塔之家. 老海龟极光 ／（美）辛西娅·劳伦特著；
（美）普莱斯顿·马克丹尼斯绘；栾述蓉译. -- 南昌：
二十一世纪出版社集团，2023.4
ISBN 978-7-5568-6915-2

I. ①灯… II. ①辛… ②普… ③栾… III. ①儿童故
事－图画故事－美国－现代 IV. ①I712.85

中国版本图书馆CIP数据核字 (2022) 第195956号

版权合同登记号：14-2022-0064

灯塔之家 老海龟极光
DENGTA ZHI JIA   LAO HAIGUI JIGUANG
[美]辛西娅·劳伦特／著　[美]普莱斯顿·马克丹尼斯／绘　栾述蓉／译

出 版 人　刘凯军
项目策划　奇想国童书
责任编辑　刘晨露子
特约编辑　郑应湘　孙金蕾
装帧设计　田丽丹
出版发行　二十一世纪出版社集团
　　　　　（江西省南昌市子安路75号 330025）
网　　址　www.21cccc.com
经　　销　全国新华书店
印　　刷　固安兰星球彩色印刷有限公司
版　　次　2023年4月第1版
印　　次　2023年4月第1次印刷
开　　本　710 mm × 1000 mm 1/16
印　　张　4.5
字　　数　20千字
书　　号　ISBN 978-7-5568-6915-2
定　　价　198.00元（全8册）

赣版权登字-04-2022-659　　　版权所有，侵权必究
购买本社图书，如有问题请联系我们：扫描封底二维码进入官方服务号。
服务电话：010-64049180（工作时间可拨打）；服务邮箱：qixiangguo@tbpmedia.com。

传世经典桥梁书

灯塔之家

⑤

小章鱼克莱奥

[美]辛西娅·劳伦特 著

[美]普莱斯顿·马克丹尼斯 绘 栾述蓉 译

21 二十一世纪出版社集团
21st Century Publishing Group

献给莉莎，她爱深海。
——辛西娅·劳伦特

献给金·萨姆·桑顿。
——普莱斯顿·马克丹尼斯

奇想国童书

项目策划　奇想国童书
责任编辑　刘晨露子
特约编辑　郑应湘　孙金蕾
装帧设计　田丽丹

目 录

1.花 园

在一座小岛的悬崖顶上，在深不可测的大海上方，一座灯塔坚实而牢固地矗立着。巨大的塔灯不分昼夜地照亮海面，灯光穿过层层波涛，指明方向，为水手们指引回家的路。

这座灯塔深受人们的喜爱，不仅仅是那些在夜里需要塔灯导航的水手们，还有住在灯塔里的一家人。

这是个幸福的家庭。潘朵拉是一只猫，海勇是一只大狗，他俩除了一起看守灯塔，还共同抚养着三个老鼠孩子——哨子、莉拉，还有婴儿小不点儿。

在这个广阔的世界里，这一家人在茫茫人海中不期而遇。在那之前，潘朵拉作为灯塔看守人

孤独地生活了四年。直到有一天，她发现了被海浪冲到岸边的海勇。暴风雨袭击了海勇和他的船，将其无情地抛掷在海岸上。

潘朵拉精心照料海勇，直到他恢复健康。就在海勇计划回归水手生活的时候，他和潘朵拉发现了孩子们——迷了路，在海上漂浮的孩子们。当时，这些小老鼠刚从孤儿院里逃了出来，和海勇一样，被风暴吹到了潘朵拉看守的灯塔——他们共同的避难所。

在灯塔看守人的小屋里，三个孩子感受到了从未有过的善意和安慰，体会到热乎乎的食物和陪伴所带来的意想不到的快乐。于是他们决定留下来，和潘朵拉生活在一起。就连习惯了浪迹天涯的海勇，也留了下来。

岛上漫长的寒冬已经过去，眼下又到了春天，有很多事情要做。一座灯塔里的生活，在春天里，充满无限生机。

哨子正在把一个豆角架修整成猫的形状，这让潘朵拉很高兴。

“到了七月，等藤蔓生长起来，”哨子说，“猫的形状看起来会更明显。”

“太棒了！”海勇正忙着种胡萝卜和甜菜，还不忘发出一声赞叹。海勇自己不太喜欢甜菜，他是为莉拉种的。莉拉喜欢把她为娃娃缝制的衣服浸在甜菜汁中，染成可爱的红色。她还用胡萝卜头把衣服染成漂亮的黄色。

婴儿小不点儿现在已经长大，可以在灯塔上的院子里玩耍了。但海勇担心一阵强风会把她吹下悬崖，于是他用一根长长的毛线把她绑在潘朵拉的晾衣绳上。小不点儿把她的木头积

木、扇贝壳和海勇做的几只小海雀堆在一起，玩得很开心。

在灯塔后面的田野里，野生鸢尾花、虞美人、报春花和风铃草正含苞待放。在海滩的沙丘上，海滩牵牛花已经开始伸展枝蔓。哨子和莉拉期待着，六月份海滩牵牛花的藤蔓变得茂密时，可以在白色的花丛中玩捉迷藏。

这会儿，他们更愿意把注意力集中在潘朵拉的花园上。当哨子搭建他的豆角架时，莉拉在用小石子给甲虫堆房子，她把集雨桶里收集的淡水装进贝壳，再把盛满水的贝壳放在房子附近，这样甲虫就能喝到水了，鸟儿也能喝到。

"孩子们，今晚是满月。"潘朵拉用围裙兜着满满一兜薄荷穿过花园时，这样说道。

"哇，太好了。"莉拉一边把一个贝壳安放在地上，一边说，"所有的东西都将闪闪发亮。"

"没错，"海勇说，"而且今晚的月亮也将带来一年中最低的潮水。"

"真的吗？"哨子问。

　　"千真万确。"海勇回答，"当潮水退去的时候，入海口应该会有一些新奇东西留下来。"

　　"我们应该去探察一番！"莉拉说。

　　"完全同意。"哨子说。孩子们喜欢在退潮时走过入海口，在泥地里踩出小脚印，看水退后留下的海星和海葵。

　　"明早潘朵拉和我修剪灯芯的时候，你们可以打包些早餐，早点儿出去。"说这话时，海勇的语气格外愉快，因为他非常喜欢看守灯塔的工作。

"小不点儿会陪着我们，是不是？"海勇补充道。小不点儿冲他笑了笑。海勇十分喜爱小不点儿，他经常在干活儿时带着她，把她塞进他毛线帽的卷边里，或是背心的口袋里。

"但是孩子们，你们必须要非常小心才行。"潘朵拉一边说着，一边把围裙上的薄荷倒进一个网格筛子，好去晾干。

"在探索入海口的时候，千万记住不要背朝着大海。"她说，"要时刻注意涨潮，一定要在潮水上涨之前回到岸上。"

"我们会小心的。"哨子说。

"我们保证。"莉拉补充说。

"你们能带些糖海带回来吗？"潘朵拉笑着问道，"做午餐用。"

"没问题！"孩子们说。

灯塔里的一家人喜欢糖海带。这将是一顿丰盛的午餐。

2.去海边

第二天一大早，潘朵拉就往哨子和莉拉的早餐袋里塞满了鹅莓饼干、小红苹果，外加一个装满茶水的木瓶。孩子们穿上雨衣，临走前分别亲了亲小不点儿。（小不点儿在厨房桌子上的筛子里，一直注视着他们的一举一动。）

"别忘了……"潘朵拉提醒他们说。

"永远不要背对着大海。"哨子说。

"没错。"海勇手里拿着几块清洁布，正从灯室的台阶上走下来。

"而且记得要安静而友好。"他补充道，"潮水很少这么低过，所以你们遇到的一些生物可能会感到紧张不安，因为他们通常都躲在水里。"

“我们会尽可能地保持安静。”莉拉说。

“我相信你们会的，宝贝们，”潘朵拉说着为他们打开门，“按时回家吃午饭。”

“好的，潘朵拉。”莉拉说。

“待会儿见！”哨子说。

孩子们背着他们的早餐袋，朝海边走去。

3. 章鱼克莱奥

当孩子们到达岸边时，他们高兴地看到海水已退出去很远，而他们可以探索的海滩面积，也大大地增加了。

"感觉我们好像拥有了一个全新的岛屿。"当他们走在坚硬的湿沙上时，莉拉这么说道。

哨子小心翼翼地绕过一只小海星。

"安静而友好。"他提醒莉拉，"安静而友好。"

莉拉指着远处的入海口边缘。那里，海水轻轻拍打着海岸，正在逐渐退去。

"我们还从来没有去过那么远的地方呢。"

她说。

"我们现在就去。"哨子说。

孩子们沿着入海口越走越远。一路上，海鞘向他们喷水，螃蟹到处乱窜，海星盯着他们看。

"沙泥越来越软了。"莉拉说着抬起她的脚。

"沙地还没有被太阳晒干。"哨子说。

哨子和莉拉停下来，看着潮水退去后留下的小水洼。

"天哪！"莉拉盯着一个巨大的绿色海葵惊叫道，"我还从来没有见过他们。"

"我也从来没有见过他们。"哨子指着一只橙色的海参说。

这时，不知是谁拍了拍哨子的腿。

"你见过我们吗？"一个声音问道。

"哎呀！" 哨子惊叫着跳了起来，"谁在说话？"

他和莉拉朝身后一个黑黢黢的小水洼望去。

"我想我看见了一双眼睛。"莉拉说，"或者

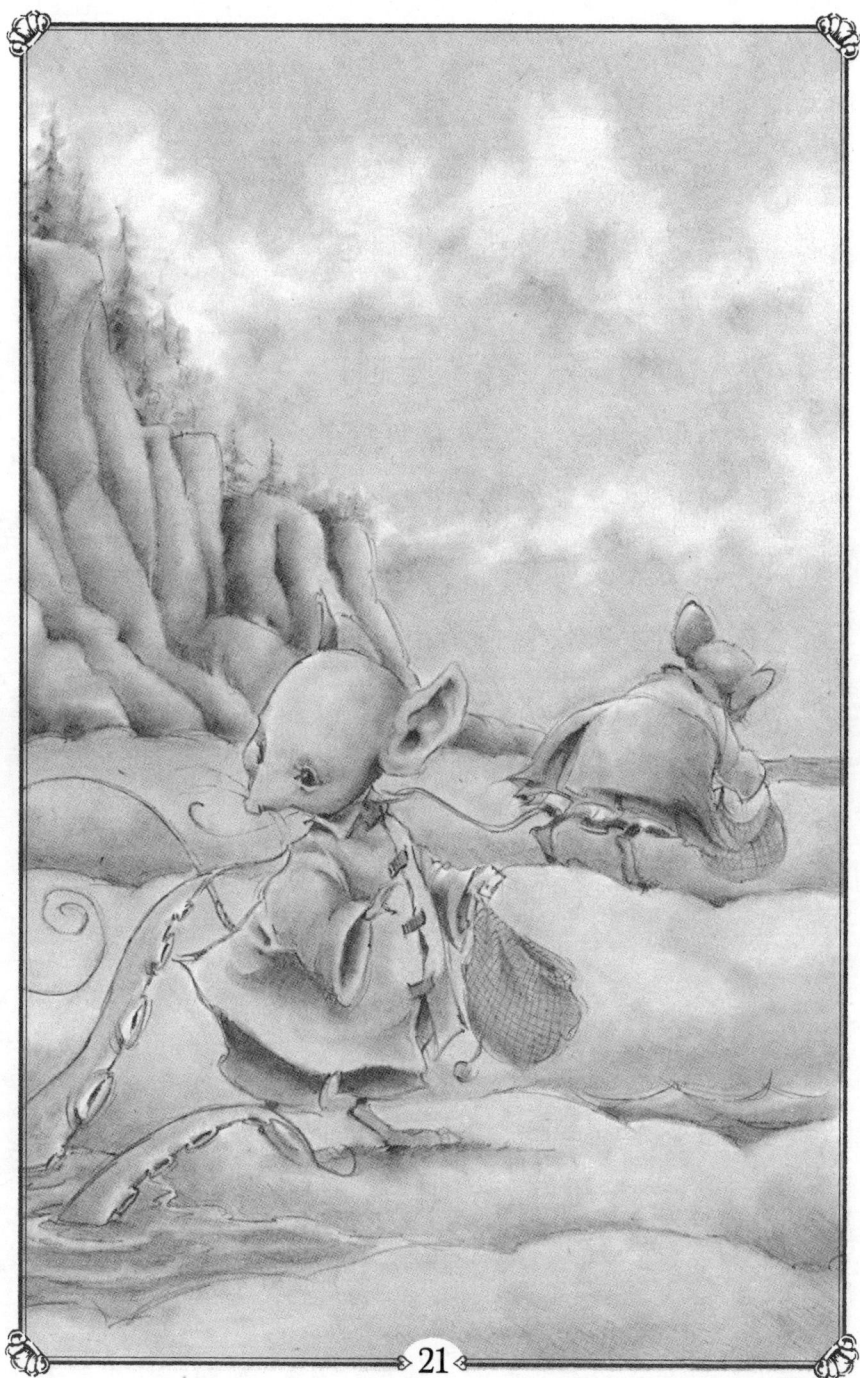

也可能是个门把手。"

"在哪儿？"哨子弯腰凑近水面，问道。

一条小触手从水洼里伸了出来，轻轻拍了拍他的鼻子。

"啊！"哨子再次跳了起来。

"嘿！"莉拉说，"是只章鱼！"

他们看着那两只黄色的大眼睛——圆圆的黄色眼睛确实有些像门把手——升上水面。黄色眼睛的主人长着一个小小的、口袋状的身体和八条长长的触手。

其中一条触手挥动着，打了声招呼。

"我叫克莱奥。"章鱼说，"对不起，吓了

你一跳。"

"哦，没什么。"哨子说，"还挺好玩儿的。我是哨子，这是我妹妹莉拉。"

"很高兴见到你。"莉拉说着，一步步靠近章鱼。当她走近时，令人惊讶的事情发生了。

"你变样了！"莉拉说，"现在你身上有条纹了！"

"哦，我是在模仿你的条纹。"克莱奥指着莉拉的雨衣说，"有时我会不假思索地根据周围的环境改变颜色。"

"太神奇了！"哨子说。

"嗯，条纹变化我还在练习中。"克莱奥说，"我最拿手的是变成红色和绿色。"

"能让我们看看吗？"莉拉问道。

"你身上有红色的东西吗？"克莱奥问。

莉拉和哨子互相看了看。

"苹果！"哨子说。

他从麻织袋里拿出一只苹果，递给克莱奥。

章鱼变成了一种奇妙的红色。

"我的天哪！"莉拉说。

克莱奥恢复了他原本的棕色皮肤。

"我喜欢各种各样的颜色。"他说，"可是我很害羞，不希望自己太过显眼。"

"我从没料到我们会在入海口遇到一只章鱼。"哨子说。

"没错。"莉拉说，"通常这里只有会喷水或瞪眼睛的家伙。"

"我犯了一个错误，"克莱奥说，"所以才被困在这个小水洼里。"

"什么错误？"莉拉问。

"潮水退得太快了，"克莱奥说，"我本来在这个洞里休息，可当我再次抬起头来的时候，大海已经把我抛在身后了！"

"啊，太不幸了。"莉拉说。

"别担心，"哨子对克莱奥说，"还会涨潮的，潮水会把你再带回海中的。"

"涨潮之前，要不要我们陪着你？"莉拉问道。

"你们愿意吗？"克莱奥问，"干坐在这里的确有点儿无聊，真不知道海星怎么能够忍受。"

"他们在解决问题。"哨子说。

"你说什么？"克莱奥问。

"我曾经问过一只海星，他整天在做些什么。"哨子解释说，"海星回答说'我在解决问题。'"

"哦，什么样的问题？"克莱奥问。

"嗯，他对我说'今天是关于一只老鼠的问题。'"哨子回答道。

"哦。"克莱奥想了想说，"我说不准，不过我觉得他可能有些无礼。"

"我也这么觉得。"莉拉说。

哨子表示赞同，随后打开自己的早餐袋。

"你吃过鹅莓饼干吗？"他问克莱奥。

哨子把一个饼干掰成四块，分别放在克莱奥的四条触手上。

吧唧，吧唧，吧唧，吧唧。克莱奥把四块饼干全都塞进嘴里。

"好吃。"克莱奥笑着说，"谢谢你。"

莉拉朝海面望了一眼，说："哨子，我感觉潮水已经开始上涨了。"

哨子看着水位线正在慢慢上升，潮水朝着岸边推进。

"哎呀，我们得走了。"他说，"克莱奥，你会找时间游到灯塔那里，去探望我们吗？"

"我会的！"克莱奥说。

"我们得快点儿了。"莉拉说，"潮水好像涨得很快。"

她拿起自己的包，试着迈了一步。

"我陷进去了！"她说，"我的脚动不了了！"

哨子跪下来，试图把莉拉的脚从湿泥里拽出来。

"你的脚一动不动！"哨子说，"拉——使劲拉！"

莉拉用尽全身力气，试图挪动她的脚。

"我陷进去了！"她说，"而且潮水就要过来了。"

“我力气很大。”克莱奥说，“也许我可以把你拽出来。”

他把一条触手缠在莉拉的腰上，往外拽。

“这不管用！”莉拉说，“我脚四周的泥已经变硬了，根本拔不出来。”

“我们必须让它变软。”哨子说，“我们必须再把它弄湿。”

“快点儿！”莉拉叫道，“想想办法！”

“我有办法！”克莱奥说着转动身体，把一个漏斗状的部位对准莉拉。

“坚持住！”克莱奥说道。随后他把水吸进漏斗里，然后对准莉拉全身，猛地喷射出一股强烈的水柱。

“太好了！”哨子说，“继续！”

克莱奥喷了又喷，直到莉拉和身边的泥地都湿透了。

莉拉从泥中拔出一只脚来——噗！然后是另一只。

她如释重负地深深叹了一口气，说："谢谢你，克莱奥。谢谢！"

　　哨子抓住莉拉的手，往岸边和家的方向跑去。

　　"来我们家做客吧，克莱奥！"他们一边跑，哨子一边喊，"明天中午就来！"

　　两只小老鼠迅速跑到安全地带，远离潮水，而克莱奥则迫不及待地要游回海里去。

4. 回 家

哨子和莉拉拖着四只沾满泥巴的脚回到了家。他们没带回糖海带，只带回了喷嚏（莉拉打的）。在门口撞见他们的潘朵拉立刻猜到，这个上午，他们的经历不同寻常。（此时海勇正和小不点儿在上面的灯室，否则他一定会说："又是一场冒险。"）

潘朵拉把孩子们领进屋，让他们坐在炉子旁，然后把他们的脚泡在一盆温水里，在他们头上裹上温暖的羊毛围巾。

"我的头没有湿，"哨子说，"只有莉拉被喷了一身水。"

"大家都喜欢头部是温暖的。"潘朵拉说着把一壶茶端到桌上，"亲爱的莉拉，你是怎么被喷了一身水的？"

"是一只章鱼。"莉拉回答说。

潘朵拉将茶壶安置好，平静地看着孩子们。

"我猜海勇可能想听听这个故事。"说完，潘朵拉把海勇从灯室叫了下来。

海勇带着站在他肩膀上的小不点儿下来了。

大家一起喝茶，孩子们讲述了他们是如何遇到章鱼，以及章鱼又是如何救了莉拉一命的。

"令人惊叹。"海勇说，"而且对于一个小孩子来说，他的主意很妙。"

"小孩子？"哨子惊奇地问。

"那是当然啦。"海勇说，"在这么小的潮汐池中发现的任何章鱼，都只会是一个小孩子。"

"你是说克莱奥会长得更大？"莉拉问。

"嗯，会大得多。"海勇说。

"我们应该设法谢谢这个小孩子。"潘朵拉说。

"没错。"莉拉说,"他是个英雄,他救了我。"

"我已经邀请他明天中午来我们家做客了。"
哨子说。

"太好了。"潘朵拉说,"我准备做一顿
丰盛的午餐——"

"他喜欢鹅莓饼干。"哨子插嘴道。

"包括鹅莓饼干的午餐。"潘朵拉笑着把刚
刚的话说完。

喝完茶后,潘朵拉让孩子们去小睡一会儿,
平复一下一个上午激动的心绪。她先把他们送
到各自的袜子床上,然后在莉拉的头上系上一
条法兰绒围巾。

"对不起,我被困住了,忘了带糖海带回
家。"莉拉轻声说。

潘朵拉轻轻应了一声,爱怜地拍了拍她。

"宝贝,你把自己带回家了。"她说,"这
才是这个家最需要的。"

莉拉笑了笑,随即进入了梦乡。

5. 章鱼一家

第二天下午，当海勇从灯室的窗户看见不是一只，而是三只章鱼的时候，十分激动。

"章鱼们来了！"他朝楼下厨房里正在给潘朵拉帮忙的孩子们喊道。

"章鱼们？"哨子重复道。

当潘朵拉准备好午餐便当后，哨子和莉拉跑到了岸边。他们看见正从海浪中游来的克莱奥，立刻知道他确实还是个小孩子——因为和他游在一起的那两个长着触手的同类，比他大得太多了。

"我把我的爸爸妈妈带来了！"克莱奥叫道。

三只章鱼尽可能近地游向岸边。哨子和莉拉很高兴认识克莱奥的父母：汉考克和弗洛伦斯。妈妈弗洛伦斯大部分时间都藏在水里，只从水面上露出她的眼睛来。

　　"我妈妈很害羞。"克莱奥说，"我们都很害羞，但我真的想让爸爸妈妈见见你们。"

　　莉拉露出最甜美、真诚的笑容欢迎他们。

　　"我们非常高兴你们能来这里，"她对汉考克和弗洛伦斯说，"你们的儿子是个英雄。"

　　一听到这句话，三只章鱼立即全都变成了红色。

　　"哎呀！"莉拉惊叹道。

　　"我们也非常高兴，小老鼠。"汉考克回答说，"我们也为自己的儿子感到骄傲。"

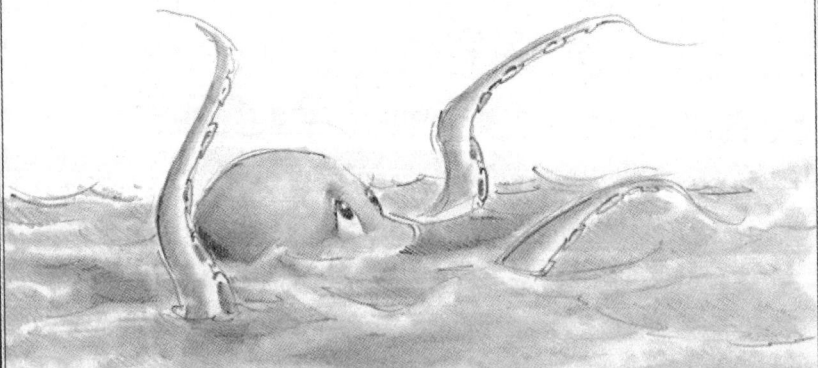

"我脸红了，所以他们也跟着变红了。"克莱奥解释说，"我们习惯模仿。"

"我们希望邀请你们共进午餐，在那边的海蚀洞里，"哨子发出邀请，"可以吗？"

弗洛伦斯抬起头来。"我们很乐意。"她说。然后她又把头低了下去。

"太好了！"莉拉叫道。

没过多久，灯塔一家和章鱼一家聚集在海蚀洞里，快快乐乐地共享午餐。

潘朵拉准备了一顿精美的午餐，包括松软的鹅莓饼干和鹅肠菜蘑菇苹果沙拉，甜点是大黄叶馅饼。

"吃了这顿饭，我再也不觉得糖海带好吃了。"汉考克边说边往嘴里又塞了一块馅儿饼。

克莱奥的妈妈弗洛伦斯送给潘朵拉一条珍珠手链，作为献给女主人的礼物。

"这条珍珠手链来自我们的沉船。"克莱奥解释说。

"你们的沉船？"哨子问道。

"我没告诉过你们吗？我们住在一艘沉船上。"克莱奥回答道。

"太棒了！"哨子说。

就这样，这些新结识的朋友们在海蚀洞里待了整整一个下午。海勇和汉考克互相讲述了他们遇到的脾气最坏的鱼的故事（海勇遇到的是条河豚，汉考克遇到的则是只乌贼）。弗洛伦斯告诉潘朵拉海胡萝卜的疗效。小不点儿则在克莱奥的触手上跑来跑去，每一条都跑了个遍。哨子和莉拉则从洞口采集了淡紫色的雏菊，送给每个人一束小小的、芬芳的花束。

这一天一切都很美好。结识新朋友，永远是
一件美好的事。

The

LIGHTHOUSE FAMILY

THE OCTOPUS

1. The Garden

Perched on an island cliff, high above the deep waters of the ocean, a lighthouse stands steady and strong. Its great lamp shines across the waves day and night, guiding sailors on their journeys home.

This lighthouse is well loved, and not only by the sailors who watch carefully for its beacon in the night. It is also well loved by the family who lives there.

This is a happy family. Pandora, the cat, and Seabold, the dog, are raising three mouse-children, in addition to keeping the light. The children are Whistler, Lila, and baby Tiny.

The members of this family somehow found each other in this large, wide world. Pandora had lived four lonely years as a lighthouse keeper when she discovered Seabold washed upon her shore, battered by the storm that had tossed him there.

Pandora tended Seabold back to health. But just as

Seabold was planning his return to the sailor's life, he and Pandora found the children, lost and adrift at sea. The little mice had fled from an orphanage and, like Seabold, had been blown by a storm to the sanctuary of Pandora's lighthouse.

Within the keeper's cottage they each found kindness and comfort and the sudden pleasure of warm food and company. And there with Pandora they decided to stay. Even Seabold, the wanderer.

A long island winter was behind them now. It was spring again, and so much to do. Spring is a lively time around a lighthouse.

Whistler was shaping a bean trellis into the form of a cat, which delighted Pandora.

"By July the vines will have grown," said Whistler, "and the cat will show nicely."

"Brilliant," said Seabold. Seabold was busy planting carrots and beets. Seabold didn't much like beets, but he planted them for Lila, who liked to dip the doll clothes she sewed into beet juice to dye them a lovely red. She also used carrot tops to make a nice yellow.

Baby Tiny was big enough now to play in the light-house yard. But Seabold was so worried a strong gust of wind might blow her off the cliff that he tied her to Pandora's clothesline with a long length of woolen yarn. Tiny happily stacked her wooden blocks and scallop shells and the tiny puffins that Seabold had made.

In the fields behind the lighthouse the wild irises were budding, as were the poppies and primrose, and bluebells. And on the dunes the beach morning glories had begun to creep. In June when the morning glory vines were thick, Whistler and Lila planned to play hide-and-seek among the white blossoms.

For now they were happy to concentrate on Pandora's garden. While Whistler constructed his trellis, Lila made beetle houses with small piles of rocks, and she collected fresh water from the rain barrel into shells, placing these near the houses so the beetles might have a drink. Birds, too.

"Tonight is the full moon, children," said Pandora as she walked through the garden with an apron of mint.

"Oh good," said Lila, settling a shell into the ground.

"Everything will glow."

"Yes," said Seabold. "This moon will also bring the lowest tide of the year."

"It will?" asked Whistler.

"Indeed," answered Seabold. "There should be new things to see in the estuary when the water pulls back."

"We should explore!" said Lila.

"Definitely!" said Whistler. The children loved walking over the estuary at low tide, making tiny footprints in the mud as they looked at starfish and anemones left behind by the receding water.

"Tomorrow morning you may pack a bit of breakfast and go out early while Pandora and I trim the wicks," said Seabold. He said this cheerfully, for Seabold quite liked his keeper duties.

"Tiny will keep us company, won't you, Tiny?" Seabold added. The baby smiled at him. Seabold quite liked Tiny, too. He often carried her about as he did his chores, tucking her in the roll of his wool cap or fitting her into his vest pocket.

"But you must be very cautious, children," said Pandora,

pouring the mint from her apron onto a netted screen to dry.

"You must remember not to turn your back to the sea as you explore the estuary," she said. "Always watch for the tide coming in, and be sure to return to the shore well ahead of it."

"We'll be careful," said Whistler.

"We promise," added Lila.

"And will you bring back some sugar kelp?" asked Pandora with a smile. "For lunch?"

"Of course!" said the children.

The lighthouse family *loved* sugar kelp. Lunch would be wonderful.

2. To the Shore

Early the next morning Pandora packed Whistler and Lila's twine bags with gooseberry biscuits, small red apples, and wooden flasks filled with tea. The children pulled on their slickers and they each kissed Tiny good-bye. (Tiny had been watching them from inside a sifter on the kitchen table.)

"Don't forget," reminded Pandora.

"Never turn our backs to the sea," said Whistler.

"Right," said Seabold, coming down the steps from the lantern room with several cleaning cloths in his hand.

"And remember to be quiet and friendly," he added. "The tide isn't often this low, so some of the creatures you meet may feel uncertain because they are usually covered by water."

"We will be as quiet as quiet can be," said Lila.

"I'm sure you will, dears," said Pandora, opening the door for them. "Just be home for lunch."

"Yes, Pandora," said Lila.

"See you soon!" said Whistler.

And carrying their breakfast bags, the children headed down to the shore.

3. The Octopus

When the children reached the shore, they were delighted to see how far away the water lay and how much more beach there was to explore.

"It feels as if we have a whole new island," said Lila as they walked out upon the hard, wet sand.

Whistler stepped gingerly around a small starfish.

"Quiet and friendly," he reminded Lila. "Quiet and friendly."

Lila pointed far out to the edge of the estuary, where the ocean gently lapped as it pulled itself away.

"We've never been all the way out there," she said.

"Let's go," said Whistler.

The children ventured farther and farther out over the estuary. As they walked, sea squirts shot water up all around them and crabs scuttled and starfish watched.

"The mud is getting softer," said Lila, lifting her foot.

"It hasn't dried in the sun yet," said Whistler.

Whistler and Lila stopped to look into the little pools of water the tide had left behind.

"Goodness," said Lila, gazing at a giant green anemone. "I've never met one of these."

"And I've never met one of these," said Whistler, pointing to an orange sea cucumber.

Someone tapped Whistler on the leg.

"Have you ever met one of me?" a voice asked.

"*Ah!*" Whistler jumped in surprise. "Who said that?"

He and Lila peered behind them into a small, dark pool of water. "I think I see a pair of eyes," said Lila. "Or maybe doorknobs."

"Where?" asked Whistler, bending closer to the water.

A small tentacle reached up from the pool and tapped

him on the nose.

"*Ah!*" Whistler jumped again.

"Hey!" said Lila. "It's an octopus!"

They watched as two large yellow eyes, which did indeed look like doorknobs, rose to the water's surface. The yellow eyes belonged to a small, baggy body that sported eight long tentacles.

One of the tentacles waved hello.

"My name is Cleo," said the octopus. "I'm sorry I made you jump."

"Oh, that's quite all right," said Whistler. "That was a good trick. I'm Whistler and this is my sister Lila."

"Pleased to meet you," said Lila, stepping nearer the octopus. As she drew closer, something amazing happened.

"You changed!" said Lila. "Now you have stripes!"

"Oops," said Cleo. "They're *your* stripes," he said, pointing to Lila's slicker. "Sometimes I blend without thinking."

"Amazing!" said Whistler.

"Well, I'm still practicing on stripes," said Cleo. "But I do reds and greens quite well."

"May we see?" asked Lila.

"Do you have something red with you?" asked Cleo.

Lila and Whistler looked at each other.

"Apples!" said Whistler.

He pulled his apple from the twine bag and held it out to Cleo.

The octopus turned a wonderful red.

"Oh my goodness!" said Lila.

Cleo assumed his original brown shade.

"I like colors," he said, "but I'm too shy to be flashy."

"I never thought we'd meet an octopus in the estuary," said Whistler.

"Yes," said Lila. "Usually there are only creatures who squirt or stare."

"I made a mistake," said Cleo. "That's why I'm here in this little pool."

"A mistake?" asked Lila.

"The tide pulled away so quickly," said the octopus. "I was resting in this hole and when I popped my head up, the ocean had left me behind!"

"Oh dear," said Lila.

"Don't worry," Whistler told the octopus. "The tide

will come back and carry you out to sea again."

"Shall we keep you company until it does?" asked Lila.

"Would you?" asked Cleo. "It's a bit boring just sitting here. I don't know how the starfish do it."

"They solve problems," said Whistler.

"Pardon me?" asked Cleo.

"I once asked a starfish what he does all day," explained Whistler, "and he said, 'I solve problems.'"

"Oh," said Cleo. "What sort of problems?"

"Well," said Whistler, "he said to me, 'Today it's a mouse problem.'"

"Oh." The octopus thought a moment. "I'm not sure," Cleo said, "but I think perhaps he was being rude."

"I think so too," said Lila.

Whistler agreed. Then he pulled open his twine bag.

"Have you ever had a gooseberry biscuit?" he asked Cleo.

Whistler broke a biscuit into four pieces and placed each piece on one of Cleo's tentacles.

Pop, pop, pop, pop. The little octopus popped each piece into his mouth.

"Mmmmm." He smiled. "Thank you."

Lila looked out toward the water.

"Whistler," she said, "I think the tide has started coming in."

Whistler looked at the line of water now slowly lapping its way to shore.

"Oops," he said. "We'd better go. Cleo, will you swim over to the lighthouse to visit us sometime?"

"I'd love to!" said Cleo.

"We'd better hurry," said Lila. "The tide seems to be edging in fast."

She picked up her bag and tried to take a step.

"I'm stuck!" she said. "I can't move my feet!"

Whistler knelt down and tried to lift Lila's foot out of the mud.

"Your foot won't budge!" he said. "Pull—pull hard!"

Lila tried with all her strength to move her feet.

"I'm stuck!" she said. "And the tide is coming in!"

"I'm strong," said Cleo. "Maybe I can lift you out."

He wrapped a tentacle around Lila's waist and pulled.

"It isn't working!" said Lila. "The mud has hardened all

63

around me and it won't let me go."

"We have to soften it up," said Whistler. "We have to get it all wet again."

"Hurry!" said Lila. "Think of something!"

"I *have!*" said Cleo. And he turned his body until a funnel-shaped part of it was pointing at Lila.

"Hold on!" said Cleo. He sucked water into the funnel, then shot it out in a strong spray all over Lila.

"Great!" said Whistler. "Keep going!"

Cleo sprayed and sprayed until Lila, and all the mud surrounding her, was soaking wet.

Lila lifted one foot out of the mud. *Thook.* Then another.

She gave a deep, drippy sigh of relief.

"Thank you, Cleo," she said. "Thank you."

Whistler grabbed Lila's hand to run back to shore and home.

"Come visit us, Cleo!" Whistler called as they ran. "Tomorrow afternoon!"

And the two mouse-children ran quickly to safety, away from the water, which the little octopus couldn't wait to swim in again.

4. Home

Whistler and Lila arrived home with four muddy feet, no sugar kelp, and some sneezes (Lila's). Pandora met them at the door and knew right away that their morning had been an eventful one. (Another adventure, Seabold would have said, had he not been up in the lantern room with Tiny.)

Pandora brought the children in and sat them down by the stove, and then she put their feet in pans of nice warm water and draped warm woolen cloths over their heads.

"But *my* head isn't wet," said Whistler. "Only Lila got sprayed."

"Every head wants to be warmed," said Pandora, bringing a pot of tea to the table. "And how did you come to be sprayed, Lila dear?"

"It was an octopus," said Lila.

Pandora set down the teapot. She looked calmly at the children.

"I think Seabold might like to hear this story," she said. And she called him down from the lantern room.

When Seabold came down, with Tiny on his shoulder, everyone gathered for tea while the children explained how they came to meet an octopus and how the octopus had saved Lila.

"Astounding," said Seabold. "And very good thinking for a baby."

"A baby?" asked Whistler.

"Yes, of course," said Seabold. "Any octopus found in a tidal pool so small would be a child."

"You mean Cleo will grow bigger?" asked Lila.

"Oh, much bigger," said Seabold.

"We should thank the child in some way," said Pandora.

"Yes," said Lila. "He's a hero for saving me."

"I invited him to visit us tomorrow afternoon," said Whistler.

"Perfect," said Pandora. "I'll make a nice big lunch—"

"He likes gooseberry biscuits," interrupted Whistler.

"—which will include gooseberry biscuits," finished Pandora with a smile.

After tea Pandora sent the children to nap away their exciting morning, first settling them into their sock-bed, then tying a flannel scarf about Lila's head.

"I'm sorry I got stuck and forgot to bring home the sugar kelp," Lila whispered softly.

Pandora purred and patted her lovingly.

"You brought home *you*," said Pandora. "That is all this family ever asks, dear."

Lila smiled and went instantly to sleep.

5. A Family

The next afternoon it was quite thrilling when Seabold spotted not one, but three octopi from the window of the lantern room.

"The octopi have arrived!" he called down the stairs to the children who were helping Pandora in the kitchen.

"*Octopi?*" repeated Whistler.

As Pandora finished preparing a picnic lunch, Whistler and Lila ran down to the shore. There they found Cleo swimming in the waves, and they knew right away he was indeed a child, for the tentacled creatures with him were *much* larger than he.

"I brought my parents!" Cleo called.

The three octopi came as close to shore as they could and Whistler and Lila were delighted to be introduced to Cleo's parents, Hancock and Florence. Florence stayed hidden in the water mostly. Only her eyes broke the surface.

"My mother is shy," said Cleo. "We're *all* shy. But I really wanted my parents to meet you."

Lila put on her best, most inviting smile and welcomed them.

"We are so very happy to have you here," she told Hancock and Florence. "Your son is a *hero*."

Upon hearing those words, all three octopi turned red.

"Oops," said Lila.

"We're just proud, little mouse," said Hancock. "We're just proud of our boy."

"They turned red because I did," said Cleo. "You know how we blend."

"We hope you'll meet us in the sea cave over there for lunch," said Whistler. "Will you?"

Florence popped her head up.

"We'd be pleased to," she said.

Then she popped it back down.

"Wonderful!" said Lila.

And before long, the lighthouse family and the octopus family were all gathered in the sea cave, enjoying lunch and each other.

Pandora had prepared a wonderful meal of fluffy gooseberry biscuits, a salad of chickweed, mushrooms, and apples, and for dessert rhubarb potpies.

"I shall never enjoy kelp again," said Hancock as he filled his mouth with another piece of pie.

Cleo's mother, Florence, had brought a pearl bracelet for Pandora, a gift for their hostess.

"The pearls came from our shipwreck," explained Cleo.

"Your shipwreck?" asked Whistler.

"We live in a shipwreck," said Cleo. "Didn't I mention

that?"

"Fantastic!" said Whistler.

And so the new friends lingered in the sea cave all afternoon. Seabold and Hancock traded stories about the grumpiest fish they'd met (Seabold: a blowfish; Hancock: a squid). Florence told Pandora about the healing properties of sea carrots, while Tiny ran up and down all of Cleo's tentacles. And Whistler and Lila gathered pale violet daisies from the cave's entrance, bringing everyone a small, fragrant bouquet.

Everything was good this day. It was always good to make new friends.

图书在版编目（CIP）数据

灯塔之家. 小章鱼克莱奥 ／（美）辛西娅·劳伦特著；
（美）普莱斯顿·马克丹尼斯绘 ；栾述蓉译. -- 南昌 ：
二十一世纪出版社集团，2023.4

ISBN 978-7-5568-6915-2

I.①灯… II.①辛… ②普… ③栾… III.①儿童故
事—图画故事—美国—现代 IV.①I712.85

中国版本图书馆CIP数据核字 (2022) 第195950号

THE LIGHTHOUSE FAMILY: THE OCTOPUS
Simplified Chinese translation copyright © 2023 by TB Publishing Limited
Original English language edition:
Text copyright © 2005 by Cynthia Rylant
Illustrations copyright © 2005 by Preston McDaniels
Published by arrangement with Beach Lane Books,
an imprint of Simon & Schuster Children's Publishing Division.
All rights reserved.

版权合同登记号：14-2022-0064

灯塔之家 小章鱼克莱奥

DENGTA ZHI JIA XIAO ZHANGYU KELAIAO

[美]辛西娅·劳伦特／著 [美]普莱斯顿·马克丹尼斯／绘 栾述蓉／译

出 版 人	刘凯军	
项目策划	奇想国童书	
责任编辑	刘晨露子	
特约编辑	郑应湘　孙金蕾	
装帧设计	田丽丹	
出版发行	二十一世纪出版社集团	
	（江西省南昌市子安路75号 330025）	
网　　址	www.21cccc.com	
经　　销	全国新华书店	
印　　刷	固安兰星球彩色印刷有限公司	
版　　次	2023年4月第1版	
印　　次	2023年4月第1次印刷	
开　　本	710 mm×1000 mm 1/16	
印　　张	5	
字　　数	21千字	
书　　号	ISBN 978-7-5568-6915-2	
定　　价	198.00元（全8册）	

赣版权登字-04-2022-658　　　　版权所有，侵权必究
购买本社图书，如有问题请联系我们：扫描封底二维码进入官方服务号。
服务电话：010-64049180（工作时间可拨打）；服务邮箱：qixiangguo@tbpmedia.com 。

传世经典桥梁书

灯塔之家

6

水獭兄妹多利多蒂

[美]辛西娅·劳伦特 著

[美]普莱斯顿·马克丹尼斯 绘 栾述蓉 译

21 二十一世纪出版社集团
21st Century Publishing Group

献给"小金块"。

——普莱斯顿·马克丹尼斯

奇想国童书

项目策划　奇想国童书
责任编辑　刘晨露子
特约编辑　郑应湘　孙金蕾
装帧设计　田丽丹

目 录

1. 救 命！

在一座高高耸立、俯瞰大海的悬崖之上，矗立着一座美丽的灯塔。灯塔里住着一个幸福的家庭。这不是一个普通的家庭，而是一个历经风险，因救助和爱而诞生的家庭。

猫咪潘朵拉曾独自在灯塔里生活了很多年，尽职尽责地守护着灯塔的光明。在那漫长的时光里，有时候，她禁不住会想，自己是否会永远这样孤独下去。

有一天，一场暴风雨带来了一个惊喜：一个叫海勇的水手和他破损的小船。潘朵拉帮海勇恢复健康，海勇则修好了自己的船，准备再次扬帆出海。海勇属于大海。

但潘朵拉和海勇还没来得及说再见，另一个惊喜就已经到来了：哨子、莉拉和老鼠婴儿小不点儿。这三个孩子是孤儿。他们置身于一个木板箱里，在海上漂流。海勇救了他们，把他们带到了潘朵拉身边，因为她能给予孩子们最好的东西——安慰和爱。

在这之后，还有一个惊喜：海勇放弃了他的航海生涯，决定继续留在灯塔里，帮助潘朵拉抚养三个孩子。海勇觉得他们可能都需要他。

这就是灯塔之家的由来。

此时正值夏天，因为没有大雾威胁航行的船只，也没有大风将船只吹离航线，所以灯塔上的工作任务得以大大减轻。

灯塔里的一家人也得以休息放松和游玩。

当然，哨子和莉拉不管冬夏，一直在玩，只不过夏天玩游戏这件事会简单些。他们爬上悬崖，采集野葱，给潘朵拉做夏季沙拉用。他们静静地坐在入海口，看着结婚多年的天鹅夫妇一起优雅地滑行。而当海鸥飞过他们的头顶时，他们则和海鸥一起欢笑。

当她的哥哥和姐姐外出探险时，小不点儿会和潘朵拉或海勇待在一起，她感到安全又温暖。潘朵拉喜欢照看她种下的毛地黄，或者烤玫瑰花松饼，小不点儿则在她的围裙口袋里呼呼大睡。而当海勇忙着修理潘朵拉豌豆地四周的石头围墙，或者用木头制作给孩子们骑着玩耍的海马时，他经常会把小不点儿放在自己帽子的卷边里。

"孩子们会非常喜欢这些的。"当海勇把一

只做好的海马展示给潘朵拉看时，潘朵拉赞许地说。

"小不点儿暂时还不能骑海马，所以我给她做了一个河豚球。"海勇说。

小不点儿把这个小球滚过小屋的门廊。

"很可爱。"潘朵拉说。

这个夏日过得如此平静，所以当海中的浮标突然铃声大作，并且疯狂地响个不停时，每个人都感到十分震惊。刺耳的声音吓得小不点儿慌忙钻进潘朵拉的围裙里，捂住自己的小耳朵。

哨子和莉拉跑进屋里。

"水獭！水獭！"他俩一起大喊道。

"你们在说什么，孩子们？"潘朵拉问道。与此同时，海勇伸手去拿他的手杖。

"一只水獭在摇浮标铃。"莉拉回答，她的眼睛因为吃惊而睁得大大的，"他在呼救！"

的确如此，一只水獭需要帮助。

而且毫无疑问，他找对了地方。

2.多蒂和多利

获得潘朵拉的允许后，哨子和莉拉跟着海勇一起从悬崖峭壁上爬下去，前往海边。

爬到一半的时候，海勇看见了海里的水獭。只见他正抱着浮标，用尽全力地来回摇晃。浮标的警铃发出震耳欲聋的声音，好似飓风在海上掀起了万丈波涛一般。

"救命啊！"水獭大喊道，"快点儿！"

海勇和孩子们加快了速度。他们爬上了海勇的船，很快就到了浮标处。

"哇，谢谢你们的到来！"水獭感激地说，"我叫多利。我妹妹多蒂遇到了麻烦。"

"什么样的麻烦？"哨子和莉拉异口同声地问道。

　　多利解释说，刚才他和妹妹在一艘停泊于蛋岛附近的废弃船上玩捉迷藏。

　　"然后，"多利表情沉痛地说道，"多蒂被水手的网缠住了，无法脱身。"

"啊，天哪！"莉拉脱口而出。她和哨子看着海勇，想知道他会怎么做。

海勇驾船去过五湖四海，经历过无数冒险。只要涉及大海或船只，无论什么问题，他都有解决办法。对于眼下这个问题，海勇有解决的自信。

"我知道怎样把你的妹妹从那张网中解救出来。"海勇对多利说。

"真的吗？"多利满怀希望地问。

"这艘船在蛋岛的哪一边？"海勇问道。

"西南方向。"多利回答说。

"你游回去。"海勇指示他说，"我们很快就会到那里。现在我需要找到几只海豚。"

"海豚？"哨子疑惑地问，"找海豚做什么呀？"

他们都看着海勇。

"比赛。"海勇笑着说，"海豚可以比赛。"

3. 海　豚！

一旦海勇拿定主意，事情的进展就会非常迅速。水獭多利游回了妹妹身边，海勇和孩子们则回到了灯塔。随后，潘朵拉跟一只海鸥交谈了一番。这只海鸥名叫鲁弗斯，喜欢在灯室外的窗台上休息。

　　"你能尽快找到海豚吗？"潘朵拉问道。

　　"我知道海豚的确切位置在哪里，"鲁弗斯回答说，"因为我们今天早上刚刚进行了一场比赛。"

　　"你能飞到海豚那里，告诉他们我们急需海豚的帮助吗？"潘朵拉问道。

　　没等潘朵拉说声谢谢，鲁弗斯就飞走了。

　　厨房里，哨子和莉拉正在打包午餐，准备

带给多利和他被渔网缠住的妹妹。

"他们可能很渴。"莉拉说着把野覆盆子果汁倒入海勇用葫芦雕刻的壶中，然后用一颗大橡子塞住壶嘴。

"还很饿。"哨子边说边拿了一条潘朵拉的茶巾，把早餐剩下的接骨木油饼包了起来。

海勇一直看着窗外，很快就看到了鲁弗斯。海鸥示意他到岸边去。

"孩子们，我们走吧！"海勇招呼道，"快点儿！"

"祝你们好运！"潘朵拉一边说，一边和小不点儿一起，向他们挥手告别。

当海勇和孩子们走到岸边时，发现有十二

只海豚已等在那里，有的不时地跃出海面，有的在水里来回转圈，有的摇头晃脑兴奋地交谈着。

"他们来了！"一只海豚叫道。

海勇、哨子和莉拉站在一块礁石上等着，海豚们游了过来。

"有什么我们可以帮忙的？"十二只海豚异口同声地问道。说话时，他们的鼻子上下晃动着。

"我们需要找到一群锯鳐。"海勇说，"你们能带我们去吗？"

"当然可以！"十二只海豚一起回答说。

很快，海勇、哨子和莉拉驾驶"探险号"扬帆起航，十二只海豚围绕在小小的船头附近，他们游起来风驰电掣、光彩夺目，他们都泳技超群，又充满特别的幽默感。

在他们的引领下，"探险号"以前所未有的速度，向着从未到过的遥远地方驶去。

哨子和莉拉这时候才发现，海豚们是如此喜欢竞速航行的比赛。

4.蛋 岛

海豚们很快就找到了一群锯鳐，所有的锯鳐都肯定地表示他们乐意帮忙。于是，海豚们游走了，继续玩耍去了。海勇、哨子和莉拉驾船开往蛋岛，一群能干的锯鳐紧跟在他们身后。

"我看到他们了！"当那艘废弃的船远远地出现在视野中时，莉拉高声喊了起来。"我们带来了果汁！"她叫道。

"还有油饼！"哨子喊道。

不一会儿，锯鳐们就开始全力以赴地锯起缠住小水獭多蒂的绳子来。

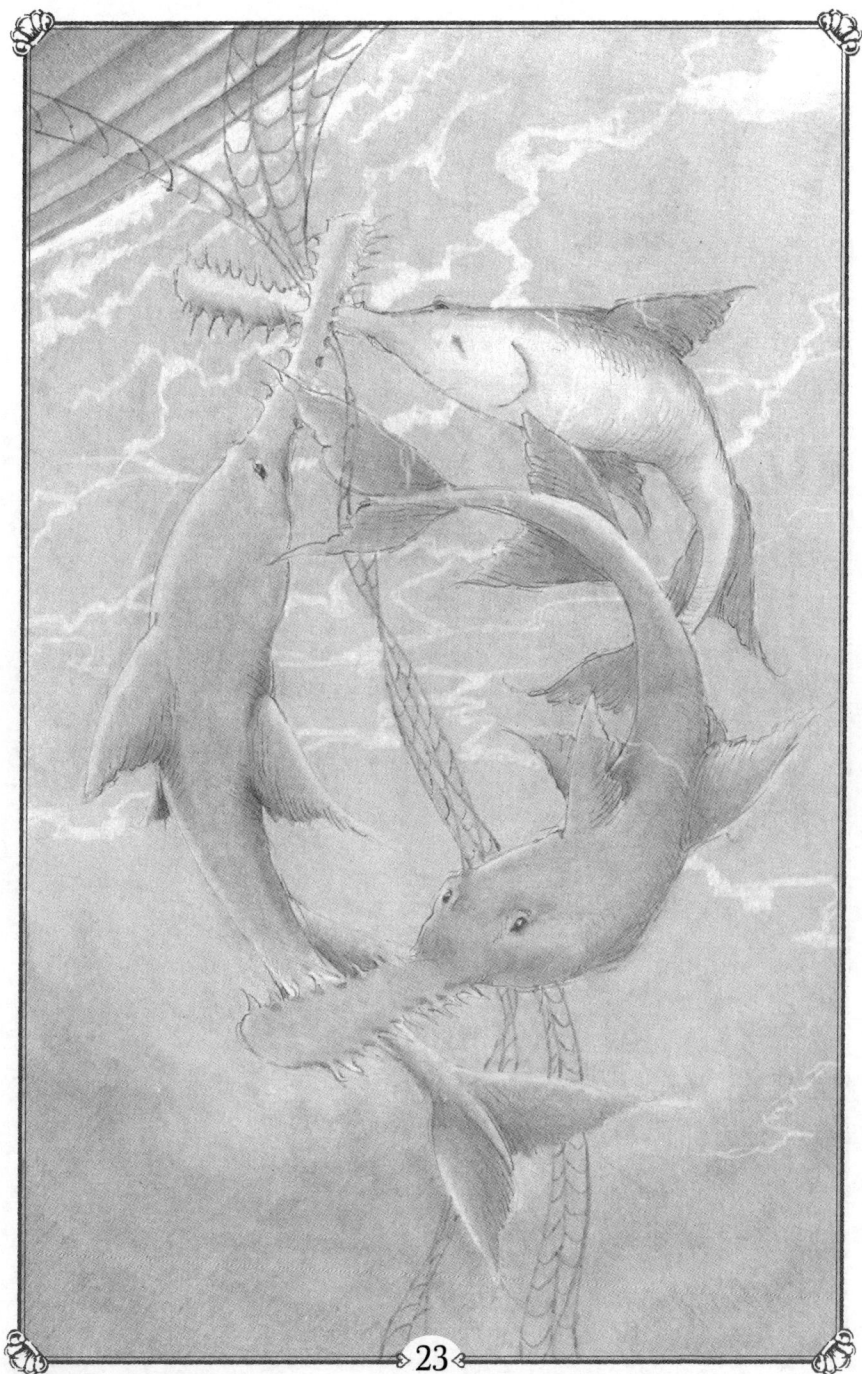

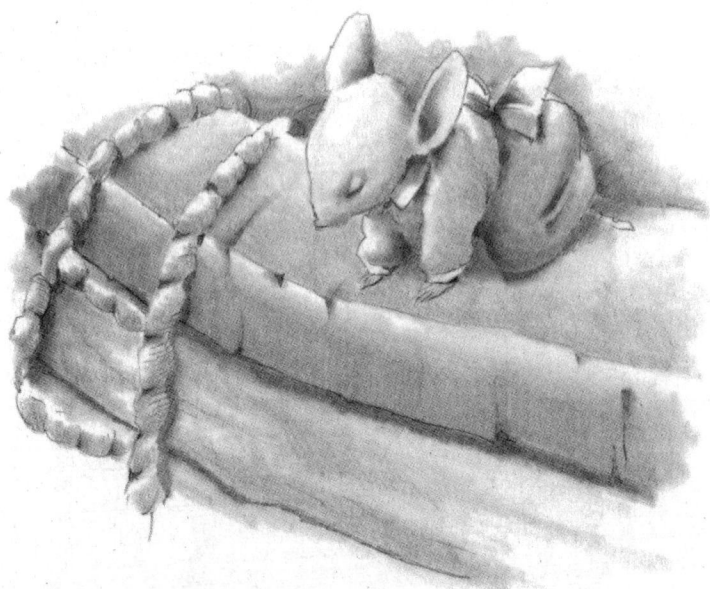

在锯鳐们干活儿的时候，莉拉尽力安慰多蒂。她给多蒂讲美人鱼的故事，缓解她的紧张情绪。

　　但是水手的网又粗大又结实，要锯断这样的绳子，锯鳐们需要花费很长的时间。

　　此时，太阳已经开始落山。很快，海面将被黑暗笼罩。

　　可怜的多蒂，被绳子缠得死死的，一动不

能动。随着太阳慢慢落山，她感到越来越害怕，开始哭了起来。

"亲爱的！"哨子、莉拉、海勇和多利同时安抚起多蒂。如果不是忙得不可开交，锯鳐们估计也会这么呼唤她。

但就在此时，在黑暗中，他们周围的海水开始闪闪发光，并且变得越来越明亮。

这样的情景让多蒂奔涌的眼泪止住了。

"是水母！"哨子叫道。

就连发光水母也来帮忙了。

每个人都竭尽全力地来帮助多蒂，终于使她重获自由。

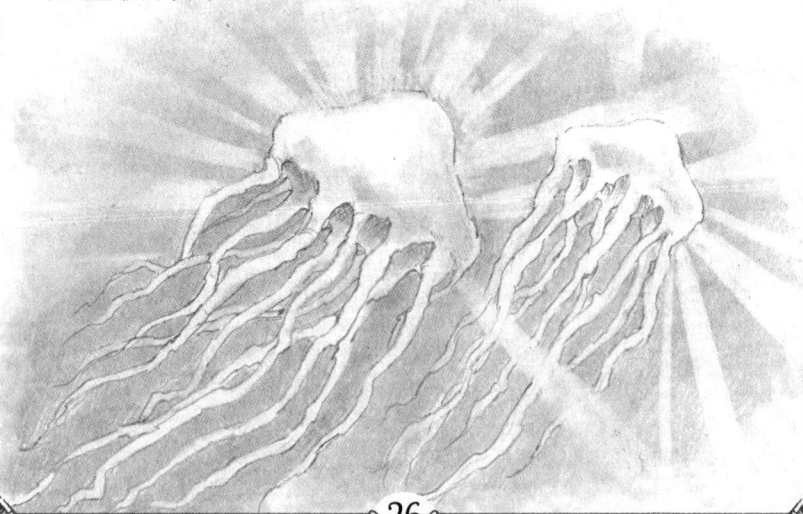

多蒂首先拥抱了哥哥,接下来拥抱了海勇、哨子和莉拉,最后给那些帮助自己的水中小伙伴们送了一个飞吻。

锯鳐和水母游走了。留下来的大家在这个美丽的夜晚,一起吃着接骨木油饼,喝着热乎乎的野覆盆子果汁。

5.朋友们和饺子

在这场紧张、刺激的夜间营救过去不久后的一个早晨，多利和多蒂出现在灯塔之家的小屋门口。两只水獭看上去非常快乐，灯塔之家的每个人都很高兴见到他们。

"我们这次来是想为你们做些事情。"多蒂解释说，"为了报答你们的勇敢和善良。"

"啊，这没什么。"哨子说，"而且说实话，能帮到你们，我们很开心。"

"不管怎样，我们不能白来一趟。"多利说。

随后，他从口袋里掏出一个小锤子，说："我对使用工具很在行。"

多蒂则从她的口袋里掏出一个针垫，说："我很擅长做针线活儿。"

"我们能为你们做些什么？"他们异口同声地问道。

　　就这样，在这一天结束时，潘朵拉有了一个漂亮的崭新的杉木桶，里面种满了小红萝卜和胡萝卜。

　　而莉拉和小不点儿的娃娃各自有了五件新
衣服。

他们每个人都吃了一大碗山药饺子。

　　然后，多蒂和多利按照水獭的习惯，手拉手离开，回自己的家去了。

结识新朋友的感觉真好！

The
LIGHTHOUSE FAMILY

THE OTTER

1. Help!

On a tall cliff rising far above the sea stood a beautiful lighthouse, and in this lighthouse lived a happy family. But this was not an ordinary family. It was a family created by adventure, rescue, and love.

Pandora the cat had lived there alone for many years, devoted to the keeping of the light, and sometimes she had wondered if she might always be alone.

Then one day a storm had blown in a surprise: a sailor named Seabold and his shipwrecked little boat. Pandora helped Seabold mend, and he, in turn, mended his boat to prepare for sailing again. Seabold belonged to the sea.

But before Pandora and Seabold could say their good-byes, another surprise arrived: Whistler, Lila, and baby Tiny, three orphaned children who had been set adrift in a crate at sea. Seabold rescued them, and he brought them to Pandora for that which she gave best—comfort and love.

After this, still another surprise: Seabold gave up his

sailing life. He decided to stay on at the lighthouse, to help Pandora raise the three small children. He felt they all might need him.

That is how the lighthouse family came to be.

It was now summer at the lighthouse, and chores were much easier, for there was no fog to threaten the sailing ships and no gales to blow the ships off course.

The lighthouse family could relax and play.

Of course, Whistler and Lila played all the time, summer or winter, but summer play was simpler. They climbed over the cliffs, collecting wild onion for Pandora's summer salads. They sat quietly in the estuary and watched the Swans— long married—glide gracefully together. They laughed with the laughing gulls when the birds flew above their heads.

Baby Tiny stayed safe and warm with Pandora or Seabold while her brother and sister were out exploring. Pandora enjoyed tending her foxgloves or baking rose-petal muffins while Tiny slept deep in her apron pocket. And Seabold often carried Tiny in the roll of his cap as he made himself useful repairing the rock walls around Pandora's pea patch or building wooden sea horses for the children to ride.

"The children will love those," Pandora said with approval as Seabold showed her one of the sea horses he had made.

"Tiny isn't quite ready to ride a sea horse," said Seabold. "So I made her a puffer-fish ball."

Tiny rolled the little ball across the cottage porch.

"Lovely," said Pandora.

This summer day was passing so peacefully that it was really quite jarring to everyone when suddenly the loud bell of a fog buoy out in the sea began frantically to ring. In fact, it was so alarming that Tiny scrambled into Pandora's apron and covered her tiny ears.

Whistler and Lila came running into the house.

"Otter! Otter!" they both cried.

"What do you mean, children?" asked Pandora as Seabold reached for his walking stick.

"An otter is ringing the buoy bell," said Lila, her eyes wide. "And he is calling for help!"

Indeed, an otter did need help.

And he had surely come to the right place to find it.

2. Dottie and Dooley

With Pandora's approval, Whistler and Lila climbed with Seabold down the rocky cliff to the shore.

Halfway down, Seabold could see the otter out in the water, hanging on to the fog buoy and rocking it back and forth with all his might. This made the buoy bell ring as loudly and clearly as if a mighty storm were tossing the water.

"Help!" called the otter. "Hurry!"

Seabold and the children hurried. They climbed into Seabold's boat and quickly arrived at the buoy.

"Oh, thank you for coming!" said the otter gratefully. "My name is Dooley, and my sister, Dottie, is in trouble."

"What kind of trouble?" asked Whistler and Lila at the same time.

Dooley explained that he and his sister had been playing tag on an abandoned boat anchored near Egg Island.

"And then," said the otter, his face looking quite

serious, "Dottie got tangled in a sailor's net, and she can't get out."

"Oh dear," said Lila. And she and Whistler looked straight at Seabold to see what he might do.

Seabold had sailed so many oceans and had lived so many adventures that whatever a problem might be, if it involved the sea or a boat, he would have the solution. And for this problem, Seabold felt sure that he did.

"I know how to free your sister from that net," he said to Dooley.

"You do?" the otter asked hopefully.

"On which side of Egg Island is this boat?" asked Seabold.

"Southwest," answered Dooley.

"Swim back," Seabold instructed, "and we will be there very soon. Right now I have to find some dolphins."

"Dolphins?" asked Whistler. "What can dolphins do?"

They all looked at Seabold.

"Race," said Seabold with a smile. "Dolphins can race."

3. Dolphins!

Things began to happen very quickly once Seabold had a plan. Dooley the otter went swimming back to his sister, Seabold and the children returned to the lighthouse, and soon Pandora was speaking to one of the gulls who liked to rest on the sill outside the lantern room. The gull's name was Rufus.

"Can you find the dolphins quickly?" asked Pandora.

"I know exactly where the dolphins are," said Rufus, "because we had a race this morning."

"Will you fly to them and tell them we need them right away?" asked Pandora.

And before she could say thank you, Rufus was off.

In the kitchen Whistler and Lila were packing a lunch for Dooley and his entangled sister.

"They will probably be very thirsty," said Lila, pouring wild raspberry juice into a pitcher Seabold had carved from a gourd. She popped a large acorn nut into the spout.

"And hungry," said Whistler, wrapping the elderberry fritters left from breakfast into one of Pandora's tea towels.

Seabold watched out the window and soon saw Rufus signaling him to the shore.

"Let's go, children!" said Seabold. "Hurry!"

"Good luck!" called Pandora as she and Tiny waved good-bye to them.

When they reached the shore, Seabold and the children found twelve dolphins leaping out of the water and spinning and bobbing and talking excitedly among themselves.

"There they are!" said one of the dolphins.

They swam up to the rock where Seabold waited with Whistler and Lila.

"How can we help?" all twelve said at the same time, bobbing their noses up and down.

"We have to find a school of sawfish," said Seabold. "Can you guide us there?"

"Oh yes!" came twelve answers.

Then Seabold, Whistler, and Lila were soon sailing in *Adventure*, its little bow surrounded by twelve speeding, dazzling, acrobatic, exceptionally good-humored dolphins.

In their wake, the little boat sailed faster and farther than ever before.

And Whistler and Lila discovered they adored racing.

4. Egg Island

The dolphins soon found the sawfish, and the entire school said that most certainly they would be happy to help. So the dolphins went off to play, and Seabold, Whistler, and Lila sailed toward Egg Island with a very capable school of sawfish following close behind.

"I see them!" cried Lila when the abandoned boat appeared in the distance. "We brought juice!" she called.

"And fritters!" yelled Whistler.

In no time at all the sawfish were sawing vigorously at the rope trapping the young otter.

Lila tried to comfort Dottie as the sawfish worked.

She told her stories about mermaids, which helped the mood all around.

But sailor's netting is very thick and strong. Sawing through such rope takes a sawfish quite a long time.

And the sun was now setting. And soon the sea would be dark.

Poor Dottie, all tangled and trapped, became more and more afraid as the sun's light disappeared. She started to cry.

"Oh dear," said Whistler, Lila, Seabold, and Dooley all together. The sawfish might have said this too, had they not been so busy.

But just then, in the darkness, the water all around them began to glow. It glowed, brighter and brighter, and as it did, Dottie's tears stopped flowing.

"Jellyfish!" said Whistler.

Even the luminescent jellyfish had come to help.

So with everyone doing everything they possibly could to help young Dottie, finally she was set free.

She hugged her brother first, and then she hugged Seabold, Whistler, and Lila. She blew kisses to the fish.

And as the sawfish and the jellyfish swam away, every-one who was left behind ate elderberry fritters and drank warm raspberry juice in the lovely night.

5. Friends and Dumplings

One morning not long after this amazing nighttime rescue, Dooley and Dottie showed up at the cottage door of the lighthouse family. The otters looked quite happy, and everyone was glad to see them.

"We have come to do something for *you* now," explained Dottie. "To repay you for your bravery and your kindness."

"Oh no," said Whistler, "it was no bother at all. In fact, we quite enjoyed it."

"Nevertheless, here we are," said Dooley.

He then pulled a small hammer from his pocket. "I am

very good with tools," he said.

Dottie pulled a pincushion from her pocket. "And I am very good with a needle," she said.

"What can we make for you?" they asked together.

So by day's end, Pandora had a beautiful new cedar barrel planted with radishes and carrots. And Lila and Tiny had five new dresses for their dolls.

Everyone ate a large bowl of yam dumplings, and then Dottie and Dooley left for home, holding hands as otters do.

It was so nice to have made new friends.

图书在版编目（CIP）数据

灯塔之家. 水獭兄妹多利多蒂 /（美）辛西娅·劳伦
特著 ;（美）普莱斯顿·马克丹尼斯绘 ; 栾述蓉译. --
南昌 : 二十一世纪出版社集团, 2023.4
ISBN 978-7-5568-6915-2

Ⅰ. ①灯⋯ Ⅱ. ①辛⋯ ②普⋯ ③栾⋯ Ⅲ. ①儿童故
事－图画故事－美国－现代 Ⅳ. ①I712.85

中国版本图书馆CIP数据核字 (2022) 第195948号

THE LIGHTHOUSE FAMILY: THE OTTER
Simplified Chinese translation copyright © 2023 by TB Publishing Limited
Original English language edition:
Text copyright © 2016 by Cynthia Rylant
Illustrations copyright © 2016 by Preston McDaniels
Published by arrangement with Beach Lane Books,
an imprint of Simon & Schuster Children's Publishing Division.
All rights reserved.

版权合同登记号：14-2022-0064

灯塔之家 水獭兄妹多利多蒂
DENGTA ZHI JIA SHUITA XIONG MEI DUOLI DUODI
[美]辛西娅·劳伦特 / 著 [美]普莱斯顿·马克丹尼斯 / 绘 栾述蓉 / 译

出 版 人　刘凯军
项目策划　奇想国童书
责任编辑　刘晨露子
特约编辑　郑应湘　孙金蕾
装帧设计　田丽丹
出版发行　二十一世纪出版社集团
　　　　　（江西省南昌市子安路75号 330025）
网　　址　www.21cccc.com
经　　销　全国新华书店
印　　刷　固安兰星球彩色印刷有限公司
版　　次　2023年4月第1版
印　　次　2023年4月第1次印刷
开　　本　710 mm×1000 mm 1/16
印　　张　3.5
字　　数　17千字
书　　号　ISBN 978-7-5568-6915-2
定　　价　198.00元（全8册）

赣版权登字-04-2022-657　　　版权所有，侵权必究
购买本社图书，如有问题请联系我们：扫描封底二维码进入官方服务号。
服务电话：010-64049180（工作时间可拨打）；服务邮箱：qixiangguo@tbpmedia.com 。

传世经典桥梁书

灯塔之家

7

小海狮托普

[美] 辛西娅·劳伦特 著

[美] 普莱斯顿·马克丹尼斯 绘　栾述蓉 译

21 二十一世纪出版社集团
21st Century Publishing Group

献给"小花生"。

——普莱斯顿·马克丹尼斯

奇想国童书

项目策划　奇想国童书
责任编辑　刘晨露子
特约编辑　郑应湘　孙金蕾
装帧设计　田丽丹

目 录

1. 秋 日

在深蓝色的大海上，矗立着一座孤独的灯塔，它曾经是猫咪潘朵拉这位孤独的灯塔看守者的家。潘朵拉发誓用生命去保护所有往来航行的船只。她忠于职守，日日夜夜看守着灯塔上那盏明灯，并且尽量不让自己感到孤独——只是要时时做到并不容易。

有一天，潘朵拉的生活发生了彻底的改变：一场暴风雨把一个名叫海勇的水手和他破损的小船"探险号"抛到了她所在的海岸上。潘朵拉从此有了同伴！

潘朵拉帮助大狗海勇恢复了健康，看着海勇整修好他的船并准备重回海上。分别的日子近在眼前。

就在海勇即将起航之前，又一次紧急救援发生了。潘朵拉和海勇发现了三只小老鼠孤儿，他们藏身于一个木板箱中，在茫茫大海上漂浮，又怕又饿。这三个孤儿——哨子、莉拉和小不点儿——十分迫切地需要一个家。

　　他们找到了一个家。这个家不仅由他们和守护灯塔的潘朵拉组成，更难能可贵的是，这个家也包括海勇。这位高尚的水手非常关心这几个孩子，所以他决定留下来，帮着照顾他们，做些自己力所能及的事。

　　这就是灯塔之家的由来。

　　灯塔附近的秋天是一年中非常美丽的时节。海面上，南下的灰鲸喷出心形的水花，向潘朵

拉问好，他们已经认识这只善良的猫很多年了。生长在茂密灌木丛中的蓝莓吸引了成千上万只燕子。燕子们俯冲下来饱餐一顿，然后再速速飞去，追赶鲸鱼迁徙的脚步。而到了傍晚，落日在高塔的窗户上，投射下深红色的余晖。

对灯塔之家来说，夏天总是轻松愉快的，而到了秋天，潘朵拉和海勇就要开始紧张地投入看守灯塔的工作中。现在，这个季节的第一场大雾随时可能降临，所以灯室的窗户和棱镜必须一尘不染。海勇总是手里拿着一块抹布，爬上爬下地干活儿。潘朵拉则把一桶桶的灯油

递给他,以便那盏巨大的灯的火焰整晚燃烧不熄,警示水手远离危险的礁石。

冬天很快就要来临,孩子们能在户外安全玩耍的日子已经所剩不多了,因此潘朵拉敦促他们去尽情探索。

"你确定不需要我们帮忙打扫吗?"每天,哨子和莉拉在出门前都会问上这么一句。

"不需要,我的宝贝。"潘朵拉总是这样回答,"你们的工作就是玩。"

哨子和莉拉笑了。这份工作可真不错。

两个孩子于是便离开了小屋。他们的妹妹小不点儿没有和他们一起去，她喜欢待在家里做家里那个年龄最小的乖宝宝。每一天，哨子和莉拉出门去，都期待会有一些新的发现。潘朵拉给孩子们的口袋里装满了用樱桃和薰衣草花制成的特殊糖果。

"这样，直到晚饭前，你们都不会饿肚子。"潘朵拉说。

哨子和莉拉喜欢四处探索。这里有这么多不同的地方可以去，你永远猜不到会有什么样的发现。

这一天，哨子和莉拉看到一只雪鸮①栖息在一个高高的山丘顶端，审视着目之所及的土地和海洋。

"他在思考这个伟大又广袤的世界。"哨子说道，莉拉点了点头。他们俩经常能看到这

_____

① 雪鸮是一种大型猫头鹰，因全身几乎为雪白色而得名。

只雪鸮，两人都很崇拜他。海勇曾告诉过他们，这只雪鸮不久就会飞回北极，不过目前他还留在这儿。

孩子们爬上了长满野玫瑰的陡峭山坡，朝着秘密海湾进发。鲸鱼妈妈们用这个海湾作为安置她们的宝宝们的日托所。鲸鱼宝宝们在这里绕着圈子游泳，而鲸鱼妈妈们则会离开一会儿，去做自己的事情。

哨子和莉拉本来盼望着今天海湾里会有鲸鱼宝宝，但他们都不在，只有几只黑尾鹿在礁石上吃海带。

两个孩子很有礼貌，尽量不发出声响，以免打扰到黑尾鹿。可是当他们走过一片岩藻时，脚下却发出了响亮的啪啪声。

黑尾鹿看到他们就跑开了。黑尾鹿总是很害羞。

"真对不起！"莉拉叫道。

"抱歉！"哨子说。

但也有一些生物喜欢孩子们的陪伴——泥滩上的扇贝就喜欢被孩子们追赶。当哨子和莉拉伸手去抓一只扇贝的时候，他就从壳里喷出一道水柱来，把孩子们浇个透心凉；他自己则

因为用力而在原地不停地转圈圈。

哨子和莉拉被许多只扇贝喷出的水淋着，最后被浇得像两只落汤鸡一样。他们一路欢笑着回家。

"你们又去跟扇贝玩了。"潘朵拉一边微笑着说，一边帮他们脱下湿毛衣。孩子们换上干爽的衣服，坐在桌前，开始吃大碗的炖甜菜和大麦。此时，小不点儿在一个装满苔藓的茶叶罐里，睡得正香。

这是灯塔里又一个美好的日子，不过孩子们仍然盼望着会有未曾谋面者到访，带给他们新奇的冒险体验。

于是，他来了。

2. 一个小宝宝！

在灯塔旁的小屋里，早晨，潘朵拉总是第一个起床，因为她喜欢在安静的独属于自己的厨房里为一家人准备早餐。在晨曦中搅动一大锅粥，让她感到快乐。

因此，在那个不速之客到来的早上，是潘朵拉先大声惊呼道："我的天哪！"她的叫喊声把所有人都吵醒了，只有那个客人例外。

灯塔之家的成员们穿着睡衣和拖鞋，目瞪口呆地盯着那个在海勇椅子上呼呼大睡的来客。

那是一只小海狮，打着呼噜，睡得非常香甜。

"我们应该叫醒他吗？"莉拉问道。她很期

待有新的玩伴。

所有人的目光都转向了海勇，因为这是他的椅子。大家似乎都认为应该由他来做决定。

海勇摇了摇头。

"让这个孩子睡吧。"他对大家说，"天知道我自己有多少回在那张椅子上锯过木头。"

"锯木头？"哨子不解地问。

海勇笑了。"我指的是打呼噜。"他解释说。

于是一家人开始吃他们的早餐。尽管锅咣当咣当地响，这个东西或那个东西不时叮当叮当地掉到地上，枫糖浆被要求递来递去的声音此起彼伏……家里一派忙碌嘈杂，但那只海狮宝宝却像所有的小宝宝一样，一直在酣睡。

终于，当哨子和莉拉在擦干最后两个早餐盘子时，小海狮睁开了眼睛。

他看到小不点儿在厨房的桌子上玩着一套木制的积木，就从海勇的椅子上坐起来，拍打着两只脚蹼，发出狮子一般的欢呼声。

"天哪！"大家惊叹道。小不点儿则对着这个会吼叫的宝宝咯咯地笑出声来。

等大家紧绷的神经都放松下来（他们还不

习惯有人在他们的厨房里吼叫），对小海狮说了一番表示欢迎的话之后，全家才得知这只海狮名叫托普，是他妈妈把他带到了这间小屋，把他放到了海勇的椅子上，并告诉他"在这里等着"。

"要等多久呢？"哨子问。

突然间，小海狮满眼是泪。

"哦，不会很久的，我肯定！"莉拉赶紧安抚这个孩子，"用不了多久的。"

"你想喝碗粥吗？"莉拉问道。莉拉一直很擅长照顾小孩子，她自己的小妹妹就很喜欢她。

托普擦了擦眼泪，点了点头。小海狮坐在海勇的椅子上，长着跟海勇一样的银色胡须，

看上去几乎就像这个家庭的另一个成员，一个小海勇。

托普的确非常轻松地就融入了这个家庭。他吃孩子们吃的东西，孩子们玩的时候他也玩（他很擅长接球），他们睡觉时他也跟着睡。每天都忙忙碌碌有事可做，让托普不再忧虑妈妈要过多久才能回来接他。

灯塔一家都非常喜欢托普，托普则对一切都充满好奇。他会用脚蹼拿起一个东西问："这是什么？"然后不管三七二十一，就扔到半空，对着它狂吠。小不点儿喜欢托普这样做，她在一旁一个劲儿地鼓掌，于是，托普就更来劲了。

托普在灯塔里住了三天之后，潘朵拉和海勇才意识到这只小海狮还没学会游泳。

"我的天哪。"潘朵拉说。

"我妈妈本来正准备教我的，"托普说，"然后她让我在这里等着。"

潘朵拉有一种非常强烈的母性本能，所以她希望托普能尽快学会游泳。

她告诉托普："这对一只海狮来说很重要。"

灯塔后面有一艘旧独木舟，多年来一直搁置在茂密的草丛中。从来没人用过这艘独木舟，因为海勇有自己的小船，而且唯一能用到独木舟的河离这儿很远，所以这艘独木舟没有什么用处。

但作为一个婴儿游泳池，它再合适不过了。

于是，灯塔里的一家人决定，在等待托普的妈妈回来的过程中，教托普学习游泳。

3. 玛丽回来了

在小海狮住下来的第七天，终于有消息传来。当时，海勇正在花园里修理门闩，一群大雁排成人字形在他头顶飞来飞去，吵吵嚷嚷，带来了消息。

每只大雁都在大声嚷嚷着，急于把消息说给他听，海勇只能听到他们七嘴八舌的吵嚷声，根本听不清他们到底在说些什么。

当雁群终于意识到这一点之后，他们推选了一位代表，降落到地面上。

"托普的妈妈需要送一只受伤的海雀到哈德利环礁，"大雁代表说，"但她已经在回来的路上了。明天就能到。"

　　这真是个好消息。为了庆祝这个消息，哨子和莉拉决定装饰一下小屋的门廊，以迎接海狮妈妈的到来。他们从盐沼的黏土中采集了天使之翼[1]贝壳，把它们挂在门廊的每根柱子上。然后，他们还用哨子收集的沙币[2]，在大门上方拼出了"欢迎"的字样。

　　最棒的是，莉拉为托普缝制了一顶海军蓝的水手帽，让托普戴着它迎接妈妈的归来。

　　第二天，托普的妈妈如约而至。她是只大

---

① 天使之翼是一种海鸥蛤，壳薄易碎，呈半透明状，两壳摊开极像天使的翅膀，所以得此美名。

② 沙币是一种圆形海胆，因为长得像银币而得名。

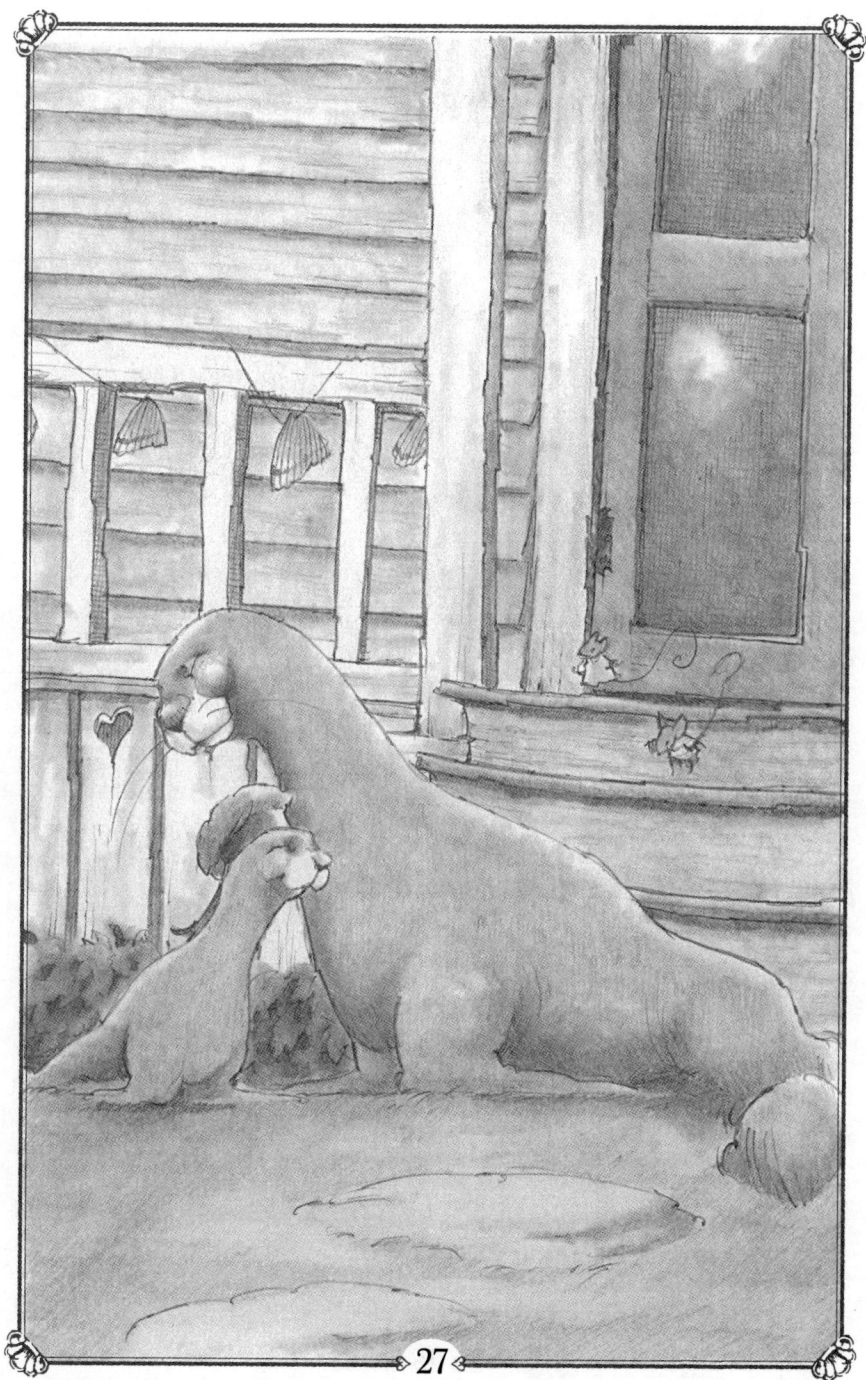

个头海狮，她那银色的胡须要比托普的长得多。莉拉认为她很美。

她名叫玛丽。玛丽已经在海上观察灯塔一家很长时间了。所以，当她突然需要帮助她的海雀朋友回家时，她确信自己的孩子在灯塔里会很安全。事实也的确如此。

"非常感谢你们，"玛丽说，"我希望托普没有总是在吼叫。"

"嗯，没有。"海勇说，"再说了，吼叫也是一种音乐。"

为了感谢他们每一位，玛丽带来了一个用熊草编织的漂亮的篮子（海雀的哥哥擅长编织篮子）。潘朵拉在篮子里装满了无花果、李子和蜂蜜小面包。

然后，所有人跟着一只非常快乐的小海狮来到屋后。

他们一起观看这只小海狮游泳。

The
LIGHTHOUSE FAMILY

THE SEA LION

1. Fall Days

There stands above the dark blue sea a solitary light-house that once was the home of only a solitary light-keeper, Pandora the cat. Pandora had pledged her life to the protection of all the sailing ships. Faithfully, night and day, she tended the lights, and she did her best not to feel lonely. But this was not always easy.

Then one day Pandora's life changed completely when a storm threw onto her shore a sailor named Seabold and his broken little boat, *Adventure*. Pandora had company!

She helped Seabold regain his health, and she watched as he repaired his boat to return to the sea. A good-bye was near at hand.

But before Seabold could set sail, there was yet another rescue. Pandora and Seabold found three orphaned children drifting in a crate in the sea, afraid and hungry. Their names were Whistler, Lila, and Tiny, and they very much needed a home.

They found one. Not only a home with Pandora in the protection of her lighthouse. But, remarkably, a home with Seabold as well. For the noble sailor came to care about them so much that he decided to stay, to help look after them, and to be of use.

And this is how the lighthouse family was made.

Fall was a beautiful time of year at the lighthouse. Out at sea the gray whales migrating south blew heart-shaped spray to say hello to Pandora, for they had known the kind cat for many years. Blueberries growing in deep thickets attracted thousands of swallows who swooped down for a big meal before flying to catch up with the whales. And in the evenings, sunsets cast a deep red glow over all the windows of the tall tower.

Summers were always playful times for the lighthouse family, but in the fall Pandora and Seabold got serious about lightkeeping again. Any day now there would be the first fog of the season, and the windows and the prisms in the lantern room had to be spotless. Seabold was always going up and down the ladder with polishing rags in his hands. Pandora passed pails of lantern oil to him for the giant lamp that burned each evening to warn sailors away from the dangerous rocks.

Because the children had only a short time left for playing safely outside before winter arrived, Pandora urged them to go and explore.

"Are you sure you don't need us to polish?" Whistler asked as he and Lila headed for the door every day.

"No, my dears," said Pandora. "Your work is to play."

Whistler and Lila smiled. It was nice to have that sort of work.

The children then left the cottage and their baby sister, Tiny, who enjoyed being the baby in the house, and they went out to see what they might find. Pandora sent them with pockets full of special candies made of cherries and lavender flowers.

"To keep you nicely fed until supper," she said.

Whistler and Lila loved to explore. There were so many different places to go, and one never knew what one might find.

This day Whistler and Lila saw a snowy owl perching at the very top of a high sand dune, surveying all the land

and sea.

"He is thinking about the great wide world," said Whistler. Lila nodded. They were both admirers of the owl, whom they saw now and then. Soon the owl would fly back to the Arctic, Seabold had told them. But at present he was here.

The children climbed the rocky slopes covered with wild roses, heading for the secret cove used by the whale mothers as a day-nursery for their babies. The babies swam in circles while the mothers went away for a little while to do whatever mother whales do.

Whistler and Lila hoped somebody might be in the cove today, but there were no baby whales, only some black-tailed deer enjoying a bite of kelp on the rocks.

The polite children tried to be very quiet so as not to disturb the deer, but they walked over a patch of rockweed, and it made a loud *pop~pop~pop* when they did.

The deer saw them and ran away. Deer were always shy.

"So sorry!" called Lila.

"Sorry!" said Whistler.

But there were others who did enjoy the children's

company. On the mudflats the sea scallops loved being chased by the children. When Whistler and Lila reached down to tag a scallop, it forced a jet of water from its shell that doused the children and set it spinning.

Whistler and Lila got very wet from so many showers, and they laughed all the way home.

"You've been visiting the scallops again," Pandora said, smiling as she helped them remove their wet sweaters. The children changed into dry clothes, then sat at the table eating big bowls of beet and barley stew. Baby Tiny was asleep in a tea tin filled with moss.

It was another very nice day at the lighthouse. But the children still hoped someone new might come along soon to give them an adventure.

And someone did.

2. A Baby!

In the cottage, Pandora was always the first one up in the mornings, as she enjoyed having a quiet kitchen to herself while she prepared the family's breakfast. Stirring up a big pot of porridge at dawn made her happy.

So it was Pandora who exclaimed "My goodness!" rather loudly on the morning that someone new arrived. And this woke everyone up except the visitor himself.

In their nightgowns and slippers, the lighthouse family stared at the visitor asleep in Seabold's chair.

It was a baby sea lion, snoring in perfect contentment.

"Should we wake him?" asked Lila, very much looking forward to a new playmate.

All eyes turned to Seabold. Since it was his chair, everyone seemed to think this was his decision.

Seabold shook his head.

"Let the baby sleep," Seabold told them. "Goodness knows I've sawed plenty of logs in that chair myself."

"Sawed logs?" repeated Whistler.

Seabold smiled. "Snored," he said.

So the family went about having their breakfast, and in spite of pans rattling and this and that dropping to the floor and many requests to pass the maple syrup, the baby sea lion, as all babies do, slept soundly through the noise of a very busy home.

Then finally, as Whistler and Lila were drying the last two breakfast plates, the sea lion opened his eyes.

He saw Tiny playing with a set of wooden blocks on the kitchen table, and he sat up in Seabold's chair, clapped both flippers, and roared like a lion.

"Heavens!" said everyone. Tiny laughed at the other baby, who could roar.

Once everyone's nerves had settled (they were not used to someone roaring in their kitchen), and welcomes had all been said, the family learned that the sea lion's name was Topper and that his mother had brought him to the cottage, put him in Seabold's chair, and told him to "wait here."

"For how long?" asked Whistler.

Suddenly the baby sea lion's eyes filled with tears.

"Oh, not long at all, I'm sure!" said Lila quickly to reassure the baby. "Not long at all!"

"Would you like a bowl of porridge?" she asked. Lila had always been good with babies. Her own baby sister adored her.

Topper wiped his eyes and nodded his head. Sitting there in Seabold's chair, silver whiskers just like Seabold's, he seemed almost like another member of the family. A little Seabold.

And Topper did fit in beautifully. He ate what the children ate, played when the children played (he was quite good at catch), and napped when the children napped. Staying busy helped keep away Topper's worries about how long he might have to wait for his mother.

The family enjoyed Topper very much. And Topper was curious about everything, so he would hold something in his flippers and ask, "What's this?" Then he would throw whatever it was into the air and bark at it. Tiny loved this. She clapped and clapped, which made Topper do it even more.

Topper had been at the lighthouse for three days before Pandora and Seabold found out that the baby sea lion had not yet learned how to swim.

"Oh dear," said Pandora.

"My mother was just about to teach me," said Topper, "before she told me to wait here."

Pandora had a very strong motherly instinct, so she wanted Topper to learn to swim as soon as possible.

"It is important for a sea lion," she told him.

There was an old dugout canoe behind the lighthouse that had been sitting in the tall grass for many years. The canoe was never used, for Seabold had his own boat, and the only river for paddling was too far away. So it was not very useful as a canoe.

But it would be a perfect baby pool.

So while they waited for Topper's mother to return, the lighthouse family saw to it that Topper had some swimming lessons.

3. Mary's Return

On the seventh day of the baby sea lion's stay, news finally arrived. It arrived in the form of a flock of very loud geese flying in a V above Seabold's head as he repaired a gate latch in the garden.

The geese were all shouting the news so loudly that it was impossible for Seabold to hear anyone because he had to listen to everyone.

When this became apparent to the geese, a representative landed.

"Topper's mother had to give an injured puffin a ride to Hadley's Atoll," said the goose. "But she's on her way back. She'll be here tomorrow."

This was indeed wonderful news. So wonderful that Whistler and Lila decided to decorate the cottage porch for the mother's arrival. They gathered angelwing shells from the clay of the salt marsh and strung them from post to post. Then they used Whistler's collection of old sand dollars to spell out WELCOME above the front door.

Best of all, Lila sewed a navy-blue sailor cap for Topper to wear for his mother's return.

The following day Topper's mother arrived just as she had promised. She was a very large sea lion, and her silver whiskers were much longer than Topper's. Lila thought she was beautiful.

Her name was Mary. From the sea Mary had watched the lighthouse family for a long time. And when she needed suddenly to help her puffin friend home, she knew that her baby would be safe at the lighthouse. Which, of course, he was.

"I am so grateful," said Mary. "I hope Topper didn't bark too much."

"Oh no," said Seabold. "And besides, barking is music to the ears."

To thank them all, Mary had brought a pretty basket woven of bear grass. (The puffin's brother was a basket weaver.) Pandora filled the basket with figs and plums and honey buns.

Then everyone followed a very happy little sea lion to

the back of the cottage.

And they all watched him swim.

图书在版编目（CIP）数据

灯塔之家. 小海狮托普 ／（美）辛西娅·劳伦特著；
（美）普莱斯顿·马克丹尼斯绘；栾述蓉译. -- 南昌：
二十一世纪出版社集团，2023.4
ISBN 978-7-5568-6915-2

I.①灯… II.①辛… ②普… ③栾… III.①儿童故
事—图画故事—美国—现代 IV.①I712.85

中国版本图书馆CIP数据核字 (2022) 第195949号

版权合同登记号：14-2022-0064

灯塔之家 小海狮托普
DENGTA ZHI JIA　XIAO HAISHI TUOPU
[美]辛西娅·劳伦特／著 [美]普莱斯顿·马克丹尼斯／绘 栾述蓉／译

出 版 人　刘凯军
项目策划　奇想国童书
责任编辑　刘晨露子
特约编辑　郑应湘　孙金蕾
装帧设计　田丽丹
出版发行　二十一世纪出版社集团
　　　　　（江西省南昌市子安路75号 330025）
网　　址　www.21cccc.com
经　　销　全国新华书店
印　　刷　固安兰星球彩色印刷有限公司
版　　次　2023年4月第1版
印　　次　2023年4月第1次印刷
开　　本　787mm×1092mm 1/16
印　　张　3.25
字　　数　14千字
书　　号　ISBN 978-7-5568-6915-2
定　　价　198.00元（全8册）

赣版权登字-04-2022-656　　　版权所有，侵权必究
购买本社图书，如有问题请联系我们：扫描封底二维码进入官方服务号。
服务电话：010-64049180（工作时间可拨打）；服务邮箱：qixiangguo@tbpmedia.com。

传世经典桥梁书

灯塔之家

8
大熊托马斯

[美] 辛西娅·劳伦特 著

[美] 普莱斯顿·马克丹尼斯 绘 栾述蓉 译

二十一世纪出版社集团
21st Century Publishing Group

献给艾迪森和艾略特。

——普莱斯顿·马克丹尼斯

奇想国童书

项目策划　奇想国童书
责任编辑　刘晨露子
特约编辑　郑应湘　孙金蕾
装帧设计　田丽丹

目 录

1. 冬天的狂风

看守灯塔往往意味着一种非常孤独的生活，这样的生活猫咪潘朵拉的确过了很多年。她努力坚守职责，让塔灯长明不熄，警示航行的船只远离岸边的礁石。但每一天，潘朵拉都暗自希望，能有人陪伴在自己身旁。

终于有一天，她想要的陪伴到来了。一场大风暴将一艘名为"探险号"的破旧小船吹到了岸上。和这艘小船一起被冲上岸的，还有同样受到风暴摧残的它的水手——海勇。

潘朵拉把海勇带到了她在灯塔旁边的小屋里，并且马上开始治疗他骨折的腿，炖肉给他吃，以增强他的体质。

过了一段时间，海勇完全康复了。他知道起程远航的时间到了，因为大海一直是他生活的全部。

然而就在海勇即将扬帆出海之时，一种完全不同性质的陪伴来到了灯塔，改变了所有的一切。

他们是哨子、莉拉和小不点儿，三个小老鼠孤儿。当潘朵拉和海勇发现这三个孩子时，他们正躲在一个木板箱里，无助地在海上漂浮。他们迷失了方向，而且饥饿难耐。

潘朵拉和海勇精心照顾这些孩子。随着海勇对孩子们的感情越来越深，他意识到自己根本无法再乘船离开。

就这样，他们一起组成了灯塔之家。

灯塔的夏天充满乐趣，秋天异常美丽，但灯塔的冬天却是一个严峻的挑战。

冬季，天空和大海总是灰蒙蒙的，狂风无休无止地呼啸着。看守灯塔的工作因此变得非常艰巨。潘朵拉和海勇不仅要保证厨房里的炉火日夜不熄，还要确保灯塔塔楼里的灯昼夜不灭。他们不断往灯里添加灯油，持续修剪灯芯，并且不停歇地清洁灯室的窗户。他们两个还必须轮流在夜里敲响雾钟，警告船只驶离危险地带。

哨子和莉拉希望能帮忙敲钟，但潘朵拉不允许。有时候风刮得太猛了，就连潘朵拉和海

勇也不得不把自己绑在树上，以免被风刮跑。

　　因此，孩子们通常待在屋里玩，比如玩跳棋，哨子和莉拉也会教小不点儿识数和认字母。

　　孩子们都着凉感冒了，他们把香蜂草药膏涂在红通通的鼻头上，大口大口喝着暖乎乎的姜茶。

　　终于，冬季的暴风雨发作的次数变得越来越少。有些个早晨，几乎没有一丝雾气。每个人都知道，春天正在悄悄地到来。

　　有一天，哨子和莉拉恳求潘朵拉和海勇让他们出去走走。

　　"我们会穿上三倍厚的衣服。"莉拉承诺。

　　"我们会遮住鼻子的。"哨子补充说。

　　潘朵拉和海勇同意孩子们出去，前提条件是孩子们必须避开多风的悬崖，紧靠森林的边缘行走，确保安全。

海勇递给哨子一个小沙漏。

"只能去一个小时，"海勇说，"然后必须回家。"

"只去一个小时。"哨子和莉拉保证道。

当孩子们走出门，踏入冰冷的空气里时，他俩都希望自己能有幸，在这一个小时里，经历一场冒险。

2. 很深的树洞

海边悬崖脚下生长着一片森林，里面布满了绿色的蕨类和苔藓，四处弥漫着雪松的芳香。哨子和莉拉喜欢这片森林。不过他们知道，这片森林纵深数千米，没有指南针的指引，他们不能冒险走进去，而应该像他们所承诺的那样，待在森林边上。

"那是什么？"哨子指着前方一样东西问道。它看起来像座小房子。

当他们走到近前时，孩子们意识到，这确实是座小房子。房子由树枝制成，非常独特。一只林鼠坐在门廊上，正在喝茶。

"早上好。"林鼠打招呼说。

"早上好。"哨子和莉拉一起回答道。

林鼠热情地请他们一起喝茶，但由于只有一个小时的探险时间，孩子们礼貌地谢绝了。

"那么下次好了！"林鼠欢快地说道。

哨子和莉拉继续向前走。当他们在一棵铁杉树旁的灌木丛中小心翼翼地采集云莓时，哨子突然对一样东西产生了好奇。

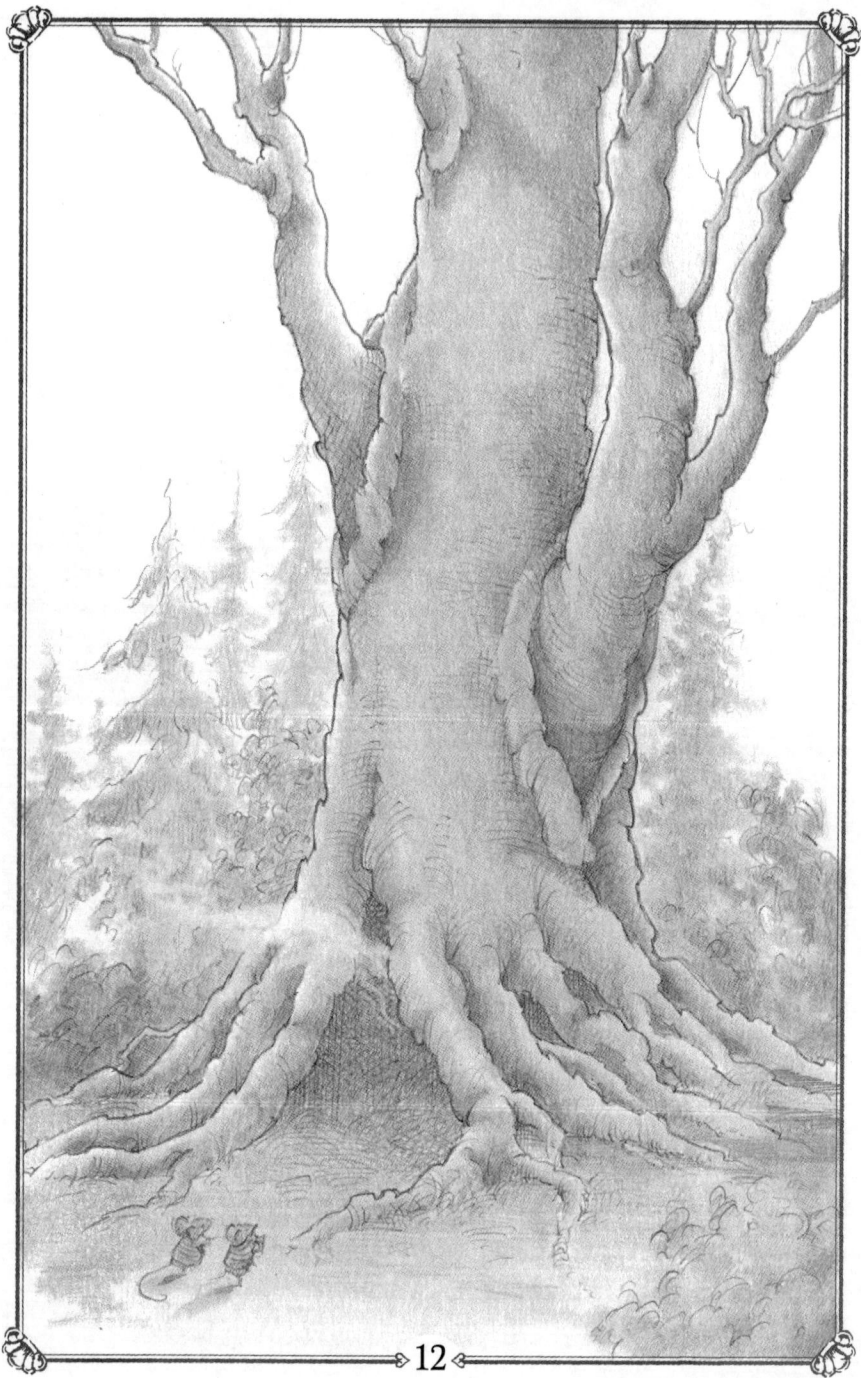

只见铁杉树粗大的根部有一个幽深的黑洞，一缕缕雾气从这个洞里不断冒出来，正如哨子在寒风中呼出的雾气一样。

"莉拉，"哨子说，"我觉得那个洞里有什么东西在呼吸。看到了吗？"他指着洞口冒出的雾气说道。

莉拉很谨慎。

"也许是只臭鼬，"她说，"我们去问问海勇。"

哨子不想惊动一只臭鼬，所以他们蹑手蹑脚地继续往前走。

孩子们回到小屋时，离沙漏计时结束只剩下了几分钟。他们向海勇描述了洞里冒出的冰冷的雾气。

"可能是只冬眠的熊。"海勇说。

"一只熊！"哨子和莉拉一起惊呼道。

孩子们还从来没有见过熊呢。

看起来，他们这短短一小时的漫步，果真是一场冒险呢。

也许还会有更多的历险在等待着他们。

3. 苏醒过来

在那只熊继续躲在树根下冬眠的这段日子里，哨子和莉拉时常带着礼物去看望他。在晴朗的日子里，他们走到森林边，把很多小玩意儿放进他的洞里：一个风干的海扇，一颗多余的跳棋棋子，一个莉拉自己做的锅架等等。其中最重要的礼物，是一个他们在夏天发现的大法螺壳。孩子们并不是经常能找到大法螺壳这样的宝贝，它们非常罕见。

邀请您
去灯塔
吃早餐

他们还给熊留下一张字条，邀请他醒来之后一起吃早餐。终于，在一个春寒料峭的早晨，这只熊醒了。

他太饿了，而且太困了，无法自己准备早餐，于是他一路跌跌撞撞地走到灯塔旁的小屋，敲了敲门。

潘朵拉打开门，看到一张毛茸茸、皱巴巴的脸，和一双带着黑眼圈惺忪的睡眼。

熊把字条递给她，竭力忍住哈欠，礼貌地说："我叫托马斯，我想我被邀请来这里吃早餐。"

潘朵拉请托马斯进屋。孩子们跑了过来，他们非常激动。

潘朵拉给托马斯做好了早餐，令大家惊叹不已的是，托马斯这顿早餐竟然一口气吃下了三十四张熊果煎饼。熊冬眠醒来以后，总是非常饥饿。

随后，海勇邀请托马斯去潘朵拉的花园看看。

作为一只彬彬有礼的熊，托马斯回答道："我非常乐意。"

说着，他打了一个大大的哈欠。

"啊，对不起。"托马斯道歉说。

托马斯在潘朵拉的花园里走了一圈。花园里有许多刚刚长出花苞和刚刚绽放的花。接着，他看见了那张吊床。

"我能试试吗？"他问海勇。

"当然可以。"海勇说。

哨子、莉拉、海勇和小不点儿（坐在海勇帽子的卷边里）看着这只熊舒舒服服地躺在了吊床上。

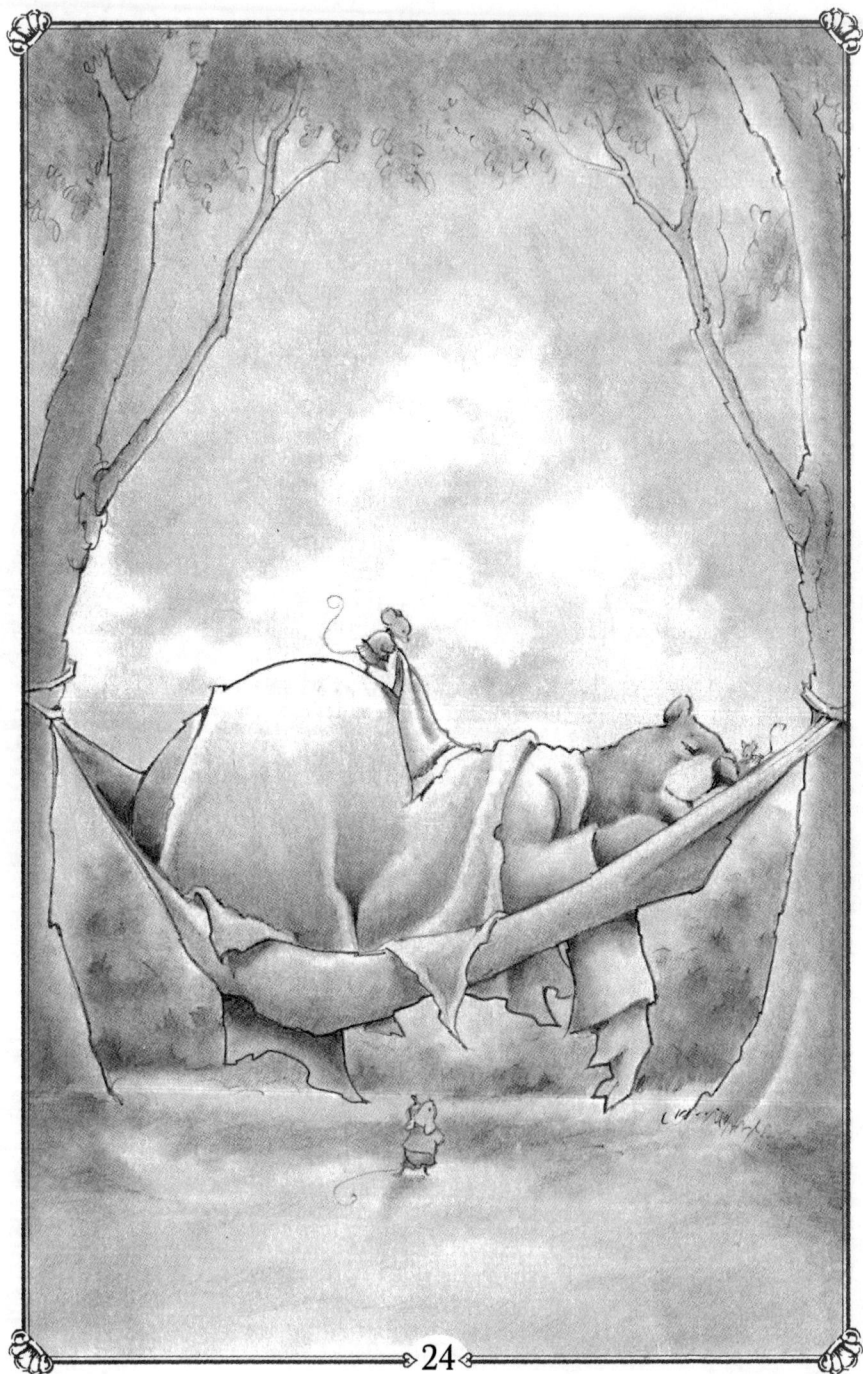

"啊!"吃饱了熊果煎饼的熊满足地叹了口气。

接着,他转了个身,立刻睡着了。

"天哪!"莉拉惊叹道。

看到这种情况,一家人只能随机应变。在寒冷的夜晚,他们给他盖上毯子;而当阳光过于刺眼时,他们把茶巾盖在他头上。小不点儿则喜欢拍他的大鼻子。

就这样,大熊托马斯在潘朵拉花园的吊床上,睡了整整四十三天。

4. 托马斯回家

终于，托马斯醒来了。他觉得很不好意思，自己作为客人，竟然在主人家里停留了这么长时间。

但全家人都安慰他说，他没有给他们增添任何麻烦。潘朵拉又做了三十四张熊果煎饼给他吃。

离开灯塔之后，托马斯回去整理了一下，把自己的东西搬到了位于一个小瀑布下方的一处环境优美的岩架上，为的是能够随时欣赏美景。然后，他邀请灯塔之家所有人到他的新家来。

"你不怕打盹儿时滚下去吗？"莉拉朝岩架外望了一眼，问托马斯。

"我怕啊，"托马斯回答说，"所以我总是在身边放一块大石头。我还从没滚下去过呢。"

　　"聪明！"哨子说。

　　"在晴朗的日子里，瀑布里会有彩虹出现。"托马斯的声音里带着一丝自豪。

　　"多么可爱的家啊。"潘朵拉说。潘朵拉很欣赏别出心裁的家居设计。

　　托马斯端来一大碗浆果，邀请大家一起吃。

然后，在他们参观新家的时候，那只林鼠来访了。原来，他和托马斯是老朋友。事实上，托马斯的早餐桌就是林鼠帮他做的。

"手艺真好！"海勇钦佩地说。

灯塔一家人准备回去的时候，托马斯给他们送上了一个惊喜。

"大法螺壳！"哨子叫道。

托马斯指着大法螺壳顶部一个新凿的洞说："一只啄木鸟帮了我个小忙。"随后，他举起大法螺壳靠近嘴边，吹了一首曲子。

"太神奇了！"孩子们喊道。

托马斯把大法螺壳递给了海勇。

"我希望听到从你们的家中传来的音乐声。"
托马斯说。

于是，整个春天，当蜜蜂醒来，蜂鸟从南方飞来，野黄菊盛开之时，悬崖上的灯塔里总是传出动听的音乐。那些美丽的音符随风飘扬，飘荡在海面上。

有时候，某只喜欢唱歌的座头鲸甚至会和着这曼妙的旋律，高歌一曲。

The
LIGHTHOUSE FAMILY
THE BEAR

1. Winter Winds

Lighthouse-keeping can be a very lonely life, and so it was for Pandora the cat for many years. She had steadily kept the lights burning to warn the sailing ships away from the rocks at the edge of the shore. But Pandora wished, every day, for some company.

Then one day company arrived. A great storm blew a battered little boat named *Adventure* onto shore. And along with this little boat came its sailor, also battered by the sea. His name was Seabold.

Pandora brought Seabold into her cottage next to the lighthouse, and she set right away to tending his broken leg and strengthening him with stew.

In time Seabold was completely well again, and he knew that he must set sail. His life had always been the sea.

But before Seabold sailed away, a different kind of company altogether arrived at the lighthouse, changing everything.

They were Whistler, Lila, and Tiny, three orphaned children drifting helplessly in a crate at sea when Pandora and Seabold found them. The children were quite lost and very hungry.

Pandora and Seabold took care of these children, and because he grew so deeply fond of them, Seabold realized he could not sail away at all.

And together they all became the lighthouse family.

Summer was fun and fall was beautiful, but winter at the lighthouse was *challenging*.

The sky and the sea were always gray and the winter gales blew endlessly. Lighthouse-keeping became very hard work. Pandora and Seabold not only kept a fire going in the kitchen day and night, but they also kept the lamps burning in the lighthouse tower day and night. They filled the lamps and trimmed the wicks and cleaned the windows of the lantern room constantly. They took turns ringing the fog bell through the night to warn ships to steer away.

Whistler and Lila wanted to help ring the bell, but Pandora would not allow it. At times the wind blew so fiercely that even she and Seabold had to tie themselves to a tree so they wouldn't blow away.

So the children kept themselves busy with inside things, like playing checkers and teaching Tiny her numbers and letters.

They all caught winter colds, and they rubbed bee balm salve onto their red noses and drank quite a lot of ginger tea.

But finally the winter storms became fewer and fewer. And some mornings there was hardly any fog at all, and everyone knew that spring was tip toeing in.

One day Whistler and Lila begged Pandora and Seabold to allow them to take a walk.

"We will bundle up three times thicker," promised Lila.

"And we'll cover our noses," added Whistler.

Pandora and Seabold agreed that it would be safe for the children to go, as long as they avoided the windy cliffs and stayed close to the forest's edge.

Seabold handed Whistler a small hourglass.

"One hour only," Seabold said. "Then home."

"One hour only," promised Whistler and Lila.

And as the children stepped outside into the cold air,

they both hoped they might be lucky enough to have a one-hour adventure.

2. The Deep Hole

The forest that grew down to the sea cliffs was thick with green ferns and mosses and the fragrance of cedar. Whistler and Lila loved it. But the forest was miles deep. The children knew that without a compass to guide them, they must not venture in but stay on the edge as they had promised.

"What is that?" Whistler asked, pointing to something up ahead. It looked like a little house.

As they drew closer, the children realized it was, in fact, a little house. It was made of sticks and was most impressive, and on its porch sat a wood rat enjoying a cup of tea.

"Good morning," the rat said.

"Good morning," Whistler and Lila answered together.

The rat graciously invited them to join him for tea.

But with only an hour for exploring, the children politely declined.

"Another time!" the rat said cheerfully.

Whistler and Lila continued walking. And it was when they were carefully gathering cloudberries from some bushes beside a hemlock tree that Whistler became curious about something new.

A deep dark hole had been made by the large roots of the tree, and from this hole a wisp of vapor was rising. It looked just like Whistler's frosty breath.

"Lila," said Whistler, "I believe something in that hole is breathing. See?" Whistler pointed to the vapor mist coming from within the hole.

Lila was cautious.

"It might be a skunk," she said. "Let's ask Seabold."

Whistler did not want to startle a skunk, so they quietly went on with their walk.

The children arrived back at the cottage with only a

few minutes left in the hourglass. They told Seabold about the frosty vapor coming from the hole.

"It is probably a hibernating bear," Seabold said.

"A bear!" said Whistler and Lila together.

The children had never met a bear.

Their one-hour walk had proved to be an adventure after all.

Maybe there would be more to come.

3. Someone Wakes Up

While the bear continued his winter sleep under the tree roots, Whistler and Lila visited him with gifts. On clear days they walked to the forest's edge and placed small things just inside his hole: a dried sea fan, an extra checker, a pot holder Lila had made, and, most important, a triton shell they had found in summer. They did not often find those. Triton shells were special.

They also left a note inviting him to breakfast when he woke up. And finally, one chilly spring morning, the bear did wake up.

Because he was so hungry and much too sleepy to find his own breakfast, he stumbled to the cottage beside the lighthouse and knocked on the door.

Pandora opened the door to see a very rumpled furry face with dark, sleepy eyes.

The bear handed her the note and, as politely as possible without yawning too much, he said, "My name is Thomas, and I believe I am invited for breakfast."

Pandora welcomed Thomas inside. The children came running. They were thrilled!

Pandora made Thomas breakfast, which turned out to be an amazing thirty-four bearberry pancakes. Bears are very hungry when they wake up.

Seabold then invited Thomas to see Pandora's garden.

Being a courteous bear, Thomas said, "I would like that very much."

He yawned a very big yawn.

"Oh, pardon me," he said.

The bear walked all around Pandora's garden, which had many flowers just coming into bud and bloom. Then he spotted the hammock.

"May I?" he asked Seabold.

"Indeed," said Seabold.

Whistler, Lila, Seabold, and Tiny (in the roll of Seabold's cap) watched as the bear eased himself into the hammock.

"Aaah," said the bear, very full of pancakes.

He then turned onto his side and instantly went back to sleep.

"Oh dear," said Lila.

The family adjusted. They put a blanket over him on chilly nights. And a tea towel on his head if the sun was bright. Tiny liked to pat his big nose.

Thomas the bear slept in the hammock in Pandora's garden for forty-three days.

4. Thomas Goes Home

Finally Thomas woke up. He was very embarrassed to find he was a guest who had greatly overstayed his welcome.

But the family assured him he had been no trouble at all. And Pandora again fed him thirty-four bearberry pancakes.

After Thomas left the lighthouse, he tidied himself and moved his things onto a very nice ledge beneath a small waterfall, for the view. Then he invited the lighthouse family to his new home.

"Aren't you afraid you might roll off when napping?" Lila asked Thomas as she peered over the ledge.

"Yes," said Thomas. "So I always put a rock beside me. I have not rolled off once."

"Smart!" said Whistler.

"There are rainbows in the waterfall on sunny days," Thomas said with some pride in his voice.

"Such a lovely home," said Pandora. Pandora

appreciated good home design.

Thomas invited everyone to share a big bowl of berries. Then, during their visit, the wood rat stopped by. It turned out that he and Thomas were old friends. In fact, the wood rat had built Thomas's breakfast table.

"Very fine work," said Seabold with admiration.

As the lighthouse family was preparing to return home, Thomas brought forth a surprise.

"The triton shell!" said Whistler.

Thomas pointed to a freshly made hole in the top of the shell.

"A woodpecker did me a small favor," said Thomas.

Then he put the shell to his mouth and played a tune on it!

"Amazing!" cried the children.

Thomas handed the shell to Seabold.

"I will listen for music from your family," Thomas said.

So all through the spring, as the bees woke up and the hummingbirds flew in from the south and the goldenrod bloomed, the lovely sound of music could be heard coming from the lighthouse on the cliff. The notes floated out and across the sea.

And, sometimes, a humpback whale who loved to sing even answered.

图书在版编目（CIP）数据

灯塔之家. 大熊托马斯／（美）辛西娅·劳伦特著；
（美）普莱斯顿·马克丹尼斯绘；栾述蓉译. -- 南昌：
二十一世纪出版社集团，2023.4
ISBN 978-7-5568-6915-2

I.①灯… II.①辛… ②普… ③栾… III.①儿童故
事－图画故事－美国－现代 IV.①I712.85

中国版本图书馆CIP数据核字 (2022) 第195946号

版权合同登记号：14-2022-0064

灯塔之家 大熊托马斯
DENGTA ZHI JIA　DA XIONG TUOMASI
[美]辛西娅·劳伦特／著　[美]普莱斯顿·马克丹尼斯／绘　栾述蓉／译

出 版 人　刘凯军
项目策划　奇想国童书
责任编辑　刘晨露子
特约编辑　郑应湘　孙金蕾
装帧设计　田丽丹
出版发行　二十一世纪出版社集团
　　　　　（江西省南昌市子安路75号 330025）
网　　址　www.21cccc.com
经　　销　全国新华书店
印　　刷　固安兰星球彩色印刷有限公司
版　　次　2023年4月第1版
印　　次　2023年4月第1次印刷
开　　本　787mm×1092mm 1/16
印　　张　3.5
字　　数　16千字
书　　号　ISBN 978-7-5568-6915-2
定　　价　198.00元（全8册）

赣版权登字-04-2022-655　　　版权所有，侵权必究
购买本社图书，如有问题请联系我们：扫描封底二维码进入官方服务号。
服务电话：010-64049180（工作时间可拨打）；服务邮箱：qixiangguo@tbpmedia.com。